I0564554

UNFIT TO SERVE

SANDRA BRETTING

A Christian Company
ElkLakePublishingInc.com

COPYRIGHT NOTICE

Unfit to Serve
First edition. Copyright © 2024 by Sandra Bretting. The information contained in this book is the intellectual property of Sandra Bretting and is governed by United States and International copyright laws. All rights reserved. No part of this publication, either text or image, may be used for any purpose other than personal use. Therefore, reproduction, modification, storage in a retrieval system, or retransmission, in any form or by any means, electronic, mechanical, or otherwise, for reasons other than personal use, except for brief quotations for reviews or articles and promotions, is strictly prohibited without prior written permission by the publisher.

NO AI TRAINING: Without in any way limiting Sandra Bretting's and the publisher's exclusive rights under copyright, any use of this publication to "train" generative artificial intelligence (AI) technologies to generate text is expressly prohibited. The author reserves all rights to license uses of this work for generative AI training and development of machine learning language models.

This is a work of fiction. Names, characters, businesses, places, events, locales, and incidents are either the products of the author's imagination or used in a fictitious manner. Any resemblance to actual persons, living or dead, or actual events is purely coincidental.

Cover and Interior Design: Kelly Artieri, Deb Haggerty
Editor(s): Peggy Ellis, Cristel Phelps, Deb Haggerty

PUBLISHED BY: Elk Lake Publishing, Inc., 35 Dogwood Drive, Plymouth, MA 02360, 2024

Library Cataloging Data
Names: Bretting, Sandra (Sandra Bretting)
Unfit to Serve
336 p. 23cm × 15cm (9in × 6 in.)
ISBN-13: 9798891341487 (paperback) | 9798891341494 (trade paperback) | 9798891341500 (e-book)

UNFIT TO SERVE

ENDORSEMENTS

With a bag of seeds and a head full of plans, a new bride follows her husband from New York to Texas where nothing about her life is what she'd planned. I related to Jo, the main character, trying to figure out where she fit in her new role as an army officer's wife. Bretting has written a strong historical, bringing the reader straight into the heat and dirt of their Texas home. Fascinating characters and a strong storyline make this historical a winner!
—**Lynn Cahoon**, *NYT* and *USA Today* bestselling author of several cozy series including the Tourist Trap Mysteries.

In *Unfit to Serve*, Bretting provides a very human viewpoint of love, war, and relationships. Readers experience an emotional roller coaster as we watch Josephine navigate being a new wife, schoolteacher, and friend all while never giving up on serving her country—whether they want her help or not! Through a new version of the military's IQ test developed by Jo and her best friend, she not only helps the war effort but, in the end, finds the courage to pursue a childhood dream and to further serve her country in the future.
—**Nicole Leiren**, USA TODAY Best-selling Author of the *Danger Cove Mysteries* and the *Sadie Sabatini Mysteries*. Upcoming in Summer 2024, Murderous CONsequesces.

When we think of Sandra Bretting, we think of her popular Missy DuBois series, and while her new historical fiction is quite different, readers have a treat in store. Her superpower has always been putting readers in her characters' worlds from page one, and she's at the top of her game with *Unfit to Serve*. Josephine and Albigence remind us that people can grow, but love remains. The book is well-researched, with Bretting choosing the most interesting historical tidbits to share. Well done!

—Lane Stone, author of the Big Picture art thriller trilogy

Jo Pembrooke and her husband, a military psychologist, encounter adversity, illness, and the horrors of war in this stirring novel of World War I. Rich with historical detail, engaging characters, and emotional depth, *Unfit to Serve* is a testament to the enduring power of faith and love.

—Ashley Weaver, author of the Electra McDonnell series

Key Words: Christian World War I women's friendship rights; First World War Jesus fairness immigrants; Historical fiction Christians early 20th century; Faith-based storytelling wartime scientific tests; Soldier fiction civilians in war America history; World War I literature untold story woman; War and sacrifice injury homecoming God love

Library of Congress Control Number: 2024943984 Fiction

DEDICATION

For my family: Roger, Brooke, and Dana. You will always be my True North.

ACKNOWLEDGMENTS

There's a famous line in an equally famous play that reads, "I have always depended on the kindness of strangers." I understand what the playwright meant, even though I usually benefit from the kindness of people I know.

How else does one account for the "beta" reader (someone who reads a book when it's in its messy, gangly phase), who agreed to review my manuscript while her husband was undergoing chemotherapy treatment? Or the daughter who spent every birthday wish on her mother's unpublished novel, hoping it would come to light? Or the grace of another daughter—one who was forced to grow up overnight when I faced a terrible illness—who never once complained about the situation?

Kindness, indeed.

I've been blessed with a trio of terrific, and terrifically kind, beta readers: Erika (Ricki) Lutjens, Kristi Jones, and Kristin Palfreyman. Thank you, ladies, for your wise input, as well as your friendship.

I owe a debt of gratitude to the late Micqui Miller, who served as my mentor during the Barbara Burnett Smith Aspiring Writers Project, many years ago. Micqui was the first published author to see a spark in my writing and to try to nurture the spark into a flame.

Likewise, for being so gracious to a newbie author who couldn't offer them anything in return, I'd like to thank Texas author Russ Hall and the legendary New York literary agent Jane Dystel. Those two literary greats helped someone who couldn't help them in return, which is very rare, indeed.

I'd like to give a big hug around the neck to my editor, Peggy Ellis, who knows the English language backward and forward. Thank you for reviewing the manuscript so thoroughly!

I also owe an enormous debt of gratitude to Cristel Phelps and Deb Haggerty of Elk Lake Publishing, Inc. for being the first Christian publisher to embrace *Unfit to Serve*. I'd love to be able to say it was the best decision they ever made, but we know that's not true. (*That* would be their decisions to follow Christ.)

To my home-away-from-home—the Cinco Ranch Public Library in Katy, Texas—my heartfelt gratitude. You offer a peaceful refuge in a crazy world. The community is so lucky to have you!

As always, I owe a debt of gratitude to my family. My husband and daughters have always encouraged me in this crazy writing life, no matter how many twists and turns it's taken.

Last, but never least, I'd like to thank my heavenly Father for his guidance and grace. Everything else is just icing on the cake.

CHAPTER ONE

JOSEPHINE

CAMP TRAVIS, SAN ANTONIO, TEXAS

SUMMER 1917

By the time the sun emerged on the horizon, the elegant Edwardian thermometer already registered a temperature of eighty-five degrees.

Eighty-five degrees!

If the heat didn't break soon, her bush beans would never flower. Jo frowned as she studied the opulent weatherglass.

"The case is rather showy, isn't it?" her new husband remarked.

"Hmm?"

He'd followed her gaze to the wall. "The weatherglass. Perhaps a portrait of the president would be better suited there."

"Perhaps." Truth be told, the elaborately carved and beveled case didn't belong on the slat-wood wall of an army cabin. "But it helps with the plantings."

She'd babied a bagful of seeds all the way from their home in upstate New York, a journey that involved no less than three separate rail lines and a dusty buggy ride. The only way she could hope to grow a victory garden in the heat of south Texas was to get ahead of the weather.

"Suit yourself." Albigence rose stiffly from the breakfast table. "Do try to cover your head next time you go outside, though. I think I spy some new freckles on your nose."

She slanted her eyes at him. "I'll try to remember. But, seriously. Will you work late again?"

"I'm afraid so. The soldiers keep coming. There's no rest for the weary. Well, off we go."

He kissed her on the cheek before turning to leave.

"By the way," he said, "I know how hard this move has been on you. But do try to get out and about today. You *are* the wife of an army officer."

An army *medical* officer, Jo wanted to add, but didn't. Albigence was so taken with his new position as a military psychologist that he couldn't be bothered with semantics.

She watched him leave, and the long, hot hours unspooled before her like an endless, empty road. A horribly straight road—with no obvious detours or clear destination. She had too much time on her hands and nothing worthwhile to spend it on, since she couldn't begin her duties as the camp's new schoolmarm for another two months.

Then again, she could always visit the post exchange. Granted, that would make it five trips this week, but another visit might allow her to feel useful.

Jo placed the breakfast dishes in the washbasin and grabbed a straw hat from its peg by the door.

Her laced boots ruffled the dust as she walked. Beside her stretched row upon row of weather-beaten army tents, which sprouted from the soil like brown sheaths of wheat. The tents belonged to the hundreds of men who hoped to join the Ninetieth Infantry Division here at Camp Travis. Most wanted to gain their citizenship papers and finally feel at home in the Promised Land.

Her brocade skirt grew heavier with each step. Jo had known enough to leave the wool party frocks behind when she left Ithaca, but she never expected air so thick with humidity she could almost wring it dry between her hands.

And the heat! Albigence had made Texas sound like a grand adventure when he first proposed the idea. Something about purple mountain majesties and amber waves of grain. As far as she could tell, the only elevation at Camp Travis came courtesy of red ant hills, which flooded her boots with sand and biting insects, should she happen to step on one. As for vegetation, there really wasn't much to see except prickly cacti and pale blue agave.

"Oh, flummadiddle," she muttered.

At least the move gave her new husband a way to serve his country. Albigence had been bothered to no end when he couldn't join the war effort because of his nearsightedness and weak constitution. As a newly minted psychologist, he could analyze those feelings all day long, but nothing cured him of the doldrums like an official telephone call from the United States Army.

That call had come only a week after their wedding. In short order, her new groom had tossed everything he owned—mostly academic textbooks, research papers, and field manuals—into a cardboard suitcase, while she lovingly layered a steamer trunk with delicate corsets, lace petticoats, and smooth kidskin gloves.

She spied the post exchange on the road ahead, and the memories vanished.

"Hello there," the merchant said when she entered. Mr. Johnson looked unaffected by the heat or humidity. "Back so soon?"

"Yes, indeed. Sure is a scorcher today, isn't it?"

"Wait 'til you've been here a while." He gave a dry chuckle. "Doesn't get any better in September. Holler if you need my help."

The merchant turned to address another customer—a baby-faced soldier with no need for a straight razor, let alone the waxed pack of Pall Malls he eagerly pointed to on a shelf.

As the shopkeeper reached for the cigarettes, the teenager plunked a few coins on the dusty plywood counter.

"American only," the merchant snarled, when he turned and realized what was on offer. "Idiot." He angrily shoved the cigarettes back in place as if the boy's coins offended him.

The poor boy slunk away, but Jo's maternal instincts bristled, since he'd reminded her of one of her students.

"You know, Mr. Johnson—"

"Say," the merchant interrupted, "I jus' got somethin' in you might like."

"Pardon?"

"That sacka flour over there." He nodded to a large sack of Bob White flour that leaned against the canvas tent. "It'd make a right fine pillowcase."

"Pillowcase? Oh."

Her anger dimmed when she followed his gaze to the sack in question. Unlike the rest of Camp Travis, which was awash in khaki, brown, and gray, the bag featured a colorful scene of green farmlands, azure clouds, and plump orange chickens.

"You're probably right about the pillowcase," she said, "and we do need flour. A few potatoes too."

"Comin' right up."

She felt the weight of a silver dollar in her pocket, which Albigence had gifted her with earlier in the week. "Three should do it. Although it's beyond me why my own vegetables won't grow here."

"You didn't try to plant anythin' now, didja? Why, everyone knows you can't put nuthin' in the ground come August. It's much too hot."

"What? Oh, of course. Everyone knows that." Jo took the tubers he placed on the counter without making eye contact. "Please send someone over later with the flour."

She'd already noted the sack's enormous size and realized her Albigence could no more lift the bag than he could thread the sewing needle she'd use on it later. Her husband was many things—brilliant, hardworking, disciplined. Strong, he wasn't.

"Of course," Mr. Johnson said. "It's six cents a pound for the flour and five for the 'taters. I'll add it to your tab."

"But I brought money with me today."

"There, there. Don't worry your pretty little head about it. By the way, the Ladies' Benevolent Society is holdin' a meetin' tomorrow night in the canteen. You should think 'bout goin.'"

"A benevolent society, hmm?" A sour taste coated Jo's throat. "Maybe I'll consider attending. Thank you, Mr. Johnson."

She hurried from the exchange before he could say more about the event in the canteen. While Jo desperately wanted to make friends at Camp Travis—which was Albigence's deepest desire for her, as well—she didn't know whether she could stomach a whole evening of nothing but idle chitchat with a roomful of women.

That was exactly what'd happened when she attended a tea party at Cornell. She'd spent the entire night hiding behind a potted fern that didn't care one way or another what she thought of the latest fashions. Jo longed to talk to someone about things that mattered, like educating America's schoolchildren, since factories now replaced family farms, or how to help the poor soldiers living in squalor overseas.

She quickly retreated down the footpath, which skirted even more rows of weather-beaten tents, until she passed the canteen. The slender planks reminded Jo of an overturned box of safety matches someone had carefully stacked to the sky, like kindling in a firewood box.

Beside the canteen ran the main road, which led to a military hospital, administrative headquarters, camp chapel, and the one-room schoolhouse. She'd oversee the latter when the children returned in the fall.

The first thing I'll teach them—

"Careful!" A woman's voice broke through her thoughts. "Or you'll be pulling needles from your skirts for days."

Jo glanced down to see a prickly pear cactus aimed at her knees. Swerving to avoid the cactus, she scanned the horizon for her good Samaritan.

A blonde girl leaned over the rail of the chapel's staircase. She looked to be about Jo's age, or some twenty years in all. She'd apparently been flaying a rag rug with a wire beater.

Like Jo, she wore a plain shirtwaist and black fan skirt, but she had fair hair and eyes, whereas Jo's coloring ran to auburn.

Jo moved closer, drawn by the possibility of friendship. "Thank you for the warning. By the way, I'm Josephine Pembrooke."

"Nice to meet you, Josephine. Whew!" The girl threw the beater to the ground. "That's enough of that. I'm Rebekkah Schmidt. I haven't seen you around camp before. Are you new?"

"We arrived a few weeks ago. My husband and I. We've been getting our cabin in order." Although, to be honest, Albigence couldn't give two figs about the state of their cabin once he'd joined the Medical Officers' Corp.

"I'm just surprised I haven't seen you at church." Rebekkah nodded at the chapel behind her. "My husband ministers to the men here. I do hope we'll see you at services this Sunday."

"What? Uh ... of course, you will." Jo's cheeks warmed even more, if that was possible. Shame on her for missing church. Albigence didn't seem to mind when they dishonored the Sabbath to unpack dishes, but she knew better. She could only imagine what the school's hiring committee would say when they learned their brand-new schoolmarm had skipped Sunday services.

"Good," Rebekkah said. "I'll watch out for you."

"Um ... do you suppose you could stay mum about my absence? The camp hired me to teach the children here, you see—"

"Say no more, Josephine." A wry smile appeared. "I'll let you buy my silence with your company. Care to join me for some ginger soda?"

"I'd love to, but please call me Jo. Everyone else does."

The girl grabbed hold of the stair rail and carefully descended the chapel's steps. Her legs seemed to trouble her, as if the back one wanted nothing to do with its mate up front. She had to practically drag the appendage along to make any headway at all.

"Poliomyelitis," she said over her shoulder once she reached the ground, as if reading Jo's thoughts. "I suffered a terrible bout when I was a child."

"Really? I hadn't noticed anything."

"Of course, you hadn't. Come along."

Soon enough, they reached a cabin that looked like every other cabin at Camp Travis. One step inside, though, and the scene changed. Somehow, the preacher's wife had turned a dull wood box into a colorful, comfortable home. A real home, with a purple velvet Chesterfield in the front parlor and lace curtains on the windows. A circle of unbleached planks near the front door signaled the spot for the newly cleaned rug.

"How in the world did you manage this?" Jo gazed high and low as she followed her hostess through the cheery rooms.

"Manage what?"

"This place. Your cabin looks like a home. Like a real, honest-to-goodness home."

"Oh, that." Rebekkah shrugged. "The curtains used to be old petticoats—don't tell anyone—and an officer's wife gave me the Chesterfield when the family was reassigned. Here we go."

She'd stopped by an icebox in the kitchen. Jo quickly intervened as Rebekkah struggled to hoist the lid and dislodge a heavy cutglass pitcher.

"Here. Let me." Jo extracted the pitcher and brought it to the kitchen table. "I guess I've been focusing more on what my cabin *doesn't* have."

"Don't blame yourself. We all need time to get used to camp life. Now, what brought you and your husband here in the first place?" She poured out the soda and offered some to Jo.

"Thank you. The testing program. My husband's a psychologist. He'd just graduated from Cornell when we got the orders to come here. Something about a new test they want to give all the men who volunteer for the army."

"Ah, yes." A dark cloud crossed Rebekkah's face. "I've heard about it. They named the quiz the 'intelligence quotient test,' you know. Rumor has it they got the test from France, where schoolteachers used it on their students."

"That's what my husband said. You don't think it's a good idea?

"Honestly? It's not up to me to decide that. I've only heard the test has caused a lot of trouble. Unintended consequences, you might say."

"Really?"

Rebekkah looked at her askance. "Now, surely, you've talked to your husband about that too. He must have strong opinions about the testing program. His thoughts carry far more weight than mine."

"Well, he's … he's been so terribly busy with work, you see." Jo squirmed on the hard seat. "I've heard about his new office, of course, and the state of the filing system." No need to discuss the delicate state of her marriage with someone she barely knew.

"I'm sure your husband's very busy," Rebekkah agreed. "They inundate the men with information once they get here. He's no doubt overwhelmed. What about you? How are you adjusting to camp life?"

"Well enough, I suppose. Other than the heat—and I can't imagine anyone ever gets used to that—they make getting around easy enough."

"The army does love order. What I meant to ask was, how are you getting along with the other wives?"

13

"The wives? Honestly, I haven't met many. But I haven't gone out of my way, either."

"Seems to me we're the ones at fault, not you. Consider yourself officially welcomed. I'm sure you'll meet plenty of other women when your husband leaves for training camp."

A beat or two of silence. "Excuse me?"

"You know, the medical officers' training camp. The place they go to in Georgia."

"Georgia?" The news struck Jo like a slap to the face. Had Albigence known about the camp all along? "That's four states away! How long will he be gone?"

"Two months, I believe." Recognition slowly dawned. "Oh, my goodness. You don't know about the training program, do you? Forget I said anything."

"No, no. It's quite all right. I need to know." If she was to lose her husband's company, what little she had of it, she'd rather find out sooner rather than later. Why delay the inevitable?

"Well," Rebekkah said, "the army sends all psychologists and physicians to a training camp before they start their service. I believe the next group leaves tomorrow. It's a terrible thing to do to the wives, if you ask me. Shipping off their husbands. But there'll be plenty of other things to keep you occupied in the meantime. You'll see."

Somehow, the drink had soured in her cup, so Jo pushed it aside. "Of course, you're right. I'm sure time will no doubt fly by."

"No doubt. You can always visit me. I'd love the company."

"Thank you. But ... but I really should be going."

Jo rose, and in her haste, nearly upended the cutglass pitcher. Her hostess had been so kind and welcoming, but she couldn't wait to get out of the cabin now. "Thank you for the soda, but the morning's half over, and I've barely begun my chores."

Tears sprang to Jo's eyes as she maneuvered around the Chesterfield. What was worse—learning about a two-month training program for her new husband or hearing about it from someone other than Albigence?

Either way, she'd never felt so abandoned in her life.

CHAPTER TWO

ALBIGENCE

SCHOOL OF MILITARY PSYCHOLOGY, CAMP GREENLEAF, GEORGIA

AUGUST 1917

Albigence had practically memorized the psychology training manual by now, but what harm could come from rereading a passage or two? He wanted to be ready for Monday's lecture, and that required an ironclad mastery of the previous week's subject matter.

If anything, he could probably teach the course on *War Psychoses and Neuroses* by now. Especially the chapter on battle fatigue—his specialty. Unlike his fellow students, Albigence refused to call the malady by its nickname— shellshock—given his healthy respect for the time and energy it took to name the various diagnoses in the first place.

No, let the other officers fritter away their time at Camp Greenleaf. He had every intention of mastering the thick syllabus in front of him and moving up in the ranks by the time he returned to Texas.

Josephine hadn't exactly embraced the training program like he'd thought she would. He'd thought she'd be happy for him. But, no, quite the contrary. She'd become almost hysterical, as if they were talking about something that lasted sixty years instead of a mere sixty days.

Maybe he could blame her female constitution for the hysteria. Everyone knew women weren't as emotionally stable as men.

"The training is only two months," he'd argued in a vain attempt to win her over.

"Why didn't you warn me? What am I supposed to do with myself while you're gone?"

"You can always visit that store you like so much. Surely you have more work to do around here." Then again, one glance around their miniscule cabin made him rethink his opinion. "Or ... what about the garden outside? I thought you wanted to plant a victory garden once we got to Camp Travis. Heaven knows you talked of little else on our journey."

"Oh, Albigence. Everyone knows you can't plant anything in the ground right now. It's much too hot for the bushes to flower."

She'd sounded like a petulant child. Not like a full-grown woman who had a household to run, for goodness' sake.

"Well, there's nothing I can do about it." He needed to end the conversation once and for all. "Every psychologist has to undergo the same training. You can't expect the army to throw us to the wolves without any training, now, can you?"

"No, I suppose not. But I never thought I'd be left alone so soon."

At that point, he'd decided the best course of action was to walk away, since there was no talking to her in her current state. Why must women be so irrational?

Since then, he'd received two perfumed letters from her—two more than he'd expected—so perhaps Josephine was over her little bout of hysteria.

He returned his attention to the syllabus. The section on *An Evacuation Hospital: Its Equipment, Use, and Internal Administration* sounded especially interesting.

A sharp knock at the door broke his concentration.

"Yes? Who's there?" he snapped.

He glanced up to see a shadowy figure in the doorway, wholly unwelcomed and altogether uninvited.

"It's me, old chap. Frank." The man moved into view, with his official necktie shamefully askew.

"Do you need something, Frank?"

"Only for you to leave your quarters and come with me. Why are you hiding in here?"

"I'm not hiding. I'm studying."

Frank, like most men at Camp Travis, was built like a stevedore, which meant he had to turn sideways to navigate the cabin's slim doorframe. He also wore a waxed moustache, much like that insufferable song-and-dance man, William F. Denny.

Albigence never did like Frank.

"Come now." The man loped into the cabin as if he owned the place. "Put those papers aside. Me and the fellas are going to the officers' club for a little entertainment."

"That's quite all right. I'm trying to get a head start on next week's lectures. I'm reading about battle fatigue … er, shellshock." Perhaps if he used the colloquialism for once, Frank would understand he was talking to a comrade, and thus leave him alone. "Would you please close the door on your way out?"

"Nonsense." Not even the most rational argument could dissuade Frank, who stood fast. "You've been working much too hard, Albie. I do believe you want to show us all up to the professors. Is that your plan? Do you want to make us look inferior?"

"Hardly." Although, truth be told, such a move would be relatively easy. "Like I said, I'm just not in the mood for entertainment right now."

Frank inched closer to the desk anyway, clearly oblivious to the situation. His broad shoulders blocked the wall sconce and dimmed the light even more.

"You're going to turn moldy in here," the intruder said. "Just once, why don't you try to have some fun?"

"Fun? What makes you think I'm not having fun?" Albigence did his best to sound lighthearted too, although the accusation stung.

"You're much too serious. I'm doing you a favor by insisting you come along."

By now, he couldn't think straight, so Albigence pulled off his spectacles and set them aside.

"Now see here, Frank. While I appreciate the invitation, I'm knee-deep in my studies at the moment. Perhaps I'll join you next time."

That promise didn't dissuade his companion, who casually toyed with the things on Albigence's desktop.

Why do men like Frank feel free to touch things that don't belong to them? A classic case of narcissistic personality disorder.

"Maybe you should try to mingle with the others," Frank said, "instead of hiding in here. Your absence doesn't look good, you know. I'm only worried about your reputation."

"I'm not hiding. I'll join you next time." Although, to be honest, he had no intention of following through on *that* promise.

"Suit yourself," Frank said. "At least keep it down in here, will ya? You're disturbing the whole camp with your ruckus."

"My ruckus?" *What a ridiculous thing to say.* "How on earth could my reading disturb anyone?"

Frank threw him an oily smile as he slithered away. At least Albigence thought it was a smile. A grimace, perhaps? He had a hard enough time reading people's facial expressions with his spectacles on, and it was nearly impossible without them.

Once Frank finally left him alone again, Albigence did his best to return to the syllabus. To no avail. The evening was ruined, and there was nothing more to be done about it.

So, he moved to the cot and flopped onto the horsehair mattress without bothering to change clothes. A new day would dawn soon enough and give him the opportunity to master the material.

Until then, he'd just have to put aside his beloved reading.

★★★

The next morning, Albigence swung his feet from the mattress and warily deposited them on the rough hardwood floor.

He missed the feel of a soft rag rug beneath his feet at daybreak. Josephine had taken great pains to create such a rug for him, which meant he always awoke with something soft to cushion his steps.

Maybe he'd answer her letters today. In them, she'd sounded a bit lost without his company. He moved to the writing desk to retrieve the papers, along with his spectacles, which weren't there. Granted, everything was blurry given his myopic vision, but he distinctly remembered placing the spectacles atop the syllabus. *Just so.* He fumbled around a bit before he dropped to his knees and dusted the floorboards with his fingers. *Nothing.* Ditto for the rest of the ground all around him.

Then, he remembered ...

Frank, standing in the doorway to his cabin. The oily smile, so disingenuous. The way he toyed with Albigence's personal effects, as if he owned them. He must have taken the spectacles without Albigence knowing.

Blast him! Now, he'd have to go to the infirmary and secure another pair, which was a colossal waste of time. Such a childish prank on Frank's part.

His mind made up, Albigence straightened his clothes as best he could, before he bumbled from the cabin. Bright sunshine greeted him, along with a wall of humidity that hit him square on.

Georgia's temperature was surprisingly like the one he'd left behind, which meant his collar felt moist and clammy by the time he reached the footpath.

The air only cooled when he entered the shade of a giant pin oak. Unlike Camp Travis, at least Camp Greenleaf had an abundance of trees, which he should've expected, given the camp's name.

Albigence followed a path dappled by piebald splotches of light and dark and blearily scanned the horizon. Although every building here looked the same—short, plain, and stout—the infirmary had the distinct advantage of hosting a large chimney on its roof, since doctors needed heat during the wintertime.

He gazed at the rooftops until his boot struck something

hard, which pitched him face first onto the ground. *Oof!* His knee hit the dirt with a sickening *thud,* followed by his chest.

He lay there, sprawled on the path, until the earth righted itself again. He rose to his knees and glanced over his shoulder to take in the culprit—the knobby root of a pin oak protruding above the ground.

Something bright and sparkly winked at him from atop the root. A round, shiny orb, which glimmered at him.

A quarter, perhaps? No, the orb was too large for a quarter. Silver dollar? He ignored the pain to reach for it, hoping for a dollar.

The truth dawned on him in fits and starts. The object was definitely manmade. A broken lens from a pair of spectacles dangled from its mangled frame.

Albigence carefully dusted the remnant and shoved it into his pocket. He couldn't decide whether to shout out in frustration or cry out in despair.

It's happening all over again.

For some reason, men like Frank couldn't help but bully him. Ruin his things and make him look foolish. They harbored an actual, physical need—one they couldn't suppress. As if his own short stature or pale complexion or advanced vocabulary gave them the *right* to bully him. The obligation even.

Maybe something else was responsible for the bullying. Something intangible. Something missing from his psyche that caused other people to treat him differently. He couldn't quite put his finger on the problem, but he couldn't deny it, either. He *was* different. That much was clear.

Which was why he couldn't believe his good fortune when he met Josephine. She resembled an angel with her auburn curls and porcelain skin. An actual angel, with brown eyes and lips stained red like port wine. The kind of angel who'd fly right past him should they happen to meet on the street instead of in a fancy ballroom at her family's mansion.

He couldn't dance, of course, or tell her any tales of derring-do, like the other men, so he decided to woo her a different way. With words. Long words, designed to show off his advanced vocabulary and scientific knowledge.

Maybe—just maybe—if he spoke long enough and ardently enough, she'd see the real man beneath the pale exterior. The man, as it were, and not the mouse. He knew of no other way to hold her attention.

Long after everyone else had deserted the ballroom, he and Josephine remained on the veranda, where they discussed what he'd studied in his classes. The effects of psychology on the very young. Psychology and the role it played in developing educational curriculum. Psychology and the current theories about psychoses and neuroses in children.

He found her surprisingly easy to talk to—given her exceptional beauty. So intelligent. Especially for a woman. Unlike other women, whom he'd always studied from afar, she didn't seem to care at all for idle talk or mindless gossip. Or anything as trivial as hearsay.

He courted her relentlessly, mindful his graduation from Cornell loomed. He did his best to talk his way right into her heart, which was the only way he knew how.

Everything happened less than a year ago. And in that year, Albigence floated along, content in the knowledge he'd received something precious from God. Something irreplaceable. An angel, no less.

Of course, he'd never say any of that to Josephine. *Oh,*

no. How could he? Saying such things aloud was unmanly. No. Emotions like those were best kept locked away. Somewhere deep in his chest, where she'd never find them.

He arose now and slapped the dust from his trousers. He scanned the horizon for the blurry outline of the camp's infirmary, where he might procure some new spectacles.

Only six more weeks to go, and he'd return to Josephine. He'd be back in Texas, where he belonged. What could possibly happen to either of them in six short weeks?

CHAPTER THREE

JOSEPHINE

CANTEEN, CAMP TRAVIS

EARLY SEPTEMBER 1917

Jo gazed at the full-length mirror while she fastened the high-neck collar of her cotton blouse. The crisp shirtwaist she'd chosen for the Ladies' Benevolent Society meeting wasn't nearly as smart as one made of taffeta or silk, but it'd have to do. Cotton was so much more practical, given the dusty boardwalks underfoot.

At least she had a reason to dress up this evening. A reason to wear something other than the black fan skirt, which had become a uniform of sorts.

Although she'd originally ignored the shopkeeper's invitation, Jo had learned the meetings sponsored by the Ladies' Benevolent Society provided the only entertainment for women at Camp Travis. Now that she had a friend in Rebekkah, it didn't seem nearly as intimidating to spend an entire evening nibbling finger sandwiches and gossiping with the other wives.

So, she resolved to attend the next month's meeting, which fell on a Tuesday.

Jo drew closer to the looking glass. She'd acquired a few more freckles on the bridge of her nose since Al's departure. He wasn't there to remind her about the sunbonnet. She'd have to explain herself later, but he wouldn't dare criticize her after the way he'd practically abandoned her. How could he?

She longed for the new school term to start, so she'd have a reason to stay inside and remain safely away from the sun. Be back in her classroom, where she belonged. She enjoyed teaching and always had. When it became clear law school was not in the cards, she set her sights on something equally fulfilling. Something she could feel good about.

Jo loved to hear the bright laughter of her students when they burst into the classroom each morning. Loved to see their eyes spark whenever they learned something new. Or to watch their confidence grow day by day.

Jo swept from the bedroom now and joined Rebekkah on the landing. Her friend wore a similar high-necked blouse and billowing cotton skirt, and she automatically linked her arm through Jo's.

"You look lovely," Rebekkah said. "It's a pity we're not going to a party tonight, instead of a boring meeting for the Ladies' Benevolent Society."

"Bite your tongue," Jo teased. "This meeting gave me something to look forward to all day. And look." She thrust out her wrist. "Perfume. I was afraid the oil would dry up if I didn't dab some on my wrist every once in a while."

"Good for you. Well, c'mon. We don't want to be late."

The women set off for the canteen, with Jo shortening her stride to match her friend's.

A stream of women soon joined them. Rebekkah seemed to know all of them by name, along with the names of their husbands and children.

Just before they reached their destination, a piece of paper fluttered across Jo's path. An announcement of some sort.

"What's this?"

She scooped up the flyer and opened it to find a picture of a yarn basket, replete with knitting needles and skeins of wool. Beneath the drawing ran a boldface slogan: Our Boys Need Socks, so Knit Your Bit!

"What do you have there?" Rebekkah asked.

"I think it's a war poster. From the American Red Cross. They're looking for volunteers. See?"

Jo tried to show her the parchment, but the line of women behind them gently surged, so she tucked the flyer into her pocket for safekeeping.

Night had fallen, and soft lamplight beckoned as they approached the canteen. The sound of cicadas preparing for an evening concert filled the air with a faint thrum.

They entered the hall together, and Jo's head immediately snapped back in wonder. The decorating committee had outdone itself this evening. Reams of red, white, and blue bunting swagged the ceiling, high and low, and even more paper bunting laced the picnic tables.

Best of all, each place setting featured a delicate porcelain teacup edged with painted roses. So refined, instead of the usual battered tin.

"Beautiful," she breathed.

"I agree," Rebekkah said. "Who would've thought they could turn our dull little canteen into an actual tearoom?"

Along the wall at the end of the room, a picnic table held delicate finger sandwiches and pastel-colored macaroons.

Yellow cornflowers sprouted from a silver ice bucket. A stack of porcelain plates—no doubt in the same pattern as the teacups—beckoned.

"I'll get us something to eat," Jo offered. "A plateful of whatever you want."

Rebekkah's eyes narrowed. "You don't have to baby me, Jo. I spent years and years taking care of myself before you came along."

"Of course, you did. I only thought you might want to chat with the other women before the program starts. You seem to know so many of them."

"I know what you thought. Don't forget I like the cucumber ones. Maybe a petit four or two."

"Aye, aye, captain." Jo snapped off a brisk salute and set off for the table of delicacies. Clumps of women stood here, there, and everywhere, and she had to maneuver around them to reach the table stocked with finger sandwiches.

"Good evening," a loud voice behind her boomed.

She turned to find Genevieve Johnson, the shopkeeper's wife, nearby. A fussy, overfed woman, she seemed to love nothing more than eating sweets and trading gossip. Or ... doing both, if she could manage it.

"Hello, Mrs. Johnson. How are you this evening?" Jo carefully reached for a porcelain dinner plate.

"Not so well, my dear. Not so well at all. Terrible gout. I would've thought the army's bland food would've cured me by now. I can't imagine why it hasn't."

Jo noticed the woman had stacked her plate sky-high. "I can't imagine why, either. But I feel for you. I've heard gout can be quite painful."

"You have no idea. Anyway, I think you're going to enjoy tonight's program. It's about embroidery knots. Can you imagine? I, for one, am keen to do something new with my needlework."

"Embroidery knots, hmm? How interesting," Jo tried to sound enthusiastic, which wasn't easy.

"Yes. We must all do our part to keep our spirits up during this terrible war. Nothing brightens our men's moods—I've found—like a well-kept home."

"Undoubtedly." While Jo longed to offer a different opinion, she knew better than to challenge the shopkeeper's wife in public. Albigence couldn't care one whit about her embroidery techniques. He wouldn't be able to tell a backstitch from a buttonhole stitch if his life depended on it. He wouldn't even notice the new pillow she'd stitched from the sack of Bob White flour when he returned.

Jo deliberately focused on the finger sandwiches— careful to select two of the cucumber ones for Rebekkah— before she returned to her friend's side.

"Why are you smiling?" Rebekkah asked.

"I just had the most ridiculous conversation. Do you think your husband cares about your embroidery techniques?"

"My Otto? Of course not. Why would you ask?"

"Apparently, we're going to hear a lecture tonight on that very subject. Which will no doubt stoke our husbands' affections for us even more."

"Now, Jo. You promised to behave. Weren't you looking forward to this meeting?"

"I was. I mean, I am. But that doesn't mean I have to love everything about it, does it?"

Her friend leaned in. "For what it's worth, I agree with you. Who cares about embroidery knots when the only thread available is black or gray? I daresay such colors would make for some rather depressing samplers."

"Exactly," Jo said, once they stopped giggling. "I do wish we'd hear a program about something that mattered. Something important."

"What did you expect? Look around. These women grew up in fancy drawing rooms, surrounded by embroidery looms and sewing baskets. They know precious little about anything else."

"Don't you suppose that could change, though? Don't you suppose they could be encouraged to care about something more important? Especially if it's presented in the right way?"

"Wait a minute. I don't like that look in your eye. What're you up to?"

"Me?" Jo feigned innocence. "I have no idea what you're talking about."

Before Rebekkah could reply, Mamie Benedict, the group's formidable president, approached the lectern.

"Good evening, ladies," she said. "It's time to call the meeting to order."

Before anyone could object, and before Jo could change her mind, she nervously stood. Butterflies roiled her insides, but that didn't stop her. "Excuse me. Madame President?"

The residual chatter softened as the audience fell silent. Horribly silent. Awkwardly silent. As silent as her father the day she announced she wanted to join his law practice when she turned eighteen. He too had stared at her bug-eyed, like the women all around her now.

"Oh, no," Rebekkah softly moaned. "Please, Jo. Sit down."

"But this is important," she whispered back.

"You there," Mrs. Benedict said. "What's the meaning of this? Do you have a question?"

"Yes, ma'am." Jo swallowed the lump in her throat. "I understand we're going to hear a lecture tonight on embroidery knots."

"Correct. I've asked our sergeant-at-arms here to read us a selection from a magazine. A magazine that comes all the way from *New York City*, I might add."

Mrs. Benedict said the town's name reverently, as if the group should feel privileged to have something—anything—sent to them from New York City.

"Which sounds delightful," Jo agreed, as she slowly withdrew the rumpled war poster from her pocket. The paper fluttered like sailcloth in a breeze. "But do you suppose we could also learn about something else? Perhaps something more practical?"

"More practical? I daresay needlepoint is one of the more practical of the household arts."

"I'm sure you're correct, but it seems the American Red Cross needs our help." Jo timidly lifted the paper higher. "They'd like us to knit socks for the boys overseas."

"Socks?" At this point, the sergeant-at-arms decided to join the fray. "For men we don't even know? And just who might you be?"

"My name is Josephine Pembrooke. My husband is away at the medical officers' training camp. I only thought—"

"Pardon me, Mrs. Pembrooke," the woman said, "but we have a system in place for this kind of thing. We ask everyone to hold her comments until the end of the meeting. That's when we open the floor to questions. If we have time, of course. Which we seldom do."

"I just thought—"

"You see, we follow Robert's Rules of Order, which was named for our very own General Henry Robert."

"Yes, I'm quite aware of Robert's Rules of Order. I found this paper on the footpath, you see. Apparently, the American Red Cross needs volunteers. To help with knitting. Socks, specifically. For the servicemen ..." Jo limped to the end of her little speech more flustered than ever.

"We don't even know those men." The sergeant-at-arms looked aghast. "What would our husbands say?"

"I think they'd understand our work is for charity," Jo said. Surely, someone else would agree with her. Even though she'd found the paper on the footpath, thoughtlessly discarded, the idea still had merit.

"That rubbish in your hands probably came from the colonel's office," the sergeant-at-arms snapped. "No self-respecting woman I know would make such an indecent proposition."

"Well, I, for one, think it's a spectacular idea," a new voice called out.

She glanced down to see Rebekkah struggling to rise next to her. The effort took a moment, which seemed to add weight to the occasion. "Why don't we put the matter to a vote? I think it would be the most democratic thing to do."

The sergeant-at-arms seemed at a loss for words.

"You see," Rebekkah continued, undeterred, "Josephine here could organize all of it. She's got quite the knack for organization. She's the camp's new schoolmarm, you see."

Rebekkah threw her a sly wink.

How crafty of her.

They'd discussed Jo's role many times over a pitcher of ginger soda in Rebekkah's kitchen. How whenever someone new learned about Jo's occupation, her demeanor automatically changed. Women would snap to attention, as if they'd suddenly become very interested in whatever the schoolteacher had to say.

People did it all the time. Mothers, in particular, stumbled all over themselves to get on Jo's good side. They wanted to help their children by ingratiating themselves to the schoolmarm. Which was ridiculous, of course. Jo would never favor one child over another, but the women in this room didn't know that.

"Yes, I'd be happy to organize everything," Jo said. "We could buy all our yarn at the post exchange." She gazed over the audience until she found who she was looking for. "Perhaps our very own shopkeeper could order the materials for us. Isn't that right, Mrs. Johnson?"

"Hmm?"

She'd startled the portly woman, who held a pale blue petit four to her lips.

"But, of course," the woman said, once she'd recovered. "I'm sure my husband would be happy to help us."

"Wonderful," Jo said. "I'll organize everything. Let's take a vote then."

With that, she sat before anyone else could object to the plan. And, before she fainted dead away.

She only basked in the glow of self-satisfaction for a moment or two.

"You were very brave, dear." A woman to her right leaned across the table to address her. "The army is so rigid, you know. They frown at women speaking their minds. I've heard they'll even deny promotions if it happens with an officer's wife."

"Promotions?" The warm glow instantly cooled. *Albigence.* She hadn't even considered him. Or his reaction. While she initially thought he'd be proud of her—after all, weren't they supposed to help the brave men fighting overseas?—nothing was guaranteed.

Perhaps she'd made a horrible mistake.

CHAPTER FOUR

ALBIGENCE

CAMP GREENLEAF, GAINESVILLE, GEORGIA

LATE SEPTEMBER 1917

Albigence was good to go the moment a clerk requisitioned him a new pair of spectacles in the infirmary.

He shoved the round lenses on his face and purposefully strode back to his quarters. Let the other psychologists fritter away their precious weekend with childish pranks. He still had work to do.

When Monday rolled around, he really *had* memorized the entire section on *War Psychoses and Neuroses*, word for word. He approached the classroom confidently the next day, looking forward to an evening lecture for once.

Even though he'd begun to miss Josephine terribly, he wanted to make her proud.

He barely waited for the instructor to ask the first question when he immediately thrust his hand in the air. Ditto for the second question. By the fifth time it happened, though, the instructor's smile thinned a bit.

"Dr. Pembrooke," the man said, "since you seem to be an expert on the material, perhaps you could join me at the lectern."

To Albigence, the man resembled a portly walrus with gray whiskers and beady eyes, and he approached the plump pinniped with caution.

"Of course, sir."

"Now then," the instructor said, once Albigence reached the lectern, "we're going to run through one of the actual intelligence tests. The very same test you will give to soldiers when you return to your own camps."

The instructor clawed a piece of paper from the lectern and held it out, along with a pencil.

"I'm going to read from the script, and I want you to pretend to be a soldier. An average soldier, of say, average intelligence. From Kansas, or somewhere else in the Midwest."

"Yes, sir."

"Attention!"

Albigence's head snapped back in surprise.

"Oh, did I forget to mention the tone?" the instructor asked. "You'll need to yell at the men to grab their attention. You should expect—no, demand—perfect order and a prompt response to all your commands. Don't settle for anything less."

"I see, sir." At this point, the room had begun to warm, and Albigence's cheeks simmered.

"Now, the purpose of this examination is to see how well you can remember, consider, and carry out what you're told to do," the instructor said. "We're not looking for crazy people here. Let me make that abundantly clear."

Crazy people? Albigence couldn't quite make sense of such verbiage coming from an official army speech. The term sounded undignified. Crass, even.

The instructor continued, undeterred. "Our aim is to learn what you are best suited to do. Your grade on this examination will be noted on your qualification card. It'll also go to your company commander. Some of the things I'm going to tell you will be *very* easy to do. Some you may find *very* hard. No one expects you to make a perfect grade, but do the *very* best you can."

A rustling of cloth sounded as someone lifted his hand. By now, sweat poured from Albigence's temples, so he welcomed the distraction.

"Excuse me," the student said from the safety of his seat, "but aren't we giving the test to soldiers to weed them out? You make it sound as if we're looking to promote them."

"I didn't write the questions," the instructor snapped. "A man by the name of Robert Yerkes did. Are you questioning Dr. Yerkes's methods?"

"No, sir. Of course not."

The student sounded deflated. They'd all heard of the renowned psychologist, and several in the audience had studied under him, Albigence included.

"We can't very well tell test-takers we're looking to eliminate them, can we?" the teacher said. "This way, every man will think he has a chance to pass the test. Even if he doesn't."

Ah-ha. That was it—the reason for the exact wording. The army wanted to lull every soldier into thinking he could do well. Recruits would then be much more likely to try their best. The technical term for that kind of trickery was "reverse psychology," but soldiers didn't need to know that.

"Anyway," the instructor barked, "soldiers are expected to listen very carefully to commands before they carry them out. Exactly so. I'm going to give you some commands. Let's see how well you can carry them out."

"I'll try, sir," Albigence mumbled.

"Now, look at your test. Each row contains several shapes ... circles, triangles, and so forth. I'll tell you what to do with the circles in question one. Then, we'll move along to question two. And so forth. When I call 'Attention,' you must stop what you're doing and hold up your pencil. Just so." Here, he mimed the act of brandishing a pencil with a fore flipper. "Don't put the pencil to paper again until I say 'Go.' Remember, always wait for the word 'Go.'"

"Excuse me," another voice interrupted, "but what if the soldiers don't understand what we're saying to them? What if their English is poor? Then, what?"

Amazingly, the instructor didn't snap this time. He smiled, or at least the expression looked like a smile, hidden as it was by the scrum of whiskers.

"An excellent question. By this point, men will be separated into two camps—those who speak English, which includes even a rudimentary grasp of the English language, and those who don't. We haven't quite figured out how to separate them, or when, but we'll deal with those pesky details later."

The instructor's smile—or what Albigence could see of it—took a sly turn.

"Sometimes, foreigners like to pretend they can't speak English. Ha! Those are the men we don't want in the army anyway. We won't abide such trickery."

"Hear, hear," a familiar voice said. The voice sounded like Frank, the slimy weasel. "I couldn't agree with you more, sir. In your esteemed opinion, aren't there some men who shouldn't even be in the army to begin with? Perhaps due to their personalities? I've heard of one man in particular who is so antisocial his behavior reflects badly on his whole unit. Would you please share your thoughts on that, sir?"

Slowly, but surely, Albigence realized what was happening. Frank was talking about him. Him!

Blast that Frank!

"Hmmm. You've raised a very interesting point." The professor sounded intrigued. "Yes, I do believe some men are ill suited for military life. Quite so. Which means they should be encouraged to follow a different path. Why don't you hold that thought for the next lecture, Doctor? We'll have more time to discuss your thoughts later. Today, we need to focus on the examination itself."

By this time, Albigence was seething. He knew Frank considered him an adversary—after the hideous incident with the spectacles, there could be no doubt—but he didn't realize Frank wanted to see him demoted. Of all the sneaky, conniving—

"Attention," the instructor bellowed. "Pencil up! Look at the circles in question one. When I say 'Go'—but not a moment before—make a figure 'one' in the first circle and draw a cross through the third. Now, Go!"

Albigence stared at the paper, dumbfounded, since he hadn't been paying attention. He hastily scribbled a number "one" in the first circle, and then he slashed a crude cross through the third. All in the nick of time.

"Attention!"

Here, Albigence froze.

"Young man! Have you forgotten the instructions already? 'Attention' means you're to put your pencil in the air. Remember?"

"Oh, um, yes," Albigence stammered. "Of course, sir. Right away, sir." Up went his pencil in the air.

"Good," the teacher said. "Much better. Now, look at the second question, where the circles have numbers in them. When I say 'Go,' draw a line from circle number three to circle number six. The line should pass above circle number four, but below circle number five."

The words tumbled end over end. Thank goodness, Albigence's reflexes kicked in at this point. He'd developed rather quick reflexes as a child, thanks to the constant bullying.

"Go," the instructor yelled.

This time, Albigence grasped the pencil with everything he had and drew a firm line over the fourth circle and under the fifth. By now, perspiration saturated his dress shirt, but he barely noticed.

So it went. By the time he finished the last question on the page, Albigence felt physically ill. Drained beyond measure.

"Remember," the teacher said, as he finally—mercifully—allowed Albigence to return to his seat, "that 'attention' always means to put your pencil up. Give the men the instructions clearly. Enunciate. Hold them to account. There will be no coddling of pretenders or charlatans."

Albigence slumped into his chair as soon as he reached it.

"But couldn't the testing conditions affect the outcome?" a student in the fourth row called out.

"How so, young man?"

"Well, if we yell at the soldiers, who's to say they might not get flustered and botch the whole thing?"

The portly walrus shrugged, apparently unconcerned. "I suppose such a thing could happen. But when you're sitting in a foxhole on the fields of France, do you think your commanding officer is going to whisper his orders delicately? No, of course not. I dare say, what we yell at the men now will be nothing compared to what they'll face overseas. Our duty—our solemn duty—is to prepare them for conditions they'll face on the battlefield."

However, at that point, a smidgen of doubt had wormed its way into Albigence's mind. While it might be true soldiers needed brusque handling, they'd never reach the fields of France to begin with if they couldn't pass the intelligence test. Albigence debated whether to voice his concerns aloud, but he had yet to recover from his exhausting bit of playacting in front of the class.

The evening drew to a close in a most unexpected way. By the time the instructor dismissed them for the night, the other psychologists crowded around Albigence and began to congratulate him. A few even slapped him heartily on the back. Either they pitied him for having to participate in the little scene with the instructor, or they thought he did quite well, considering the circumstances.

Could it be some people thought he deserved to be in the army? No matter what Frank said? Well, by golly, he'd accept their pity, or their congratulations. Anything to feel like one of the men.

For the first time in his life, Albigence felt like part of a team. A hastily assembled team of intellectuals, but a team, nonetheless.

Which was a wonderful feeling. Something he wasn't about to give up. Not for anyone, or anything.

CHAPTER FIVE

JOSEPHINE

IMMIGRANT ENCAMPMENT, CAMP TRAVIS

LATE SEPTEMBER 1917

By the time the meeting of the Ladies' Benevolent Society drew to a close, Jo felt weak with relief. She'd managed to speak her piece and escape the hall unscathed, which wasn't easy, considering her status as a newcomer or her unbridled nerves.

"Well, that was something," Rebekkah said, as they moved away. By now, the sawing of insect wings filled the night air.

"I know. I thought for sure one of the women was going to banish me to the rafters. Pin me up there with all the froufrou."

Rebekkah laughed. "You're something else, Jo. We should probably hurry, though. They could change their minds and run after us."

The women hurried down the path, with Jo helping Rebekkah along like always. They didn't stop rushing until a strange noise reached them.

Someone, somewhere, was playing an instrument. A harmonica, perhaps?

They scanned the horizon. Apparently, the sound came from a far-off campsite, where a trio of men sat before an open tent. They perched on overturned apple crates and used an Indian trading blanket on the ground as a table. One of the men held a harmonica to his lips, while the others tossed playing cards to the ground.

"Good evening," Rebekkah called as they approached, since she seemed to know the men.

"*Su'mae.*" The musician waved the mouth organ in greeting, his thick Irish brogue unmistakable. He wore baggy khaki trousers and a flat cap—all of which looked timeworn.

Rebekkah moved even closer, which gave Jo no choice but to follow along.

"Hello, Euyon," Rebekkah called. "And Derwyn. Who have we here?" She nodded at a third man, who ducked his head shyly.

"His name's Glyn, don't you know," the harmonica player—apparently named Euyon—said. "Fresh off the boat. Speaks mostly Welsh, so go slow with him."

"I see. Su'mae, Glyn."

Jo blinked when the man turned to acknowledge the greeting. The stranger was remarkably handsome. He had eyes the color of delft, a strong jaw, and hair like burnished copper.

"Su'mae," the man said, shyly.

"The two of them are playing Whist," the musician explained with a nod. "Though not very well, mind you. Care to join the lads for a round?"

"No, thank you." Rebekkah shook her head. "We're on our way home."

Instinctively, Jo understood why Rebekkah couldn't accept the man's offer. To speak to a man who wasn't one's husband—at night, no less—was one thing, but to play cards with him, in public, was quite another. While Rebekkah enjoyed a fair amount of immunity as a preacher's wife, she couldn't control everything people said about her.

"Who might this lovely lass be?" Euyon asked, with another wave of the harmonica.

"This is our Josephine," Rebekkah said. "Josephine Pembrooke. She's new to camp too. But, Euyon, let's be serious for a moment. How are your papers coming along?"

"Only fair," he admitted. "I have scads left to do for me citizenship. Still a bit o' trouble with the language, I'm afraid."

"Well, we need to fix that. Come by the parsonage tomorrow morning with your forms, and we'll get you sorted."

"A thousand thanks. Maybe I can teach you a tune on the gob iron for your kindness."

"That'd be lovely."

As usual, Rebekkah had completely charmed the man. The more time Jo spent around her friend, the more she realized people blossomed in Rebekkah's presence. Like morning glories in sunshine, they couldn't help but open up around her. Such graciousness was a skill Jo longed to learn and one she hoped to emulate.

"Perhaps I ... I could help," she sputtered. She'd directed the comment at Euyon, who seemed to be the group's ringleader.

"Aye, 'tis fair kind of you," he said. "It's our Glyn we worry for. Derwyn here speaks well enough, and he knows how to set the bones and such. They'll have want of him in the operatin' theatre when he passes the tests. Not so our Glyn. He doesn't know many words. Not many a'tall."

"I could fix that," Jo said. The words flew from her mouth before she realized what was happening. Graciousness was one thing, but helping a strange man was something altogether different. Especially one with such a handsome face, which made her heart flutter.

Glyn responded with another shy smile. She hadn't noticed the dimples before. He had deep groves at the corners of his mouth, as if a midwife had pinched his cheeks there when he was born and left thick thumbprints.

"You see, I'm a schoolmarm," Jo hurried to say, her thoughts aswirl. "It's what I do. I teach people. You know, things."

"T'ings?" Now, the handsome face looked confused.

"Yes, things," she said. "Like math, reading—all sorts of things."

"You see," Euyon said to his friend, "she's a schoolteacher. *Athro ysgol.*"

"Ah. Athro ysgol." Another shy smile. *"Angel trugaredd."*

Euyon laughed. "He called you an angel of mercy, miss. You seem to have already bewitched our Glyn."

"Um … tell him we can use the schoolhouse." Had the weather warmed over the past few moments? For some reason, her cheeks felt even hotter now, and her collar pinched.

"That so?" Euyon said.

"Yes. Now, mind you, the schoolhouse isn't much to look at." Maybe if she kept talking, she could talk herself right out of this awkward situation. "But there are plenty of books. No shelves for them, but plenty of books."

"'Tis an interesting proposition." Euyon cocked his head. "Well, the saints are on your side today, miss. Glyn here happens to be fair handy with a hammer."

"He's a *saer*," Derwyn explained. "How do you say, a … a carpenter."

"A carpenter?" Jo said. "That's wonderful!"

"Well, then, it's settled." Rebekkah beamed at them. "This arrangement will no doubt suit everyone. I'm so glad we stopped by to speak with you."

"Aye," Euyon said. "I'll see you at church tomorrow, Miss Rebekkah."

"Perfect. Goodnight to you all." Rebekkah deftly stepped away from the trio. "Sleep well. Who knows what tomorrow will bring?"

"Yes, goodnight," Jo mumbled, as she followed her friend's lead.

No matter what happened between now and then, it looked like she'd gotten herself into a tricky situation. While she welcomed the help of a carpenter, did the help have to come from someone with such a fine face and strapping physique? What would Albigence think?

There was no telling. And, like Rebekkah said, anything could happen.

CHAPTER SIX

ALBIGENCE

CAMP GREENLEAF, GAINESVILLE, GEORGIA

LATE SEPTEMBER 1917

Albigence wearily approached the cabin after yet another long evening lecture. The instructors demanded so much of them, but then again, perhaps he couldn't blame them.

They'd finally arrived at the end of their training. Six long weeks had passed in a blur. The days had been hard, but at least his instructors had prepared him for whatever he might face when he returned to Camp Travis.

Which reminded him of something else. He'd received another letter from Josephine yesterday, which arrived by rail. The perfumed envelope sat on his desk, unopened, because he'd been too tired to read the letter yesterday. He worried she might complain again about the shoddy living conditions at Camp Travis or a general lack of activities or the terrible food in the camp's mess hall.

Didn't she know airing those complaints publicly, in an actual letter, was dangerous? Everyone knew the army read their letters. It was common knowledge. He really couldn't blame them, since the whole country was at war. The military had every right to go through his personal effects and read whatever it wanted. Still ...

He retreated to his cot, grasping Josephine's letter in one fist. He gazed at her handwriting for several moments. She had the delicate, elegant script of a learned woman. One glance at his name—the way she gently arched the "A" above the smaller letters—and his resolve softened. Perhaps she'd found a way to make peace with her role at the camp by now. Perhaps she wanted to tell him about her latest adventures at the post exchange, since she seemed to enjoy shopping there. *That was it.* She wanted to provide him with lighthearted vignettes of camp life whilst he was away.

In any event, they'd be together soon enough, and all would be forgiven then.

He calmly took hold of the envelope and lifted the flap, which someone had sliced through with a pen knife.

Dearest Albigence,
The most incredible thing happened last week. I do hope I've made you proud.
I attended a meeting of the Ladies' Benevolent Society, although I hadn't planned to go at all. Do you remember the group I told you about? They hold their meetings in the canteen, and I must say the decorating committee outdid itself. Between the colorful adornments and pretty porcelain tea sets, they transformed a dreary army canteen into an actual tearoom, which looked divine. Simply divine.

Albigence lowered the letter as he considered it. As best he could recall, she'd wanted no part of the group when they first arrived at camp. In fact, she'd accused the group of being "silly," "frivolous," and "decadent."

My, how things have changed.

Up went the letter again.

I do believe I was wrong, Albigence. Terribly wrong. The women are much friendlier here than I expected. Of course, it may be due to my companion. Everyone seems to love my new friend, Rebekkah. I'm sure you will too. She possesses the incredible ability to put people at ease. It's really quite magical. People feel drawn to her —like flies to honey.

Regardless, I had my own success whilst at the meeting. I managed to screw up my courage and suggest we do something different. Something more edifying than learning about embroidery techniques. Can you imagine? They wanted to teach us how to knot our threads when our poor soldiers are sacrificing their lives for us.

As luck would have it, I'd come across a war poster from the American Red Cross whilst on my way to the meeting. I suggested —oh, you would have been so proud of the way I stood my ground—that we undertake a service project at the meetings. Miracle of miracles, the women agreed with me. Such an amazing thing to behold. You could've heard a pin drop when I spoke.

To wit, I'm going to organize supplies for the first project, and we'll take up the craft at our next meeting. Isn't that exciting? What a wonderful feeling to be useful again. On so many fronts.

I miss you, and I pray daily for your return.

Your loving wife,

Josephine

Albigence slowly lowered the letter. What did she mean, "you could've heard a pin drop when I spoke?" Surely, Joesphine didn't make her little speech in front of an entire hall full of strangers? But the letter suggested as much. A speech? She didn't even know these people, and she had no standing with them yet.

Could it be she commandeered a whole meeting for her own purposes?

Oh, Josephine.

He didn't expect this when he suggested she become more entrenched in the camp's community. No, this wasn't what he had in mind at all. Not at all. To draw attention to herself like that—at her very first meeting no less—was horrifying.

He arose from the cot now and began to pace, too upset to sit still. His Josephine. Interrupting a meeting. Speaking her mind.

What would his superiors say? He could only imagine what they'd think when they heard about his wife's behavior. They'd think he possessed a wife who couldn't control herself in public. Oh, the embarrassment!

Perhaps worst of all, she expected him to be proud of her behavior. He couldn't fathom it. They'd discussed Albigence's desire to move up in the ranks—and at great length. Josephine seemed to agree that any promotions he received would only help their union. Perhaps the army would make him a supervisor soon. Chief medical officer, even. Which would secure their financial future and allow her to quit her teaching position as soon as the babies arrived.

After all, once they began a family, she couldn't very well work anymore, could she? No, they'd need the extra income a promotion would provide. A large salary from the military to support them and their equally large family. She'd agreed to the plan. Wholeheartedly. Or so he thought.

After pacing a bit more, he finally stopped. No, she was mistaken if she thought he'd be proud of her for speaking her mind. There was no telling who else knew about her indiscretion. No telling which attaché had read her letters in the army's communications office.

Thank goodness he was going home next week. Who knew what other trouble she could get herself into?

CHAPTER SEVEN

JOSEPHINE

SCHOOLHOUSE, CAMP TRAVIS

OCTOBER 1917

Only one more week to go until Albigence returns, and only one more week until the officers' children descend on the schoolhouse.

The building looks so much better now, Jo thought. Thanks to Glyn. He'd taken a dreary schoolhouse and completely transformed it. First, he added fanciful trim to all the windows and doors. Then, he shellacked the walls until they shone, before he did the same with the floorboards. He even made a giant chalkboard out of leftover two-by-fours, which he mounted to the wall.

Those changes were just the beginning. A few weeks later, when he moved on to the exterior of the building, he noticed something she hadn't. The schoolhouse lacked a belltower. The building was a hastily-built plain wood box, like all the other buildings at Camp Travis, with no extras. This meant Jo had no way to call the children to their lessons each morning.

So, Glyn worked until the wee hours one night to create an arched tower for the imagined bell, replete with gothic swirls and crossed tin rods for a weathervane. Where on earth he managed to find the right poles to construct a weathervane was beyond her, but he took so much care with the project, his efforts touched her heart.

Afterward, Jo brought the camp's requisitions officer to the site and politely requested a copper bell, taking care to sound respectful, since she wasn't used to telling a man what to do. The bell was due to arrive from San Antonio any day now.

Jo looked forward to each new day more and more. Granted, Glyn wasn't the easiest pupil to teach, since he toyed with the cuffs of his shirt whenever he got the slightest bit bored, but she enjoyed a good challenge.

Before the sun barely cracked the horizon, she'd roll off the horsehair mattress in the cabin and race to the schoolyard, which looked so much better now. Like an honest-to-goodness schoolhouse with white milk paint on the walls, a half-moon deck that offered a bird's-eye view of the schoolyard, and a jaunty belltower, just waiting to be filled.

For her part, Jo created a deck of flash cards which included simple English words and phrases. Much like those creative Parker brothers had done with the *Game of ABCs for Little Ones,* she filled the cards with fanciful colors and drawings. She didn't include anything too difficult, only the basics, which the army would employ on tests. She wished she had more time to teach Glyn something beyond the basics, but at least he'd have a general foothold in the English language.

Time had flown. The past months of summertime had dulled her memory of how much she loved teaching people—how much she enjoyed sitting on a bench with a student and watching his eyes spark.

The only time Jo felt uncomfortable with her pupil was when he fell into a funk. This happened whenever Glyn tried to tell her about his past. Using hand gestures and words, he clumsily explained how he lost both parents while still a child. He almost starved on the streets of Wales, he mimed, until a kindly carpenter took him in. A carpenter who later lost his own life in a woodworking accident, which left Glyn homeless once again. So, he hopped aboard a steamship bound for America, which he'd heard was the Promised Land for someone like him. Someone orphaned, hungry, desperate. He wanted to become a soldier, earn his citizenship papers, and then he'd enjoy the good life. At least, that was the plan.

"Aren't you getting a little attached to him?" Rebekkah asked, at the end of another day. They sat in Rebekkah's kitchen with yet another jug of ginger soda in front of them. "I don't have to remind you about what happened with King David and Bathsheba, do I?"

Jo flashed an eyeroll. "I have no idea what you're talking about."

"Think about it. King David saw Bathsheba from the rooftop at the palace. He risked everything he had to pursue her, but the woman was married. That union ended in tragedy, if you'll recall."

"Why, Rebekkah. Get your mind out of the gutter. I'm giving the man English lessons. Nothing more and nothing less."

"Are you, now? I can't help but notice the way he looks at you. Or the way you look at him. You're treading on thin ice, Jo."

"Nonsense. You sound like one of those women's magazines we read after our meetings in the canteen."

Lately, the Ladies' Benevolent Society had ordered more magazines, beyond ones focused on needlework, for the group's members. The women gathered around the group's secretary and listened to her breathlessly recite the latest news from New York. All the stories involved scandalous celebrities or fallen politicians. Although Rebekkah didn't seem the type to enjoy such salacious things, she might have overheard them a time or two.

"I wish you'd think about it," Rebekkah said, more firmly this time. "There are other ways to cheat on your spouse that don't involve anything physical. If you focus your attention on another man, you might as well be cheating. That's not fair to Albigence, since he's not even here to defend himself."

"I don't think that's what I'm doing." If Jo sounded defensive, so be it. She couldn't help herself. After all, Rebekkah introduced her to Glyn in the first place. Rebekkah came up with the plan to trade English lessons for carpentry. Rebekkah spoke to strange men around a campfire. At night, no less! How dare she criticize Jo now.

"All right, all right." Rebekkah threw up her hands. "I'll drop it. If you say nothing's going on, then nothing's going on. Just don't let some foolish infatuation come between you and your husband. After all, look what happened to King David."

They'd had that conversation more than a week ago, and Jo had avoided Rebekkah ever since. Not because she thought Rebekkah was right, but because Rebekkah had hurt her feelings. Those bruised feelings had yet to heal.

Although ... it was all she could do sometimes to concentrate on the flash cards when she was around Glyn. By mid-afternoon, as the temperature soared, he'd sometimes remove his work shirt to expose a sleeveless one beneath it. She tried not to stare, but the man had the muscled arms of a stevedore. The way he casually hoisted a two-by-four onto his shoulders left her weak in the knees.

But, then … as soon as they started their lessons, her infatuation would cool. As strong as he was—and he was strong enough for two men—Glyn couldn't comprehend the most basic rules of the English language. "I before e," for one thing. Which wouldn't have been so bad, but he didn't seem to care. He seemed more curious about the wood pencil in his hand or a dust mote floating through the air. Anything but the flash cards, which she'd worked so hard to create. The lessons bored him.

He was so different from Albigence. While her husband couldn't compete with Glyn physically, he was intellectually superior in every way. He loved learning for learning's sake, something she wished Glyn would try to emulate at least once in a while.

Each day followed the same schedule—two hours' worth of tortured English lessons, while he fiddled and squirmed on the hard seat—followed by two hours' worth of carpentry. While he rebuilt the schoolhouse, Jo organized the bookshelves, rubbed linseed oil onto the benches, or copied the lesson plans until lunchtime arrived. Then, they'd spread the Indian trading blanket on the ground and eat in companionable silence until it was time to repeat the process.

Some nights, she returned to her cabin so exhausted, she collapsed onto the cot fully clothed. Drained by another long day of tutoring. Those were the best nights, though, because she could forget how lonely the cabin was without Albigence. How dark the rooms had become without anyone there to light the lamps. How thick the silence grew.

She'd return to the cabin and fall straightaway onto the mattress after dinner, where she slept soundly, dreamlessly ... until the morning sun roused her for yet another day.

At the end of the week, Jo approached the schoolhouse with her usual sense of optimism.

She was about to enter the schoolyard's gate when something caught her attention. A dark form appeared on the horizon—a gray splotch against pastel sky. A band of soft pink underlined the clouds and made them glow from within. The splotch wore a bowler hat she thought looked familiar, and he carried a battered cardboard suitcase at his side.

Could it be? Was it possible?

Albigence? But he wasn't due home for—what?—two more days? She quickly calculated the time in her head and realized she must've been wrong. She must've lost track of time, with the changes at the schoolhouse and the daily English lessons.

Meanwhile, the figure moved closer. When she couldn't wait one ... more ... second, Jo ran down the path and flung open her arms. "Albigence!"

He hurried to meet her, as well, but just before they hugged, he stopped.

"Hold on, dear," he said, with a wary glance over his shoulder. "People could be watching us. Let's save our greetings for the cabin, shall we? Oh, Josephine. I've missed you."

"Have you? I couldn't tell by the tone of your voice."

"Oh, but I have," he insisted. "I thought about you every day. More than once a day, sometimes."

"Well, that's something. I've missed you too."

She waited for him to hug her. While the military didn't approve of overt affection in public, an embrace was the least he could do. They'd been apart for almost two whole months, for goodness' sake.

"Aren't you going to even take my hand, Albigence?"

"Yes, of course, but let's wait until we're alone. Now, what have we here?" he asked, as he glanced at the schoolhouse—an obvious ploy to change the subject. "I see you've made additions to the building. The facade looks completely different. What a marvelous transformation."

"Yes, isn't it?" Jo followed his gaze. "I've—we've—been working very hard to get the place ready for the children. Oh, Albigence, you should see the inside. It's as lovely as the outside."

"We?" he said, picking up on something. "You've had help with it, then?"

Just then, Glyn rounded the corner of the building with his battered tin lunchpail in hand.

"Over there is the person who's responsible," she said, as she pointed toward him. "Come and meet Glyn. He's a Welsh carpenter, and he did all the work you see here."

"He did?" Albigence squinted. "Well, I suppose the army's paying him for his trouble?"

"Oh, no, Albigence. We've worked out a barter. I provide English lessons, which he'll use later when he takes the tests, and he repairs the schoolhouse."

"Such a cozy arrangement. I hope it won't set tongues to wagging."

"Why should it? We've always been aboveboard. We've always worked in plain sight."

"Hmph. No doubt." Albigence tugged at his vest and hoisted the cardboard suitcase. "All right, then. Let's go meet the man."

Together they walked to the building, with Albigence careful to keep some distance between them, lest their hands touch and set people to talking. Goodness knows she didn't want to upset Albigence more than she already had.

By the time they reached Glyn, he'd already set down his lunchpail.

"Hello, Glyn," Jo said, brightly. "I'd like to introduce you to my husband, Albigence."

"It's nice to meet you, son." Albigence's tone sounded as stiff as his posture.

He didn't shake Glyn's hand. Instead, he quietly studied the man, as if he was a specimen he'd like to put under a microscope.

"Glyn is a wonderful carpenter," Jo said, hoping to ease the way. "He's done a marvelous job with the schoolhouse."

"I can see that. Thank you for helping my wife."

All the while, Glyn frowned, as if he couldn't keep up with the conversation.

"He likes what you've done to the schoolhouse," Jo said, more slowly. "He admires your carpentry." She mimed a hammer hitting a nail. "He wants to thank you for your carpentry."

"Ah. *Creoso*," Glyn said. "How do you say you're ... you're welcome."

"Very good," Jo enthused. "You see, we're trying to get Glyn ready to take his citizenship test. Along with all the other tests he'll need to join the army. I think he's almost ready, don't you?"

"Perhaps." Albigence nodded. "I'll no doubt see you in the testing quarters, son. Best of luck to you."

Her husband turned to leave, but Jo quickly took hold of his arm.

"Hush," she whispered, under her breath. "Stop calling him 'son.' He's not a boy. He's a grown man. You're the same age, no doubt."

Glyn had moved away by this point, so he had no idea they were talking about him.

"It's all right," Albigence said. "I don't think he minds. He doesn't seem very bright, does he? Are you sure he's all right, here" ... "He tapped his finger against his skull. "... upstairs? You know. Mentally?"

"Of course, Glyn's all right," she snapped. "He's just uncomfortable with English. That's all. I find it helps to speak to him slowly and deliberately."

"I see. Well, off we go."

Albigence finally placed his hand on top of hers—his first show of affection all morning—and guided her away from the schoolhouse. She would've protested, since she'd promised to give Glyn their usual lesson today, but her husband seemed intent on getting her away from the property.

Instead, she called out her goodbyes and allowed Albigence to lead her down the path to their own cabin.

Once inside, he sniffed the air, as if he detected a bad odor. "You haven't made many changes in here, have you? I thought for sure you were going to get the household in order whilst I was away."

"But everything *is* in order. See?" Jo pointed to one of the windows, which she'd covered in a frilly white curtain. Granted, she'd used an old petticoat, following Rebekkah's lead, but no one would know. "Come into the kitchen. There's more."

She pulled him toward a shelf anchored above the stove. "I've placed all the bottles in alphabetical order. 'A' for allspice, all the way down to 'Y' for yarrow."

"How nice," he said, with barely a glance. "So very industrious of you, dear. I'm proud."

He didn't sound proud, but perhaps he was only hungry from his long journey, which would account for his sour mood.

"Would you like some eggs this morning?" she asked. "Or perhaps some oatmeal?"

"No, that's quite all right. I'm not hungry. We have something more important to discuss." He pointed to one of the kitchen chairs.

"Oh? Like what?"

"Well, dear, I received your letters while I was away."

"Wonderful! I was afraid they might have gotten lost in the post. Did you enjoy them?"

"I did ... all except one. The one where you talked about the Ladies' Benevolent Society."

"Benevolent Society?"

"Yes. I thought you promised you wouldn't make a spectacle of yourself while I was away. Didn't we agree on that?"

"A spectacle? I ... I don't understand."

"I dare say. The letter made it seem like you'd made a 'scene,'"—here, he flicked his fingers in the air to indicate quotation marks—"which would qualify as a spectacle. In fact, I found it a little embarrassing for you to speak your mind so freely. Whatever possessed you to do that, dear?"

"But I didn't—"

"Now, just a moment. You may think no one noticed, but the walls in this camp have ears. Very large ears. If I'm ever going to be promoted to supervisor, or chief medical officer, even, we need to be discreet about how we act in public. I want you to promise me you won't speak up like that again."

"But everyone loved the idea. Maybe not at first—"

"I need you to promise," he repeated. "We can't have people talking about us behind our backs."

"Us?" By now, she could barely breathe. "You've been home for less than ten minutes and already you've scolded me for something I didn't do. At least, not in the way you've made it sound. You're treating me like a child."

"I'm not treating you like a child. Although, I suppose I'll have to treat you like one if you insist on acting like one. There's no need for hysterics."

"I ... am ... not ... hysterical. I will not be spoken to as such."

She couldn't bear to sit next to him, so she quickly rose from the table.

What's happened to us?

When did married life become so difficult? So stifling. Does every man at Camp Travis talk down to his wife this way? If so, no wonder the lovely Bathsheba allowed herself to fall under King David's spell. Apparently, it was the only way to ensure a soft word from a man.

CHAPTER EIGHT

ALBIGENCE

BUILDING TWO-A, CAMP TRAVIS

NOVEMBER 1917

Perhaps he'd been too hard on her.

Albigence stopped before the testing room's door as he remembered the look on Josephine's face that morning. She'd stood stock-still in the doorway of their bedroom while he stiffly rolled off the cotton Chesterfield. She'd seemed completely disinterested in his awkward movements after he spent the entire night on the uncomfortable sofa.

Her stony silence meant she expected him to apologize. But for what? He'd only said what every other man in the camp would've said. Right or wrong, that was how things were, and who was he to fight the status quo?

In the end, she'd been the one to go behind his back and do something totally unexpected when she spoke up at the women's meeting. She'd jeopardized their position at the camp, and perhaps their entire future with the military.

Thank goodness the schoolhouse was set to open today. While he administered the very important IQ test to a new crop of enlistees, she'd be safely ensconced in her classroom, where she couldn't get into any more trouble. Teaching might be just the thing she needed to divert her attention from his shortcomings as a husband.

Inside the test-taking room, he found a ragtag group of fifty or so men lounging about on the floor, their arms and legs akimbo. They warily studied him as he threaded his way through the throng and toward the front of the room, which was threadbare, to say the least.

The requisitions officer at Camp Travis had provided each psychologist with a bald-faced clock, one battered lectern in serious need of repair, and one table on which to place the pencils and tests. Nothing more and nothing less.

He straightened his already straight tie. Despite the stifling temperature, he wore the official uniform of the psychology staff—thick olive-green jodhpurs, crisply pleated at the sides; a knitted necktie, which fell to his waist; and an officer's campaign hat, its brim round as a dinner plate. All of which he topped off with a pair of brand-new spectacles provided by the camp's infirmary. An extra pair he had every intention of keeping close at hand. Let the other men slouch about on the floor in dirty trousers and frayed work shirts. He wanted to set an example of military decorum and proper comportment.

"Attention," he snapped, in perfect imitation of his professors at the military camp.

Nothing but mute stares all around.

"When I say the word 'attention,'" he explained, "you should put your pencils in the air." He paused when he realized something. "Um, I see we have a problem."

The men had yet to retrieve their pencils from the battered tin cups he'd placed on the writing desk. He'd jumped the gun on the instructions. Now, he'd have to go back to the beginning to set things right again.

"First, you'll need to get a pencil," he said, as he pointed to the cups beside him. "After you've taken one, please return to your spot on the floor, so we can get started."

A chain of whispers passed back and forth as the men relayed his instructions. He heard snippets of Spanish, Italian, and what sounded like Yiddish, of all things. Afterward, the group stiffly rose as one and shuffled to the writing desk.

He used the opportunity to study the men as they moved. He'd been warned about a general lack of vigor among the young men hoping to join the army. Many of the candidates had escaped indescribable poverty—starvation, even— in their own countries, which showed in their emaciated bodies.

Ireland alone faced a terrible famine because of an ongoing civil war between the Parliamentary Party and Sinn Féin. Not to mention the citizens of Mexico, who faced their own war involving the Constitutionalists and Zapata's followers. Almost to a fault, the ragtag group in front of him looked pale, malnourished, and generally unkempt.

All but one. Albigence realized with a start he recognized a certain test-taker by the desk. The tall redhead he'd met through Josephine. Unlike the other men, this one—his name was Glyn, wasn't it?—took control of the situation by grabbing a fistful of pencils and calmly passing them out to the others. He looked hale and hearty, no doubt due to the hours he'd spent with a sledgehammer and chainsaw.

Yes, this was the Welshman he'd met the day before. A strapping, vigorous specimen, who looked ten times as strong as everyone else around him.

Come to think of it ... Albigence remembered a look that passed between this man and Josephine at the schoolhouse yesterday. He didn't quite care for it, to be honest. There was an intimacy in the glance which passed between Glyn and Josephine that stopped his own heart from beating. Flustered him. Made him desperate enough to hurry Josephine away from the situation.

Albigence had seen the look before—the same one worn by the lineup of men who'd wanted to dance with his Josephine at her cousin's debutante ball. Those men gazed at his angel with pure longing, their eyes made shiny by hope and unfettered desire. He'd thwarted their plans, of course, back there on the marble dance floor, and he wasn't about to repeat the scene here at Camp Travis.

No, he'd stop it by any means necessary.

He glanced away, and the memory vanished. Once Glyn dispersed the pencils and took his place on the floor again, it was time to begin the test anyway.

"Attention," Albigence barked.

He used the same harsh tone the men could expect to hear on the battlefields of France.

"Look at the first line. When I say 'go'—but not a moment before—make a figure one in the first circle and draw a cross in the third. Now ... go!"

About half the men responded right away, and the *scritch* of pencil leads filled the air. The other half whispered back and forth, which was a clear violation of military policy.

"Silence!" Albigence commanded. He addressed his comments to Josephine's "friend" in particular. "Do *not* talk to anyone else. Keep your eyes on your own paperwork and your mouths closed. I will not tolerate fraternizing during the test."

So it went for the first few questions. At one point, a gray-haired man with a studious look about him cautiously raised his hand.

"*Mi scusi*, kind sir," he said. "But how do you say number three again?"

"Hmph." Although talking during the test flew in the face of military policy, Albigence took pity on him since he was so much longer in the tooth than the others. Perhaps Albigence could bend the rules just this once.

After all, he wasn't a monster. Far from it. In fact, he prided himself on being a gentleman. Quite fair-minded too.

He calmly stated question number three again, which he addressed to the group at large. He noticed the foreigner named Glyn still looked confused, since he studied the ground rather than his paperwork. As a matter of fact, the boy hadn't written a single thing on his test paper. Not a single thing.

"You there!" he barked at Glyn. "Is there a problem?"

The fellow's head snapped up, as if he wanted to say something—he really did—but he couldn't quite work up the courage to do so. Albigence saw the struggle in his eyes.

No matter. He'd already bent the rules once. If Josephine's friend had a problem with the test, so be it. Charity was one thing, but he couldn't repeat every question on the test, now, could he? It wouldn't be fair to the others.

He decided to move forward. In the interest of the group at large, of course.

"Onward!" he commanded. "Now, for question nine. If you buy two packages of tobacco at seven cents apiece and a pipe at fifty-five cents, how much change should you receive from a two-dollar bill?"

Once more, a little over half the men responded quickly, while the others languished.

Did they really not understand the questions? But they were so simple. Ridiculously simple. Even a small boy in short pants could perform the math. Why, Albigence would've sailed right through this test had they given it to him in primary school.

Finally, after what felt like forever, the test drew to a close. By now, heat rose in waves from the floorboards. Albigence wouldn't be surprised if the temperature registered more than a hundred degrees. The obvious solution was to open a window, but there wasn't one. The army hadn't seen fit to install a single pane of glass in the boxy room. Perhaps they didn't care enough to do so.

Albigence loosened his necktie—ever so slightly, so as not to dishonor the uniform—and finally commanded the group to stop.

"That's enough. Pencils down."

He'd done his best. He silently collected the questionnaires from the men and dismissed them in groups of five.

No, he had nothing to feel guilty about, he thought, as the last man disappeared. He hadn't created the questions—or the strict protocols that governed them. He wasn't even responsible for the oppressive heat in the testing room. Everything was the military's doing, not his.

But if it were true, why did a flicker of guilt prick at the edges of his conscience? Did he actually feel sorry for the men? Especially Josephine's friend? Perhaps. But he'd already wrested his wife's affections from a line of suitors once before, and he wasn't about to repeat the scenario.

No, he had nothing to feel guilty about.

CHAPTER NINE

JOSEPHINE

CANTEEN, CAMP TRAVIS

NOVEMBER 1917

The canteen once more beckoned on the horizon, its windows aglow with lamplight and the promise of good cheer inside.

Jo had looked forward to the meeting all day. She longed for a distraction, and a way to escape a tense evening with Albigence where they both tiptoed around the cabin like strangers.

He'd wounded her pride with his words, and he wouldn't even apologize afterward.

So, she plucked up the basket of yarn and disappeared through the back door as soon as seven o'clock arrived.

Rebekkah helped her carry the heavy basket down the path by letting Jo balance it between them.

Tonight, there'd be no unplanned speeches on her part. Albigence had seen to that. He'd made her promise, in no uncertain terms, to keep her opinions to herself and do her best to blend in with the crowd.

"Do try to behave yourself," he'd warned, as he watched her dress for the meeting.

"But, of course, dear," she'd replied, barely favoring him with a glance. "Why wouldn't I? I do think you're making too much of this. Who cares what I say or do at a meeting of the Ladies' Benevolent Society? We're at war, for goodness' sake. Men are dying overseas. No one cares what I do or say at a military camp thousands of miles from the front lines."

"I don't know, Josephine. The walls here have—"

"I know, I know. The walls have ears, and the rafters have eyes. Or, so you've said. What will you do tonight while I'm gone?"

"I plan to review the men's test scores. The preliminary results don't look good. Not for a lack of trying on my part, but it won't do for the men to put in such a poor showing at the very beginning of the program."

"I suppose," Jo murmured, as she placed a cloche on her head. "But what happens to the men who don't pass the test? Surely, there must be some provision for them. A chance to retake the test and improve their scores, perhaps?"

"I'm afraid not. The army doesn't have enough time. Or patience. No, the men will be dismissed and sent back home to their own countries. Wherever they may be."

"But what happens if they can't go back home? A lot of those countries are at war. Several countries can't even feed the citizens they already have."

"I have no idea," Albigence admitted. "I suppose the army deals with it on a case-by-case basis. Why do you ask?"

"Oh, no reason. Seems to me the army hasn't put a lot of thought into the program—hasn't considered every possible angle."

"Well, it's not really our concern. And don't forget … there will be no speeches tonight. Try to control yourself."

"Yes, dear. No speeches."

The more she thought about it, though, as she patted the cloche in place, the more she realized the truth in her argument. She'd seen the hunger on the immigrant's faces, when they first arrived at camp, and the quiet desperation in their eyes. The way they spoke about the United States in hushed, reverent terms. As if the country was the Garden of Eden, Valhalla, and the Promised Land all rolled into one. What would happen if the military took their dreams away?

Her melancholy disappeared when she joined Rebekkah on the footpath. Together, they moved toward the canteen with the heavy basket of yarn between them.

"There you are." The group's president, of all people, greeted them happily the moment they stepped into the canteen. "I hoped you'd join us tonight."

"But, of course, Mrs. Benedict," Jo said, as she hefted the basket onto a nearby table. "I promised I'd deliver the wool, now, didn't I?"

"Look at you—a whole bushel full. I'm not really surprised, though. Rebekkah told us all about your great talents at organization."

"Well, the shopkeeper was surprisingly generous," Jo said. "He provided enough wool for a hundred pairs, at least."

She followed Rebekkah afterward to a picnic table near the front. Once the conversation around them settled down, the president strode officiously toward the lectern, as usual.

"Welcome, ladies. Do take a seat if you're still standing. I'm sure you've noticed the piles of yarn on your way into the meeting this evening. Our very own Josephine Pembrooke has managed to secure all the supplies we'll need for the knitting project. Do give Mrs. Pembrooke a hearty round of applause for her efforts."

Jo ducked her head at the polite smattering of applause.

"Now," Mrs. Benedict continued, "I daresay we have another topic to address before we start the meeting. You'll notice there's a vacancy at the head table."

Jo surveyed the table. An empty chair stood near the middle.

"Unfortunately," the president said, "our dear Mrs. Trudeau had to vacate her position as sergeant-at-arms. Her husband was reassigned, you see, and the family shipped off to Kentucky yesterday."

A wave of whispers washed over the room as everyone considered it. At one point, Mrs. Benedict lowered her gavel to silence the chatter.

"Now, now," she said. "Her leaving is not the end of the world. Not at all. We just need to appoint someone new to the position. Do I have any recommendations from the floor?"

A woman near the front immediately thrust up her hand.

"The floor recognizes Mrs. Dempsey." *Bang* went the gavel. "What say you?"

"I nominate Josephine Pembrooke. A schoolteacher is the perfect person to keep our meetings on track."

Jo's eyes widened. "Oh, no. No, no, no," she whispered, under her breath. She couldn't possibly agree to such a thing. Albigence would be horrified.

"Everyone, settle down," the president said. "We have a motion from the floor to appoint Mrs. Josephine Pembrooke as our new sergeant-at-arms. Do I have a second?"

A swift blur moved in Jo's periphery.

"I second the motion."

"Rebekkah!" Jo hissed. "Stop that! Albigence will kill me if I'm elected. It's only going to make things worse."

"Nonsense," her friend whispered back. "He should be proud of you. This means everyone thinks you're trustworthy."

"Mrs. Pembrooke," the president called out. "Would you like to address your comments to the room at large?"

"Excuse me?"

"Your comments. Perhaps you'd like to say a few words to our members."

Slowly, but surely, Jo rose to her feet, her cheeks burning with both fear and embarrassment.

"I'm ... I'm honored you'd think so much of me," she began, as she took in the smiles all around her, "and I'm touched by the gesture. I really am. But I can't possibly accept it. I have too many responsibilities at the schoolhouse and too much to learn here before I take on such an important position."

"Nonsense!" someone in the back of the room yelled. "We need you."

"But—"

"Charlotte is correct," the president said, as she prepared to lower her gavel once more. "You'd be doing us a great favor, Mrs. Pembrooke."

"I'm truly flattered—"

"It's settled then." *Bang.* "All those in favor of having Mrs. Josephine Pembrooke, our esteemed schoolmarm, serve as the next sergeant-at-arms, say 'Aye.'"

A thunderous chorus of "ayes" arose.

"All those opposed," the president continued, "by the same sign."

There was silence except for the chirps of the ever-present cicadas on the other side of the wall. Even the normal clatter of teaspoons striking porcelain cups had fallen silent.

"The membership has spoken." Mrs. Benedict beamed at her. "Mrs. Josephine Pembrooke shall serve on the board by unanimous election of the membership. Hear, hear!"

Slowly, but surely, Jo sank back to the bench.

"Congratulations," Rebekkah whispered.

"For what? You know Albigence is going to kill me. Not literally, of course, but he might as well. I'll never hear the end of it."

"Nonsense. Give him some credit, will you? Besides, this isn't about Albigence. It's about you. Such a privilege. It's an honor. You should be pleased everyone thinks so highly of you."

"Oh, that's much better. I'm sure he'll understand everything now." Jo rolled her eyes. "Why on earth would you second such a motion? I ought to—"

"You ought to what? Thank me? Well, then. You're welcome."

"That's not what I was going to say, and you know it."

Despite her best intention, a tiny smile finally wormed its way onto her lips. She couldn't stay mad at her best friend. Especially since the whole audience seemed to be watching them. "You're a fine one, Rebekkah Schmidt. A fine one, indeed."

"Thank you. I'll take that as a compliment."

Before either of them could say more, a loud noise sounded at the back of the room. Someone had thrown open the heavy oak door.

Bang!

A lone figure stood under the transom.

The man wore black from head to toe, and he gazed about the hall frantically.

"Now, see here—" the president sputtered.

"Allo!" From the cut of his coat and strong accent, Jo could tell he was a recent immigrant.

"What do you want?" the president demanded.

"Mrs. Schmidt." He desperately scanned the audience. "Rebekkah Schmidt."

"I'm over here, Milo." Rebekkah planted her palms on the table and awkwardly rose. "What's wrong?"

"'Tis a body, ma'am. They found a body in a back field."

Rebekkah didn't hesitate. "Where is he?"

Strange how Rebekkah automatically assumed they were talking about a man.

"He's in a field out back, he 'tis. Please come."

For some reason, Jo felt compelled to rise, as well. Something terrible had happened. Something terrible—and terribly close to home.

She hurried behind Rebekkah as they left the building. Her thoughts tumbled end-over-end as they emerged into the night air, which was dark as pitch. She lurched forward blindly, trusting her feet to find their way, since her brain was of no help at all.

They headed to the encampment occupied by the Welshmen. Everyone knew the men stuck to their "own kind" when they arrived at Camp Travis—Italians with Italians, Dutch with Dutch, Texans with Texans, even—and Glyn and the other Welshmen were no different. They banded together as if their very lives depended on it. Perhaps they did.

After a moment, the one named Milo silently pointed to a field on his right.

Unlike that first night, no one played the harmonica now or slapped playing cards on an Indian trading blanket or laughed. Nothing sounded but an urgent thrum of voices, which came from an open field.

Jo hurried past the others—who tried to stop her, of course—to approach the group. Once there, she forced herself to look down to where a body lay in the scrub grass with something dark and wet beneath his head. The figure had lush copper hair—she could tell as much—and an open carpenter's pouch beside him. The familiar awl, now coated with blood, nestled in his hand.

Glyn had turned his beautiful face sideways, away from the camp. Apparently, he'd taken the awl to his own neck and used it to meet his Maker. There, in the middle of a dusty army field, with nothing for company but towering cacti and skeletal prickly pears.

"Oh, my Lord," Rebekkah breathed as soon as she reached the same spot. She must've spoken to one of Glyn's friends by now, because another man hovered near them. A single tear rolled down the stranger's cheek.

Nothing Jo saw made sense. Why in the world would Glyn—the kind-hearted carpenter who could construct a weathervane from copper tubes—do this?

"He found out tonight he was being deported," Rebekkah whispered, apparently reading her thoughts. "Your husband had to deliver the bad news. He was being sent back to Wales."

"Wales? But there was nothing for him there."

"Albigence didn't know that. No one did."

"But he should've known. Why didn't he know?"

"Now, please don't blame your husband. Glyn's death is not Albigence's fault. I'm sure the army insisted he reject Glyn."

"No." Jo spoke more firmly this time. "You're wrong, Rebekkah. Albigence could've said no. He should've stopped this from happening. Refused to go along with ..." She motioned to the ground. "... with whatever *this* is." She couldn't stop the words, which came hard and fast. "Why, if he was half the man Glyn was—"

"Don't you dare say that." Fire flashed behind Rebekkah's eyes for the first time. "You can't compare two completely different people. You haven't heard your husband's side of the story yet. You're jumping to conclusions."

"Why are you defending him? Just ... don't."

With that, Jo slowly backed away, shocked at Rebekkah's attitude. Now was not the time, nor the place, to worry about Albigence, for heaven's sake. Not when an innocent man lay in a pool of his own blood, far away from anyone or anything else.

A supposedly safe field, miles away from the fighting overseas.

The irony wasn't lost on her. Weren't the military recruits supposed to be safe here? Nothing bad would happen to a soldier as long as he remained on American soil. No one would die here. Wasn't that the unspoken promise?

Jo stumbled away from the carnage, blinded by fury and an aching sense of helplessness.

CHAPTER TEN

ALBIGENCE

OFFICE OF MAJ. GEN. HENRY ALLEN, HEADQUARTERS, CAMP TRAVIS

LATE EVENING, NOVEMBER 1917

A sharp rap on the cabin door woke Albigence from his sleep. A loud, incessant knock, which he couldn't ignore.

He rolled off the Chesterfield and sleepily opened the screen. "Hello? Who's out there? Show yourself."

A figure moved from the shadows. "Hello, Doctor." The man wore the navy uniform of the Military Police Corps.

"Yes, Officer. What's happening?"

"You need to come with me. You've been summoned to the major general's office."

"Major gen—"

"Now, sir. They said I was to bring you there straightaway."

Albigence debated his next move. On the one hand, he'd been roused from his rest by a messenger who wouldn't even state his business. On the other hand, the army often ignored basic manners to operate efficiently. The man's methods *were* efficient. He had to grant him that.

"All right. Give me a moment," he said, fully awake now. "Let me tidy up a bit."

"I'm sorry, Doctor. But my orders were to bring you to the major general's office immediately."

"Now see here—"

"Immediately, sir."

Albigence debated whether to protest again, but the solider seemed set on his mission. Not that Albigence could blame him. Orders were orders, and they all obeyed them as best they could.

"I see. Well, at least let me leave a note for my wife."

"There isn't time, sir."

"No time? But she's at a meeting in the canteen. She'll wonder where I am."

"No time, sir."

"I know. You have orders." Albigence sighed heavily. "All right, then. Let's get going."

He closed the cabin as best he could, although he couldn't imagine what Josephine would think when she returned from the meeting. She'd come home to find an empty cabin, a rumpled bedsheet on the Chesterfield, and a pile of his reports scattered about the desk.

Then again, she'd been so angry with him lately, she might not even notice his absence. Or worse, she might welcome it. Neither of those two scenarios provided much comfort as he trudged away with the military policeman.

After a few moments, they arrived at the base's headquarters, which towered over the other buildings on the main road. At three stories tall, with elegantly finished windows and doors, the administrative office was the most complete building around. Albigence had never been there, save for one awkward tea ceremony when his commanding officer inducted him into the Medical Officers' Corps. He hadn't noticed the building's accoutrements then—bloodred mahogany trim around the windows and doors, rectangular flowerboxes which sprouted bulbs under the sills, a columned portico to grandly announce the front entrance.

The officer escorted Albigence into the lobby and up the stairs, which served as the official office and residence of Major General Henry Allen.

A stern-faced individual sat behind an imposing mahogany desk. The commanding officer had slick salt-and-pepper hair parted severely down the middle and deep crevices between his eyes. Not for naught had he earned the nickname the Comandante.

He didn't even bother to put aside his paperwork when Albigence approached the desk, which gave Albigence no choice but to shift his weight from one foot to the other while he waited. Much like at the tea ceremony, he felt out of place and underdressed.

After what felt like forever, the major general deigned to acknowledge his guest. He set the papers aside and fixed Albigence with a glare that could melt an ice floe.

"Do you know why I've sent for you, Doctor?"

"I have no idea. I was asleep on the Chesterfield, you see—"

A sharp *thwack* sounded. The man had slapped the desk with his open palm.

"I don't care one whit about your sleeping arrangements," he barked. "You've presented me with a very serious problem this evening. Very serious, indeed."

Albigence blinked. "Problem? I don't understand."

"Yes, problem."

The man moved his focus to a military policeman standing nearby. One curt nod, and the soldier disappeared. Apparently, the mistake was too awful to broadcast in front of anyone else.

"You see," the commanding officer said, as soon as the door swung shut, "one of our recruits died tonight. A recent immigrant, as it turns out. Perhaps you know him."

Albigence gasped. *Of course, he knew him.* Out of all the visits he paid to would-be soldiers this evening, only one man's reaction surprised him. The Welshman—an odd choice for Jo to befriend—had crumbled to his knees when he heard the news and then pressed his forehead to the dirt. It was quite undignified. Everyone else who failed the test seemed resolved to pack his bags and leave the army in the morning, as well he should, but this one refused to do so.

"Perhaps there was foul play involved, sir?" Albigence offered.

"Negative." Another *thwack*. Like everything else about the man, the noise was violent and unpredictable. "We've already determined the death was a suicide. That's not at issue here. What the devil did you say to that young man, Doctor?"

"Um, well ... just what I was supposed to say. Soldiers who can't—or don't—pass the intelligence test must leave the army. I believe I used the words, 'post haste,' sir."

"Post haste?" The man winced, as if Albigence had uttered an epitaph in church or done something equally horrible. "I see. Well, then." He shouted for the policeman and the door once more opened. "Bring in the other doctor, soldier."

Apparently, someone had been waiting in the wings all along. When the mahogany-trimmed door opened yet again, a shrouded figure appeared.

The swish of the man's army jodhpurs—so familiar amongst the psychology staff—sliced the air.

"Good evening, sir." Frank offered a brisk salute as soon as he reached the desk.

He seemed at home in the commander's office, as if he'd visited the room many times before.

"At ease, Doctor," the commander said. "I know you've already advocated for this man's general discharge from the army, but I'd like you to repeat what you told me earlier. The charges, as you see them. Why do you think the army should separate—nay, *must* separate—this man from his service?"

"Of course, sir." Unlike Albigence, Frank didn't bat an eyelash. "I—actually, we as a whole—have good reason to believe Dr. Pembrooke misused his position with the Medical Officers' Corps. It's been reported his wife spent an inordinate amount of time with the young man who committed suicide tonight. A *suspicious* amount of time, if you catch my drift."

Albigence gaped. *What in the devil was Frank implying?* What other doctors had joined in this evil cabal against him? The questions kept coming, none of which offered a ready answer.

"Now, see here, Frank—" Albigence sputtered, compelled to say something, anything, to defend his wife's honor.

"Silence!" *Thwack.* "This is a very serious allegation, Dr. Beauchamp. Very serious, indeed. Are you telling me Dr. Pembrooke unfairly failed a potential soldier to even a romantic score?"

"Yes, sir. That's exactly what I'm saying."

"Interesting." The major general leaned back in his chair. "What do you have to say for yourself, Dr. Pembrooke?"

Albigence's whole body tensed. Only his thoughts moved freely, and they bounced around the room willy-nilly. *How'd they ever get mahogany trim for the windows in here? There's no forest for miles. And why is the room so bloody hot? As hot as Hades.*

"Cat got your tongue?" the major general asked. "Well, to be fair, this is not unlike a certain situation I faced in Alaska last year. Quite so."

Alaska? Did he say Alaska? I must be dreaming. Wake up, wake up, wake up!

"Yes, quite so," the officer continued, unconcerned with anything but the sound of his own voice. "An Inuit girl was accused of entertaining two suitors, neither of whom knew about the other. Rather than have two men fight over her, I brought the fair maiden into my office to explain herself. Which she couldn't do, of course. She ended up jumping through the nearest window, and that was the end of that."

Oh, no, Finally, his thoughts settled down long enough for Albigence to understand. The man was talking about bringing Albigence's wife in for questioning. Now. At midnight. To tell her side of the story.

Please, no. Josephine already was furious with him. To bring her in, under police escort no less, would only stoke her fury. She'd never talk to him again. There must be another way.

He cast about frantically for an answer. An answer to this horrible predicament. Suddenly, he caught the tail end of a memory which whizzed through his mind. Granted, the memory was hazy, since the incident happened many months ago and many miles from here, but none of that mattered now. Albigence seized on the idea with everything he had.

The debutante ball for Josephine's cousin. The line of elegant suitors, who queued up in a line to woo his wife.

Since he couldn't compete with them on looks or vitality, he chose a different path. He would win her with words. An amazingly long string of words, which he'd use to buy some time until her heart softened.

"You see, sir," Albigence began, his mouth working furiously to keep up with his brain, "I believe what we have here is a common psychological phenomenon, which involves, um, transference. Yes, that's it. Psychological transference. The condition is a lot more common than one might think."

He took a quick breath. "By ingratiating himself to my wife, the recruit hoped to secure his position here at the base. He was *transferring* the power meant for his superiors, you see, and giving it to another person. The person on the receiving end was my wife. As a schoolteacher, she represented a higher authority to this young man." He chuckled dryly, but it sounded about as false as his instant diagnosis. "Theirs was a purely platonic relationship, but he mistakenly awarded her the awe due his superiors— all because of the psychological phenomenon known as transference."

He paused for dramatic effect. Whether he believed a single word he was saying was beside the point.

"As a trained psychologist," he continued, breathlessly, "I immediately recognized the problem. I knew we were dealing with an unstable character. Therefore, I knew I had to protect my wife at all costs. Which I did, sir. I made certain Josephine was involved in other activities— just this evening she attended a meeting of the Ladies' Benevolent Society—and I forbade her from ever visiting the Welshman's camp again."

"Transference, hmmm?" The major general looked intrigued by the notion. "Can't say I've ever heard of it. What an interesting concept."

"Yes, it is," Albigence readily agreed. "No less than Sigmund Freud himself devised the term at the turn of the century. You see, Freud believed repressed trauma from one's childhood could manifest itself in unnatural attachments to others. Yes. That's it. Repressed trauma from childhood, indeed."

Another quick breath before he continued, "Freud believed the actual basis for this affliction went back to one's earliest days. People who lacked strong parental support—such as orphans—often transferred their feelings of affection to strangers."

"Transference, hmmm?" The major general repeated the term, as if mesmerized by the sound of it. "Quite interesting. I do enjoy learning about new phenomena." He turned to the military policeman. "Find out if the good doctor is telling the truth, soldier. Go and speak to the boy's associates. Ask about the soldier's homelife—in Wales, wasn't it?—and find out whether the suicide tonight was an orphan. If he was, I owe you an apology, Doctor. And, if he wasn't? Well, we'll cross that bridge when we come to it."

"Yes, sir."

At this point, Albigence was so relieved, he nearly fainted. He'd babbled on and on about a psychosis he knew little to nothing about. But, how else could he explain his wife's affection for a stranger ... and someone who took his own life? It was the only way he could think of to present Josephine as the victim here—not the instigator.

"We're done for now, Doctors," the major general snapped. "This mess will sort itself out soon enough. Return to your cabins and await further instruction."

Albigence stumbled away from the desk. He studied the carpet as he made his way to the door, because he could only imagine the look on Frank's face right about now.

If such looks could kill, Albigence knew he'd soon be six feet under the ground.

CHAPTER ELEVEN

JOSEPHINE

CABIN NUMBER P–79, CAMP TRAVIS

LATE NOVEMBER 1917

The striped cardboard suitcase was the first thing to go. Jo hurled the bag through the front doorway, where it landed upside down on the porch.

She took a certain satisfaction in that. After all, the blasted suitcase had witnessed some of her marriage's most stressful moments. The bag deserved rough treatment.

The first time the suitcase interfered in her life happened when they were on a train leaving a perfectly wonderful home in upstate New York, only to arrive at a dusty, God-forsaken military outpost. Most recently, it witnessed the scene at the schoolhouse, when Albigence refused to shake hands with her friend. A young immigrant he insisted on calling "son" in a misguided attempt to belittle him.

No, the suitcase had seen far too much drama for Jo's liking, so she swiftly kicked the bag's side for good measure.

If Albigence thought he could talk his way out of this one when he returned home tonight ... well, he had another think coming. The moment she found out he played a role in Glyn's death, she knew she had to do *something*. She couldn't very well sit by and let her husband destroy another man's life, could she?

If he'd destroyed Glyn's life, who's to say he wouldn't destroy other immigrants' lives? Smash their dreams and leave them so despondent, they'd rather die than face uncertain futures?

Albigence didn't create the intelligence test which killed Glyn, but he might as well have. She'd seen the papers scattered on his desk when she dusted the front parlor. The thick paragraphs of type provided instructions for mathematical equations. All of them written in English, and all of them like hieroglyphics to someone who didn't even speak the language.

How unfair. It ran counter to everything she knew about right and wrong.

Since her husband was involved in the tragedy ... well, he had to pay a consequence. She'd never feel comfortable again in the same cabin with his personal effects lying around. On the tables, in closets, under her bed.

She'd relied on her schoolteacher's training to come up with a solution. A wholly rational one, since Albigence disliked anything irrational.

She'd read about the solution whilst at the teacher's college in North Carolina. She'd come upon a copy of *The Compendium of Native American Peoples,* which described a fascinating Cherokee tradition. Apparently, when a squaw by the name of Making Out Road chose to divorce Kit Carson, the famous frontiersman, she employed a tried-and-true method used by the tribe. She simply tossed the adventurer's belongings—one cotton bedroll, a kerosene lamp, and two Remington rifles—out of her tepee. Such a bold move told the rest of the tribe she wanted nothing more to do with the man.

Voilà. Problem solved.

Now, here she stood. Surveying all Albigence's worldly belongings, which she'd stacked in three sloppy piles on the porch.

"What's all this?" A soft voice emerged from the darkness.

"Oh, I see you've finally come home."

"What have you done, Josephine?" Her husband emerged from the shadows, his face drawn.

"I thought you'd want your personal effects when you move to new quarters," she said. To her credit, she didn't apologize—she *wouldn't* apologize—for what she'd done.

"New quarters? I ... I don't understand."

"It's quite simple, really. I think we should spend some time apart. I know what happened with Glyn Firth tonight. I can't live under the same roof with a person who would treat another human being that way. Someone who could be so inhumane. How could you, Albigence?"

He bumbled toward her, clearly exhausted. "So, that's it, hmmm? What this is all about? My failures as a husband?"

"Quite so. I think it's best for us if you move to new quarters for a time."

"I see."

Slowly, but surely, something new crossed his face. A dark look, and one that was quite uncharacteristic for him. He still looked sad, to be sure, but his eyes had narrowed.

"Are you sure this is about me?" he asked. "Or is this about you and the dead man?"

"I ... I don't know what you're talking about."

"I think you do. Did you fall in love with the Welshman, Josephine?"

The question shocked her. "Wh ... what? Whatever are you talking about?"

"It's a simple question, really. Did you fall in love with the Welshman?" He obviously couldn't bring himself to say Glyn's name aloud.

"I'm not even going to dignify that with a response. And I'm not in the mood to stand out here and air our dirty—"

"I need to know," he snapped. "Why are you doing this? Because you fell in love with another man?"

"No, of course not. No! Don't be silly. I grew quite fond of him, of course. We spent so much time together, and you were never home." She paused to let the implication sink in.

"Ah, I see. So, it's my fault. My fault you sought another man's company when you couldn't have mine."

"I wouldn't put it like that—"

"No? Then how would you put it?"

She didn't have a ready answer. She couldn't think clearly, to be honest, and the look on her husband's face chilled her.

"Cat got your tongue?" he asked. "Don't worry. I won't make a scene. I'll go. Apparently, you're the one calling the shots here, not me. Which is quite different from how things used to work."

He stooped to throw his belongings into the dented suitcase as best he could.

"You don't even know where I've been tonight," he said, as he closed the lid. "What I've done to protect your honor. I don't expect you to thank me, but I'm not the monster you make me out to be."

"Oh, Albigence." She softened her tone. "I never said you were a monster. I do think you've lost your way, though. I think *we've* lost our way. And we're not going to find it by going at each other's throats, are we?"

"I don't know what to think anymore." He stepped away from her once he'd finished. He looked lost now, as if he didn't know which way to turn.

"Goodbye, Albigence," she whispered. She reluctantly moved toward the cabin door and the cold comfort it offered on the other side.

For some reason, every man she cared about ended up disappointing her—one way or another. Why should Albigence be any different?

CHAPTER TWELVE

ALBIGENCE

MEDICAL INFIRMARY, CAMP TRAVIS

DECEMBER 1917

He'd gotten used to the loud *crick* in his spine whenever he shifted his weight on the mattress now. Three weeks on a lumpy bluetick mattress would do that to anyone. He wasn't exactly complaining. At least, they'd given him a sturdy roof over his head and an enamel washbasin with which to tidy himself.

He'd appeared at the door of the infirmary without warning after the fracas with Josephine. He didn't know what to expect when he knocked on the door. Would they send him away too, or would they recognize a man in need of healing? Even if it wasn't the sort of healing which they normally provided?

In the end, a night watchman pointed out a spare closet. A miniscule room with a rusted cot and lumpy mattress, a shard of broken glass over the washbasin, and a bare lightbulb that flickered on and off, as if possessed by a spirit.

Apparently, the person who used to live in the closet—a high-ranking officer with a mistress, whom the watchman shrewdly didn't name—had left the premises to return to his own quarters. Albigence was free to use the frugal accommodations, such as they were, for as long as he needed them.

He rolled over again on the mattress, which smelled of rot and mold. Three long weeks had passed since he'd last slept comfortably in his own bed. Three long weeks since he'd felt a soft rag rug beneath his feet when he awoke. Three long weeks since he'd heard his wife's sweet voice, like a soprano song in his ear.

Unfortunately, there'd be no more sleep for him tonight. Between the broken bedsprings, which poked his sides like a cattle prod, and the memory of Josephine when she threw him out of their home, he couldn't possibly manage it.

Instead, he raked his hand though his rumpled hair and reached for the spectacles he'd placed on the mattress.

At least, he still had his position with the Medical Officers' Corps. The army couldn't take that away. Not after the military policeman's report, which stated in no uncertain terms that the suicide victim had, in fact, grown up on the streets of Wales as an orphan. The major general probably still enjoyed saying the word "transference" to himself whenever he was alone.

Albigence stretched and nearly boxed the hanging lightbulb. The only thing to do at times like this was to visit the infirmary's washroom, which offered much better lighting and an equal amount of solitude. The night staff would be napping at their desks by now, and none of the patients were ambulatory, so he'd have the whole place to himself. He would commandeer a trashcan, which he'd flip over to create a desk, and then he'd prop a textbook against a perforated pail he'd pilfered from the supply closet. Although he'd read every textbook available, he might as well take another crack at *Studies on Hysteria*. Perhaps Freud was onto something when he blamed early childhood trauma for hysteria later in life, particularly amongst the female population.

Perhaps that's what ailed Josephine now. Maybe some childhood trauma had caused her to banish him from their home. He wouldn't bet against it.

He lumbered to the washroom with the textbook in hand. Once he sat on the cold tile floor, with the familiar trashcan desk in front of him, he began to feel marginally better. He wouldn't doubt if someone in Josephine's childhood had unwittingly—or worse, with full knowledge—abused her in some way. Abuse, however minor or major, could be the reason for her current bout of hysteria.

An interesting hypothesis, to say the least.

He sat there contemplating the ramifications of his hypothesis when someone new burst through the washroom's doors.

"Allo!" The greeting came from a young man in a dirty butcher's apron. The newcomer held a slim glass jar in his hand, which he lifted high. "Didn't know the room 'twas taken."

"Well, 'twas." Albigence didn't mean to sound sarcastic, although it probably came off as such. "My apologies. Please come in. Don't mind me."

The man appraised the strange desktop. "'Tis an on odd place to do one's reading."

"Yes, well. I'm in need of a reading light, you see, and this one suffices."

"Och. Indeed."

Judging by the vessel in the man's hands—filled with a thick, brown gravy—he no doubt worked as a cook. He probably spent his days with a whisk in one hand and meat cleaver in the other.

"Yes, do come in," Albigence repeated. "I truly don't mind."

"Aye. I still say ye could do better for a library."

"You'd understand why I'm here if you saw my current living conditions. By the way, I'm Dr. Albigence Pembrooke. I'm a psychologist here with the Medical Officers' Corps."

"I know who you are," the man said. "We all do."

"You do?" *How on earth does this man know my name, when we've never met before?* "Are you sure? Perhaps I resemble someone else you know. I don't believe I've had the pleasure of making your acquaintance."

"Och, but you have." The gentleman—still unnamed—moved further into the washroom, which caused the fluid in his jar to slosh back and forth.

"We've met?' How so?"

"You were there that night. 'Twas three weeks back now. You came to our tents with your papers and such."

Oh, no. He should've suspected as much. The accent, the coppery hair, the pale skin. The man looked like a Welshman. No doubt a friend of the recently deceased. The thorn in Albigence's side, even after his untimely death by suicide.

"Yes, I was there," Albigence grudgingly admitted.

"Just so. You know our Glyn wasn't an eeijit, right? He 'twas smarter than most of the men here."

"Really? Well, I'm afraid his test scores were abysmal. He couldn't answer a single question."

"Och, that I can believe. The boy didn't know much English. Not much a'tall."

"Then what makes you think he was so brilliant?"

"Why, look at 'is handiwork. The man could build a castle from a corn crib, dontcha know. A few more weeks with his tutor, an' who knows what could've happened?"

Albigence wasn't surprised. He'd seen the woodwork in the schoolhouse and the casing for the bell. The Welshman knew his way around a hammer and nails. That much was true, but it didn't mean he had the smarts to join an American Army regiment, did it? Especially if the troop was under fire on a battlefield.

"Again, that may be so, er ..."

"Derwyn. Mah name's Derwyn. Pleasure ta meetcha." He leaned over to shake his hand.

Albigence returned the gesture, even with the less-than-sanitary conditions. "Yes, well, Derwyn, it's not my fault your friend couldn't pass the army's intelligence test. If he'd only studied, you see—"

"He was tryin' to. But then you come along and put a stop to it."

"Look, here. I'm very sorry about what happened to your friend. Really, I am. But I don't make up the questions. I didn't write the test. My role was to administer it and let the chips fall where they may."

"Dat's how it is, izit? Well, t'anks to your papers, our boy Glyn has gone up to the saints. You might think a wee bit more 'bout your test. Won't be many soldiers left by the time you're done with 'em."

With that, the man dumped the full contents of his glass jar into the washbasin. A waterfall of cloudy, clotted fluid flowed into the bowl.

Is that blood? No, it couldn't possibly be.

"If you don't mind my asking, Derwyn, just what do you do around here?"

"Me? Och, I'm a poor country lad from Scotland. Do a bit o' this and dash o' that in the operatin' theatre."

"Operating theatre?" Albigence blinked. "Pardon me?"

"Aye. 'Tis a surgeon, ya see. Me specialty is fixin' faces and settin' bones. Do a right fine job o' it, if I do say so me-self."

"You're a surgeon? Surely—"

"Aye. Trained at St. Andrews. Put aside me Gaelic to make me-self useful here in America. Too many lads coming back wit' only parts o' their faces left. 'Tis a right shame."

"My apologies, Doctor." Albigence immediately sprang to his feet, which knocked aside the improvised desk. Never in his wildest dreams did he imagine the boy in front of him was a surgeon. A medical doctor with even more advanced training than himself.

The man surely didn't look like one. Or sound like one, either.

"I ... I saw your apron," Albigence sputtered, "and I assumed you worked in the mess hall."

"'Tis all right." The doctor casually wiped his hands on the oilcloth. "You might want to give the lads 'round here a bit more credit nex' time, though. Some of 'em are right smart in the head. Like our Glyn."

The surgeon turned on his heel, the faint scents of rubbing alcohol and iodine following him as he left the washroom.

Albigence was too surprised to say goodbye to him. He couldn't decide what was worse—the way he automatically assumed the physician worked as a cook or the way the lad didn't take offense to it. Had the tables been turned, Albigence would've thrown a royal fit if someone mistook him for a simple camp cook.

Time would only tell, but he felt there must a lesson in there for him somewhere.

CHAPTER THIRTEEN

JOSEPHINE

SCHOOLHOUSE, CAMP TRAVIS

DECEMBER 1917

He appeared at the edge of the schoolyard one morning, his path evident by soggy footprints he left behind in the frost. She watched him curiously from her perch on the porch's rail. Noticed the bedraggled clothes and off-kilter bowler. The sallow face, darkened by patches of stubble on his cheeks and chin.

Albigence?

After only three weeks apart, her husband already looked the worse for wear.

Jo longed to rush over to him and throw her arms around him. Let him know the worst was over. They'd come to an understanding soon. They *had* to come to an understanding, didn't they? She couldn't imagine what would happen if they didn't.

Oh, how she missed him. The first few days passed easily enough, since she did her best to stay away from the cabin as much as possible. When she did return home, she found she cooked only half as much at mealtimes and rarely dusted or mopped the floors. But those petty bonuses couldn't eliminate the heavy silence that clung to everything and grew more oppressive over time. After a while, every sound was magnified, from the *scritch* of the sewing needle biting into fabric to the *thunk* of the icebox lid as it slammed closed. The noise echoed through the empty house like canon fire shot into a void.

Not only that, but Jo's curiosity about her husband's circumstances grew stronger day by day. Where on earth did Albigence rest his head at night, and who else was there? He didn't have any close friends at Camp Travis, or at least none she knew of, and his coworkers didn't seem especially friendly.

But if she knew one thing, she knew this—her husband would never spend his nights with another woman. Not only was her Albigence bright and industrious, but he was faithful to the core. Too bad she'd never given him any credit for his faithfulness when he was around.

"Hello." Jo quickly rose from her perch and strode to the schoolyard gate. Better to meet him at the pass. "What're you doing here?"

An awkward shuffle or two. "I've come to talk to you."

"So I've gathered." She gently swung open the gate. "Why don't we move inside? The children will be here soon, but the schoolroom's empty now."

She led him into the schoolhouse, where morning sun warmed the floorboards. Jo remembered his admonition about the walls at the camp having ears, so she swiftly closed the door behind him. She would've made a joke about it while she did so, but this didn't feel like the time, nor the place, for anything remotely lighthearted.

Instead, she quietly sat on one of the benches near her desk. "Now, please tell me why you've come."

"I've realized something." He cautiously sat next to her, as if he might spook her should he move too fast. "I've realized something about you."

"About me?" In an instant, any warm feelings brought on by his sudden appearance cooled. If he was going to upbraid her again about her relationship with Glyn ... well, she didn't have to stand for it. He'd come all the way to the schoolhouse to speak with her. *He* was the stranger here, not her. He had no right—

"I'm sorry, Josephine," he said. "I never told you how I felt about that night. How sorry I was about what happened to the Welshman ... er, Glyn."

"Excuse me?"

"Yes, I never told you." He worried the brim of his bowler while he spoke. The fabric was shiny from use. "I made a mistake. I should've told you how I felt. You deserved to know."

"Go on." Jo breathed the words, because it seemed so unnatural to hear her husband apologize. For anything. In all the time she'd known him, Albigence had never once said he was sorry for a mistake on his part. He usually ignored his missteps or pretended they hadn't happened.

"That night must've been horrible for you," Albigence continued. "I heard you were one of the first people to come across the body. I'm sure you saw devastating things. My dear, if there's any way that I could take away those memories—take them on myself—I would. As God is my witness, I would."

"But you can't, can you? I'm afraid no one can." His mention of Glyn's death sobered her. "That wasn't the worst part, though. The worst part was I thought you didn't even care. I thought you'd be glad for his death. One less problem to deal with."

"I didn't care? How could I not care? His death was a tragedy. A horrible thing. Just because I didn't know him as well as you did, his death still affected me. I'm not a monster, you know."

"I never said you were." When she finally looked him in the eye, Jo noticed something new there—a small tear. Tiny, but unmistakable. This stoic man—her husband—was on the verge of tears.

"I'm so sorry," he softly repeated. "I wish I'd told you earlier."

Jo gently placed her hand on his. "It's all right. I forgive you. But I need to ask for your forgiveness too. I never should've let my friendship with Glyn come between us."

She paused before saying, "Nothing happened between us, mind you. But I let myself get carried away by his appearance, and the way he treated me. I suppose I needed to feel important. Valued. Like I was worth spending time with. Tutoring Glyn gave me a reason to feel good about myself. Which was selfish on my part. I know that now."

"But I understand why. I was away so often I shouldn't have been surprised."

"I did wonder whether your work had become more important to you than anything else. Me, for example."

"Oh no, my dear. Nothing has ever been more important to me than you. There's something else I should've said to you then. You see, I understand why you'd be attracted to someone like Glyn. I know I can be difficult to get along with. Awkward, or stiff at times. Perhaps that's why I chose to study psychology in the first place. Perhaps I hoped to fix some part of me that was broken."

Jo couldn't help but smile. "There's nothing wrong with you, Albigence. You're just different, and that isn't necessarily bad. I daresay your difference was why I fell in love with you in the first place. I knew what I was getting myself into."

He squeezed her hand then, as if to emphasize whatever he said next. To imprint the words on her heart.

"To be honest," he said, "most people don't know what to make of me, which made your love all the more amazing. You saw past my shortcomings."

"You're much too hard on yourself, Albigence. You've always been too hard on yourself. Did you really think I was oblivious to your ploy the night we met? When you talked on and on about psychology? You say you're not brave, but you are. I could've left you standing out there on the veranda at any moment. I could've walked away and embarrassed you in front of my family and friends. But you took a chance. You touched my heart in the process. I chose to be with you, Albigence. I didn't choose anyone else."

His gaze turned solemn. "Not even the Welshman for a while?"

"No, not even him. I always thought I wasn't interested in outward, physical things. How people looked. Or what they wore. But I let a perfect stranger turn my head. Someone I didn't know very well and could barely communicate with. The attraction was all smoke and mirrors. I blame myself, though, because I should've realized how shallow my feelings were. It was a fantasy, plain and simple, but one I could've stopped. I didn't. For that, I owe *you* an apology. I really don't know what came over me."

"We've both made mistakes, and wasted a lot of time in the process." His throat moved when he swallowed. "Do you think there's a chance we could start over? Go back to the way things used to be?"

"I think so. At least, I hope so." Jo glanced at the doorway. "We have so much more to talk about, but I'm afraid my students will be here soon. They'll be shocked if they see you here with me. I do believe they think I live in the schoolroom by myself and somehow manage to eat, sleep, and live here." Such a wonderful change to be able to say something lighthearted for once.

"All right, then," he said. "I'll leave you. I don't want to, but I will."

"Wait a moment." Jo pulled something from the pocket of her skirt. She held her favorite linen handkerchief, which she'd monogrammed with her new initials once Albigence made his intentions known. She pressed it into his palm as a sign of her affection. "I think you should keep this. I think you should move your suitcase back to our cabin too. But only if you want to."

"Of course, I want to, Josephine. Desperately."

"Okay, then. Please come to the cabin after work. I'll help you unpack."

Albigence carefully placed the handkerchief in his breast pocket, where it lay against his heart.

"Thank you, darling. Now ... I think I'd like to kiss you." He leaned forward and impulsively kissed her on the lips. It was the first kiss they'd shared in weeks.

I really do love this man.

"I'll see you tonight," he whispered, earnestly. "At the cabin."

He quickly moved to the doorway before the children could see them. Sure enough, a few moments later, the panel opened with a resounding *whoosh*.

The first children to enter were the Myer twins, who barreled through the doorway and launched themselves onto the bench reserved for the youngest children. They reminded Jo of whirling dervishes with their spinning arms and legs.

"Whoa!" she said. "Hold on a moment, boys. I haven't even rung the school bell yet. Where are your manners? Haven't you forgotten something?"

"Yes, ma'am," they cried in unison. "Good morning, Teacher."

"That's better. Good morning. Now, put your lunch pails under your bench and take off your coats while I ring the bell. There's not a moment to waste today, so chop-chop."

The children did as they were told, and soon a dozen others joined them. The children thundered through the doorway like a herd of wild horses, bringing with them shrieks of laughter, stomping feet, and clattering lunch pails.

"Take your seats, please," Jo yelled, above the din.

When the noise didn't abate, as she knew it wouldn't, she set two of her fingers against her teeth and let loose with a high, shrill whistle. Not for naught had she followed her older brother around the family's stable whenever he summoned the hunting dogs. He'd taught her to whistle in secret, in the hayloft, so her mother wouldn't find out and punish her for such unladylike behavior.

The shrill noise immediately quieted the children.

"Much better, class. Now, as I told the twins, we have a lot of information to cover this morning. Today, we're going to study history. Specifically, Western European history in the nineteenth century."

"Ugh," the children cried in unison.

"Now, class. Don't despair. History can be fascinating if you know where to look."

"Do you want us to separate into groups?" Cecil, one of the older boys, called out.

Normally, Jo split the children into two groups whenever she taught a new lesson. First, she'd corral the older children at the back of the room, near the bookcase. She'd teach them the material first, using more mature terms and precise definitions.

Then, those students returned to their seats and taught the material to their younger classmates. The smaller children received the same lesson, but in simple terms they could understand.

"No, not today," she said. "Today, we'll have a combined class. Now, everyone, please fetch a blackboard from the pile. They're freshly washed, so don't dilly-dally."

Ever since Albigence had moved away, she'd found herself with more time on her hands, which she'd used to clean the classroom—scrubbing blackboards, washing curtains, mopping floors. She'd been terribly industrious during their three weeks apart and, in truth, ridiculously bored.

"All right, class," she said, when they all returned, "today, we're going to talk about the Irish potato famine. Which happened roughly seventy years ago, in eighteen-forty-five. Can anyone tell me what happened?"

The children either stared into space or played with their hands.

"Now, surely one of your parents must have told you about the famine," she said. "The event decimated the entire country of Ireland. Anyone?"

Finally, one of the older boys lifted a hand. Only instead of answering the question, he giggled into his palm.

"What are you laughing at, Cecil? Whatever could be funny about the Irish potato famine?"

"I'm not laughing," he lied, as his shoulders shook even more.

"Yes, you are. You most certainly are. I will not tolerate lying in my classroom. Now, out with it."

"It's ... it's just something my dad says," he finally confessed.

"I see." Unfortunately, a sinking feeling washed over Jo. She had a sneaky suspicion he was about to repeat something off-color about the Irish. But she'd be darned if she'd let one ill-mannered child sway the discussion with his antics.

"Well," she continued, "since you seem to find today's topic so terribly humorous, please tell us why. Just what does your brilliant father have to say about the Irish potato famine?"

She didn't mean to be cruel. After all, everyone knew the boy's father was a terrible drunk. But she didn't have the time—nor the patience—for this conversation today. If she didn't nip such talk in the bud, the children would only whisper about it later on the playground. No, a better tactic was to drag such ignorance out into the open, rather than let it fester in the dark.

The boy sat taller in his seat, as if he enjoyed the attention.

"My pa says Irish bathe in their own piss."

The class erupted into laughter, especially the older boys. To be fair, the youngest ones looked more shocked than amused.

"Well, we all know your father's wrong," Jo said. "Don't we, class? Think of all the wonderful Irishmen—and women—we have in this country. An Irishman harnessed the power of radiant heat. This is why your mother can fill your washbasins with warm water—not piss—every morning. Or look at the submarine. The very tool used by the United States Navy to fight the Germans. An Irishman invented submarines."

She took a steadying breath, hoping to control her irritation. "Now, because you have befouled our classroom with such talk, Cecil, go stand against the wall. Nose and toes against the boards. Nose and toes. Don't move until I say so."

"Yes, ma'am." The boy finally stopped grinning long enough to slide off the bench and slink to the wall. Now that he'd relinquished his moment in the spotlight, he didn't seem nearly as enthusiastic.

"There," she said. "That's better. Yes, Timothy?"

"But my dad says it too." Unlike Cecil, though, young Timothy sounded more confused than anything else. As if he honestly didn't know what to believe. "He said people from Ireland are dirty, and they smell bad."

"He did, did he? Well, what do you suppose everyone says about us? About us as Americans?"

Again, the children simply stared into space or fiddled with their fingers.

"You see, prejudice works both ways, children. To some of the Irish, we're no doubt gluttonous and lazy. But are we?"

Some of the children shook their heads vigorously.

"Of course, it's not true. Just because one person acts a certain way or does a certain thing, it doesn't apply to everyone from the same country. I'm not gluttonous," here, she turned sideways to show off her trim waistline, "nor lazy. But I'm proud to be one-hundred-percent American. You can't paint every American with the same brush. Or, every Irishman, either."

"But why do they smell, then?" a tiny voice asked.

This time, the speaker was Imogene Morgenstern, a sweet-natured child who sat in the front row. The little girl didn't possess a mean bone in her body, which meant she honestly didn't know the answer.

"I'll tell you why," Jo said. "Many people arrive here from far away. They travel by train or boat, which don't offer good washing facilities. I daresay I was in need of a good bath when I first arrived in Texas. I no doubt stunk to high heavens."

The little girl's eyes widened at the thought. But if such familiarity allowed a lesson to stick with her pupils, so be it. She'd use herself as an example all day long to drive home a point she was trying to make.

After that little incident, the rest of the day passed uneventfully, hallelujah. By the time Jo dismissed the class, she was mentally and physically drained.

She watched her students leave the room with a sigh. While she could control what they heard *inside* the classroom, she couldn't control what they heard outside it. She wasn't there at night or on weekends, and she only hoped and prayed people wouldn't fill her young students' heads with garbage by the time they returned to class Monday.

Jo locked the schoolroom door behind her and headed for the post exchange. While she'd promised to meet Albigence at their cabin as soon as possible, he wasn't due home for another hour or so. She had plenty of time to pick up groceries for their dinner tonight.

She wanted him to have a nice, homecooked meal. Although she still didn't know where he'd stayed during their separation, she doubted his accommodations had a fully stocked kitchen and someone who knew how to use it. Her husband was overdue for some sourdough bread, cured ham, and leafy vegetables, all of which she'd find at the exchange.

Mr. Johnson stood at his usual spot next to the counter when she arrived.

"Hello, there," he called out. "Got more supplies in. Let me know if you need help gettin' anythin' off the shelves."

"Thank you." Jo purposefully kept her tone cool, since she couldn't forget the way that he'd mistreated the young soldier earlier.

She quickly moved to the vegetable bin and plucked out a head of lettuce. Once she grabbed a loaf of sourdough and canned ham, she marched to the counter and laid everything out.

"Have any plans for the holidays yet?" the shopkeeper asked, as he tallied the items on a notepad.

"Hmph. Not yet. I've been too preoccupied to think about it."

Before either of them could say more, something banged on the other side of the tent. The noise accompanied a scuffle of some sort.

"What the devil—" Mr. Johnson sputtered.

Jo reacted more quickly. She hurried through the tent flap and stepped onto the landing. A small crowd had gathered in an open space next to the exchange. She pushed her way to the front and saw two teenagers holding a smaller boy down. Their victim wore an army uniform splotched with mud.

One of the boys, a strapping cowboy in leather chaps, leaned over to punch the soldier in the gut.

"Stop it!" Jo shouted. "Stop what you're doing right now."

No one listened. Instead, the cowboy hit the soldier again, and the young man's skull fell against the hard ground.

"I said to stop it," Jo yelled.

She glanced around helplessly. *Why isn't anyone doing anything?* Several grown men stood nearby, but they seemed more amused than anything else. One even slipped his neighbor a silver dollar in an apparent wager.

That was the last straw. Jo immediately shoved two fingers in her mouth and let loose with a high-pitched whistle.

The boys immediately stopped fighting. Even the one who held the young soldier still finally released him, which caused the boy to collapse in a heap.

Jo hurried to his side. He'd flung one arm across his chest in a vain attempt to protect his ribs.

"Are you okay?" she whispered.

When he didn't answer, she glared at his attackers.

"What's wrong with you two?" she yelled.

The cowboy looked especially sheepish, with his head hung low. Meanwhile, his friend studied the sky, so he wouldn't have to meet her gaze.

"Someone, run and get the MP," Jo yelled, to no one in particular. "Now!"

Fortunately, a young girl next to her nodded and scampered away.

"I'm so sorry," she said, as she returned her attention to the injured soldier. The poor lad was struggling to catch his breath.

"*Gracias*," he mumbled.

But of course. He's not from around here. She should've guessed as much.

"Can you stand?" she asked, softly.

"*Sí.* Yes." He groaned as he straightened, one arm still crosswise over his ribs.

Jo gently took the other one and helped him to his feet.

"All right then," she said. "What happened?"

The soldier shook his head. He was either too embarrassed or too upset to say.

"You can tell me," Jo said. "Please. They won't hurt you anymore."

When he still wouldn't speak, she shifted her attention to the bullies. She'd get to the bottom of this if it took her all night.

"Start talking," she spat. "What happened here?"

"Nuthin', ma'am," the cowboy said. "We were just teachin' him some manners. Didn't mean nuthin' by it."

"First of all, your grammar is atrocious," she said. "And, you've probably broken one of his ribs. I daresay the major general will lock you up in the garrison for this."

Someone snickered behind her.

"You think this is funny?" she asked the other one.

"He won't do nuthin'."

"We'll see about that. You can't just beat up a soldier and get away with it."

The injured boy finally spoke up. "No. *Por favor*. No police."

"But they've hurt you. They must be punished."

She deliberately turned her attention to the one who'd punched him in the stomach.

"All right, young man. You have two seconds to tell me your side. You'd better start talking."

"We were jus' joking around." Another halfhearted shrug. "I asked him to move aside and he wouldn't. Started gibber-gabbering at me."

"He was speaking Spanish, you idiot." Although she knew it was wrong to call someone stupid, she didn't feel very charitable at that moment.

"Don't give him no right to ignore us," the other boy said.

Jo was about to yell at him, when she realized something. She knew the boy. Even with a felt hat smashed low over his eyes, it was hard to forget his nose, which he'd broken in at least two places.

"Michael Hollingsworth. Is that you? You were in my class a few months ago."

The boy had dropped out of school unexpectedly. One day he was there, and the next, he wasn't.

"S'pose so," he muttered. "My pa got deployed overseas, so I stopped goin'."

"Your grammar is terrible too. You should've stayed in my class. You know you're not supposed to fight. What will your mother say when she finds out?"

"She don' care 'bout no Mexican."

"Stop it," Jo shouted. "Don't say another word, or I'll punish you myself."

With that, she carefully draped her arm across the injured boy's shoulder. For some reason, the MP still hadn't arrived, and she wanted to get him to the infirmary as soon as possible.

A sinking feeling washed over her, though, as she moved through the silent crowd. They knew something. Something ominous.

No one was coming. No one wanted to get involved when the victim was a foreigner.

Her plans for the evening had taken a most unexpected turn.

CHAPTER FOURTEEN

ALBIGENCE

CABIN P-79, CAMP TRAVIS

DECEMBER 1917

Albigence practically ran to their cabin once the workday ended. He'd left his desk a full half-hour early tonight, so he could hurry home and set things right with Josephine as soon as possible.

He longed to make a good impression. If he were to win her back—really win her back—then he must change the way he treated her. Keeping a better schedule was one way to start. No more rushing out of their cabin as soon as he breakfasted. No more returning home after dark. No more poring over test results at the end of the day while Josephine quietly read in a corner. If that was how they spent their nights, they might as well live in separate cabins.

During their separation, he'd come to an amazing realization. He longed to spend more time with her. He'd been so focused on moving up the chain of command— since the first day at camp, to be honest—he'd shunted aside everything else.

Even tonight, he had to fight to keep his new resolution. Since his supervisor always positioned himself near the main door to the psychology offices, there was no coming or going without the man's notice. His supervisor used a railroad steward's pocket watch, of all things, to monitor the staff as they entered or left the building. If some poor soul tried to leave before six o'clock at night, Dr. Humphries quickly noted the offense in a thick leather binder he kept at his desk.

Albigence knew he'd have to outwit the man if he wanted to leave the office early. But how?

Since the first floor offered exactly one exit, which Dr. Humphreys monitored, he realized he'd have to escape the building some other way. Ah! He remembered a washroom on the second floor with a window that offered an intriguing possibility.

Of course, the window was barely three feet wide by two feet tall, so he'd have to employ some gymnastics to use it.

After studying his options, he decided the best way to escape the building unnoticed was to shimmy through the opening, and then twist around and grab the windowsill with his fingertips. Once he steadied himself, he could release his grip and fall gently to the ground below.

Fortunately, the gardener had planted a leafy pittosporum bush beneath the window, which would cushion his fall.

The plan worked beautifully in theory, of course. The first time he tried it, during the sleepy lull of midafternoon, he froze with his fingers glued to the windowsill—too afraid to let go. On his second attempt, though, at the end of the day, he closed his eyes and willed his hands to relax.

Whoosh!

His knees took the brunt of the impact, but at least he managed to stay upright. For someone who wasn't at all athletic—and never had been—his escape was quite the feat of derring-do. Too bad he couldn't tell the others about it, especially that *H. neanderthalensis* named Frank, who would surely turn him in for insubordination.

Now, here he was, unpacking his faithful cardboard suitcase back at their cabin and listening for the soft swish of his wife's petticoats across the floorboards, which came a moment later.

"I'm in here, Josephine," he called out. "In the bedroom."

Jo swung through the doorway with a heavy sigh, her picture hat askew. She didn't even bother to remove the chapeau before she fell face-first onto the horsehair mattress.

"Heavens to Betsy." She spoke into the pillow, her voice muffled. "What a day I've had."

"Really? Well, it sounds like we both ..."

He stopped midsentence. He'd had another epiphany whilst living in the supply closet, which came rushing back. What would happen if he let his wife speak first, without interrupting her—without him trying to steer the conversation back to himself?

The thought occurred to him one lonely night when even his textbooks offered no consolation. Maybe, just maybe, Josephine might enjoy taking the reins of their conversation for once. Granted, this was not how things usually worked, but the idea warranted further study. The payoff would be an even closer union with her, which he desperately wanted.

He solemnly cleared his throat. "I'm sorry. I've interrupted you. Please tell me about your day."

Jo immediately rolled over. She also cocked an eyebrow, as if she couldn't decide whether he was serious.

"You want to hear about *my* day?" she said. "Hmm. Well, all right then. Three boys were fighting by the post exchange, and no one tried to stop it."

"Oh, no. That's terrible. What happened?"

"Well, I had no choice. I somehow got them to stop, and then I walked the injured one to the infirmary. His only crime was to be born in Mexico. Those two brutes pummeled him half to death because of it."

"My dear Josephine. You could've been injured! I only wish you would've sent for me."

"There wasn't time. Everything happened so quickly, I didn't know what to do. Turns out one of the brutes is a former student of mine. He obviously should be back in the classroom, because he doesn't know how to behave in public."

Albigence gently took her hand. Josephine really did have the most exquisite sense of right and wrong. No doubt, that's what led her to become a teacher in the first place. She couldn't help but restore order to a universe that constantly veered off-kilter.

"Go on, please," he said.

"Well, then there was this morning. I tried to give a history lesson to my class, and it turned out badly."

"Badly? How so?"

He knew he was employing a psychological tactic called "mirroring," whereby one person repeats what the other has just said, but it seemed appropriate this time. He really *did* want to know.

"Are you feeling all right, Albigence? You haven't taken ill, have you?"

"What? No, of course not. I'm fine. I'd just like to know what happened with your students today."

"Huh. Well, everything started when I brought up the topic of the Irish potato famine. Now, I didn't expect the children to know everything about it, but I also didn't expect to hear them spout such rubbish. Pure, unabashed rubbish."

"Rubbish? How could anyone argue with an actual event in European history?"

"You'd wonder, wouldn't you? Well, one child didn't doubt it happened, but he blamed the Irish for it. Said the famine was caused by their poor hygiene."

"Balderdash. A famine has nothing at all to do with personal hygiene. How could it?"

"Exactly." She paused to lay her free hand against his forehead. "You're sure you're feeling well? You're not feverish?"

"I said I'm fine, Josephine. Can't I ask you about your work?"

"Yes, you can. But you haven't shown much interest in it until now. Why the sudden curiosity?"

"I've had an epiphany." No need to hide the truth. "I believe I talk too much sometimes. It's time for me to cede the floor to you and allow you to participate more fully in our conversations."

"Me? Well, isn't that something. I really could use a sounding board. You see, I've developed a theory. I believe the parents at Camp Travis have filled my students' heads with nonsense. They tell the children all Irish people are dirty, poor, and lazy. Not to mention, odorous. Then, the children either take out their ignorance through physical violence, or they mock them behind their backs. Both are quite upsetting."

"How did you leave it with your class?"

"I did the best I could, but I don't think I convinced them. I'm afraid my students are only mirroring the prevailing attitudes at the camp. People are incredibly prejudiced here, in case you haven't noticed."

"Oh, I've noticed. The major general does nothing to stop it. He told me he lived with the Inuit for a while, but he spoke about them as if they were savages."

"Yes, and from there, it's only a hop, skip, and jump for people to feel the same way about other races. The prejudice here flows from the top down, and ends up funneling right into the minds of my students."

Albigence thought it over. "No doubt prejudice is due to the sheer number of nationalities we have at the camp. The air is full of Spanish, Italian, Dutch, French ... you name it. With so many languages, there's bound to be confusion and distrust."

"You're right." Josephine suddenly sat up. "Please repeat what you just said."

"I only meant to say, people don't trust each other because they can't speak the same language. It's just like the story in the Bible. The people of Babel only got along when they spoke the same language. Everything fell apart when God scrambled their languages."

"You're right." Jo repeated herself and rose from the bed, completely forgetting her earlier exhaustion. "People here don't trust newcomers because they don't understand them from the start. I tried to help someone with his English once, but I didn't take it far enough."

"Far enough?"

"Yes. The real problem occurs earlier," she continued. "When people first get here. If we wait until after they've been here awhile, they've already separated themselves into groups. Oh, Albigence. You're brilliant!"

"I am?"

Jo quickly kissed the crown of his head, which felt wonderful. Although he didn't know why, who was he to question it?

"What we need is a plan." She began to pace now, her movements methodical. "A way to bring people here together from the very beginning."

We? Albigence had been happy to listen to her concerns— he was especially thrilled to receive the kiss—but he didn't expect to be included in her soliloquy. His heart could take only so much excitement in one day.

"What if we came up with a way to educate the men here when they first arrive?" she asked. "Prejudice wouldn't have a chance to take hold. We'd show people our foreign guests are doing their best to assimilate."

"Just what are you proposing, Josephine?" After all, the last time she attempted to tutor someone in English, things didn't go very well. "I don't want to be indelicate, but don't you remember what happened the last time you tried to teach someone English?"

"That was a totally different scenario." She'd walked to a corner of the room and pivoted on her heel. "I'm talking about inviting large groups of people—men of all colors and creeds—to come to a rally and learn English alongside their fellow recruits. The moment they arrive."

By now, Jo was so excited, she forgot to pace altogether.

"We could use the canteen," she said. "We'll hold weekly gatherings. All free of charge, of course. For everyone. No matter the nationality. Now, what could possibly go wrong with such a plan?"

What indeed?

Albigence didn't dare say so, though, since he was thrilled to be back in her good graces.

For one thing, they'd have to use government property—the canteen—and the army was *not* known for being generous with its property.

"Now, dear. Let's think this through. We'd have to get approval from the major general, and he's a very stern man. Not to mention, he's incredibly busy."

"But I thought you knew him."

"I do. In a way." He was too embarrassed to admit his one-and-only meeting with the commander consisted of Albigence rambling on and on about something called transference.

"Then, why don't you ask him?"

Her soft brown eyes bored straight into his soul, which melted his resistance.

"Well, I suppose I could. I could make an appointment to see him." A new thought struck him, though. "But what about your time? I know how tired you are at the end of the school day. Just look at you now. You took straight to your bed. Do you really want to add another commitment to your schedule? Especially since you have the Ladies' Benevolent—"

"That's it!"

Again, she gazed at him in wonder, as if he'd said something brilliant. And, again, he had no idea why.

"Now, what?" he asked.

"I never mentioned what happened at our last society meeting. Now, don't look at me like that. I meant to tell you. I really did. The women of the Ladies' Benevolent Society elected me as their new sergeant-at-arms. I didn't even ask for the honor. The election was their idea, not mine."

"Congratulations, then."

"But it's better than you know," she said. "The sergeant-at-arms can requisition the canteen any time she wants. The major general doesn't even have to know about it."

"Are you certain?"

"Positive. The president said the sergeant-at-arms secures the canteen for all official functions. If one of those functions happens to be a large gathering of immigrants ..."

Jo didn't finish the sentence. She didn't need to. Josephine intended to go through with her plan, no matter what.

"Hmm," he said. "Perhaps it could work."

"It could, couldn't it? Oh, Albigence. An event like that might be just what this place needs to bring it into the twentieth century. To improve the lot of all newcomers without challenging the old order. After all, what could possibly go wrong?"

What, indeed!

CHAPTER FIFTEEN

JOSEPHINE

CANTEEN, CAMP TRAVIS

LATE DECEMBER 1917

Butterflies swirled in her stomach the moment Jo spotted the canteen. Dusk had fallen by now, and soft lamplight once more poured through the canteen's windows like liquid gold.

She scurried along the footpath, the new brocade shawl snug against her neck—a Christmas gift from Albigence, which he'd ordered all the way from New York City.

Normally, she'd have chosen a heavier fabric for the blouse beneath it, like boiled wool or tweed, but tonight she wore layers of silk and velvet. The very best of what she owned. She wanted to look refined and dignified, so the audience would give her its full attention.

The rally in the canteen took forever to plan. Although she didn't need the major general's permission, she still had to convince the president of the Ladies' Benevolent Society to go along with the idea.

Mrs. Benedict, whom Jo always assumed to be a decent Christian woman, turned out to be surprisingly bigoted in the end. She insisted such an audience would "dirty" the hall and ruin it for future events—spread disease and filth in a hundred different ways. Her reaction was quite disappointing, to say the least.

After listening to the matron's diatribe, Jo finally convinced her otherwise by promising to scrub the canteen from top to bottom once the event concluded.

Moving on, her next challenge was to decorate the hall. She wanted everything to be beautiful, yet functional. To make the space feel warm and welcoming—much like Rebekkah's home had felt to her when she first arrived—but also serve a practical purpose.

To that end, she painted a dozen colorful banners with English words. She used the phonetic spellings for everyday words, like hello—huh-loh—and good-day—gud-dā—which she then applied to butcher paper in bright crimson paint.

The banners reminded her of those colorful *papel picadors* she'd seen in pictures of Mexican fiestas.

Jo had put her heart and soul into planning the event. Just when she was about to open the door to the canteen and finally enter the hall, a slew of new worries assailed her.

What if no one comes? What if they're too frightened?

Or what if they thought they'd be punished for coming? Perhaps mocked if they did?

Maybe they didn't even know about it. She'd posted flyers all over the camp, including every door, wall, and flagpole she could find. But what if the men didn't even notice the flyers? Or couldn't read them?

She knew it wouldn't do any good to write the posters in English, so she searched high and low for people to translate the words. But she couldn't find translators for every single language, which left entire swaths of Europe and Asia unaccounted for. What if someone's native tongue was obscure, like Yiddish? What, then?

Stop it, Jo.

With a steadying breath, she swung open the door to the hall, where she beheld a wonderland of red, white, and blue. Best of all, the air smelled of cocoa and melted butter, since dessert tables spread along both sides of the canteen. Women who were sympathetic to her cause had piled them high with sugary treats. The first thing the audience would see when they entered the hall was an abundance of cookies, cakes, and pies—all made by members of the benevolent society.

Not everyone was willing to participate. Some people, like Mrs. Benedict, wanted nothing to do with it. Others, however, thought her idea made perfect sense and were only too happy to help.

One of those was Rebekkah, who stood by the dessert table with her back to the door.

The sight gave Jo pause. Although they'd spoken to each other since that horrible night in the bloody field, they still tiptoed around each other, as if they were afraid to do or say something to trigger another fight.

"Hello," she finally said, once she decided to approach Rebekkah.

Her friend turned. "Josephine. How are you?"

"I'm fine. A little nervous about tonight, but that's to be expected."

"Don't worry. Everything looks wonderful. And do I spy a phonograph in the corner?"

"Yes. I thought we'd play some records halfway through the program. A little Elsie Baker, or maybe the American Quartet to get things going."

"Perfect. You've really thought of everything, haven't you?"

"I hope so. Well, uh, I should—"

"Wait. Don't go." Rebekkah reached for her arm. "Please. We never really talked about what happened that night. You, know ..."

"I understand. You don't have to say anything."

"But I *must* ask. Why were you so angry with me?"

"Because you sided with Albigence." She spoke honestly, frankly. "Which crushed me. I never expected your reaction."

"I only did it because you blamed your husband for Glyn's death. Even before you knew the circumstances."

"I knew enough."

"Yes, but you took out your anger on Albigence."

"Which was understandable, given the circumstances."

"Was it? Look, Jo. I know what it's like to suffer a terrible loss. I spent a whole year of my life lying in bed with nothing for company but books. I can relate to Albigence on some level, because we both see ourselves as outsiders. I had to stand up for him. You wouldn't, so who did that leave?"

"So, that's why you took his side instead of mine?"

"I only wanted you to stop blaming him for everything. You know, Glyn chose to kill himself. He could have taken another route."

"Rebekkah, he only committed suicide because of what my husband told him, which makes Albigence partly responsible."

"Partly. But I choose to forgive people, even when they make terrible choices. Otherwise, I'm no different from all those people who say there is no God. Have you even talked to Albigence about what happened in the field? Have you forgiven him for his part in it?"

Jo lowered her gaze. "You might be surprised, but I did. Forgiving him took a long time, but I finally did."

"Good. That's what I was hoping you'd say." She glanced over Jo's shoulder. "By the way, we might have to finish this some other time. Look."

Jo turned to see a clutch of men shyly enter the canteen. Each one wore a frayed cap, heavy wool coat, and work boots of some kind. The men cast furtive glances at the heavily laden dessert tables, wondering whether they could approach.

Rebekkah didn't hesitate. She immediately grabbed a porcelain plate, loaded the dish up, and then offered the sweets to the first man she came across. Once the other women realized what was happening, they did the same.

Afterward, it was only a matter of time before dozens of other men joined them. Tall ones and short ones, middle-aged men and teenagers. Some wore newsboy caps, like the early-birds, while others sported cloth bowlers, berets, or fedoras. Most of the men dressed in thick black coats, although Jo spotted a well-worn sack suit or two in the crowd.

Ten minutes later, it seemed half the camp had piled into the canteen. When the picnic tables had filled, men took to standing with their backs against any open spots on the walls, grazing the raw wood slats, or they broke off into groups and formed tight circles around the periphery. People glanced around, not quite sure what to expect.

Jo spotted Albigence standing next to one of the windows, so she rushed over to greet him.

"I'm so glad you're here."

"Me too. I thought you might have a big audience, but nowhere near this size."

"Isn't it wonderful? There must be three-hundred people here."

"Congratulations, Josephine. You've done it." He leaned over and kissed her heartily on the lips.

He's come so far, hasn't he?

Once he leaned away again, she sucked in her breath. "Guess there's no time like the present."

She forced herself to turn around. Somehow, she found the courage to put one foot in front of the other until she found herself at the front of the hall.

A metal thingamajig—she'd heard someone once call it a speaking trumpet—waited for her there. She'd found it in the supply warehouse, where a requisitions officer entrusted the gadget to her. She didn't worry about testing out the apparatus first, though, and found it weighed twice as much as she expected.

"Hello," she said, her arm trembling from the effort. "Can everyone hear me?"

Even with the speaking trumpet, no one paid any attention. They were too busy talking, laughing, and passing cigarette butts back and forth. If anything, the din had grown even louder over the last few minutes.

By now, everyone had begun to form tight circles. Rings of men clustered along the back walls, while others pushed picnic tables together to accommodate the newcomers. She recognized the Welshmen right away, since they all hovered around Euyon, who'd tucked a harmonica into the band of his cap.

Determined to try again, she lifted the trumpet once more. "*Hola*," she screamed. Just when she was about to give up and finally shove her fingers in her mouth for a nice, loud whistle, another voice broke through.

"*Fermata*," someone yelled at the back of the room.

She smiled. She knew a smattering of Italian, and the speaker was telling his comrades to stop. How kind of him to try and quiet the crowd. Maybe he could convince them to finally settle down and pay attention to her.

But, no. Instead of waiting for the crowd to simmer down, the man continued to yell. Then, he punched someone in front of him as hard as he could. His victim dropped to the ground like a rag doll. The assault was the opening salvo in a war that'd apparently been brewing at the back of the hall.

People came from all four corners to join in on the fracas. Jo desperately scanned the crowd, searching for Albigence. *Where is he?*

Before long, a new sound rang out. She heard the *smash* of delicate bone china hitting the concrete floor. Men had taken the china plates and delicate teacups and whatever else they could find on the dessert table and hurled them across the room. Others scrabbled on the ground for the broken pottery, which they then brandished like knives.

In a matter of seconds, the hall became a bloody battlefield. Someone hurtled past the podium with his forehead split wide open. Bright red blood flowed onto his shirt, as if he'd walked under one of her beautiful crimson banners before the paint had dried.

Even those who ended up on the ground continued to roll around, their faces and clothes smeared with fresh blood.

Jo thought about screaming—a piercing, female scream, which no man could ignore—but then she finally found Albigence. He stood by the door with another man, who looked oddly familiar. The man wore the same uniform as Albigence, only he sported a shiny waxed mustache.

The two had been arguing, apparently, because the man with the moustache violently shoved her husband out the door.

Just when she thought all hope was lost, someone in her periphery hopped onto a picnic table next to her. The man had a familiar face, and he kept a shiny harmonica tucked into his hatband.

"Stop!" Euyon yelled from his perch. "*Fermare.*"

Which did nothing. The combatants couldn't hear him, or, if they did, they didn't care. They were too busy fighting each other to listen to someone on a picnic table.

Jo had never seen, or heard, anything like it in her life. The *thud* of a closed fist against a jawbone. The *craaaccckkk* of a skull bouncing off the hard floor. A loud *oof* when someone fell face-first onto the stone-cold concrete. The chaos was all around her.

Suddenly, Euyon screamed again. "*Polizia,*" he yelled.

Then, he pointed to the window, as if he spotted one of the MPs outside. That got the group's attention. One by one, the men stopped fighting when they realized the police were on their way.

All at once, the men charged the exit. Convinced they were only seconds away from being arrested, they pushed and shoved their way out of the hall. They couldn't get away fast enough.

One moment, a deafening roar filled the room, and the next, an eerie silence fell over it. Augmented by a few rough coughs from the injured men on the floor.

Jo crumpled. The crowd had destroyed everything she'd worked so hard to create. Leaving nothing in their wake but a pile of broken tables and chairs, ripped banners and slashed bunting, and telltale blood splatters on the walls. In short, hard evidence from a night gone horribly awry.

She glanced at Euyon. He'd remained on the picnic table, too stunned to move. Then, he dropped from the bench and walked away. She wanted to call out to him. To thank him for what he'd done. Heaven only knows how much worse things could've been if he hadn't intervened. But she didn't have the energy. She could barely see straight, and she didn't trust her voice to work, anyway.

Two thoughts kept scrolling through her mind.

What will they do to me? What will the army do to us?

She had no idea. Since she wasn't in the military, she wasn't subject to its laws. But Albigence was. He'd signed a contract the moment he'd joined the Medical Officers' Corp. A contract which stated he would never, ever disrespect the army's property. Of course, they'd hold him accountable.

She couldn't bear the thought. Not only had she ruined things for herself at Camp Travis, but she'd taken Albigence into the pit with her. She didn't know if she could ever forgive herself for that.

CHAPTER SIXTEEN

Approaching the major general's desk this time was much harder than before. At least the last time it happened, right after the Welshman's suicide, no one could prove his wife was involved in the tragedy.

The accusations against her then were ephemeral. Hearsay. Difficult, if not impossible, to prove.

But tonight was different. Tonight, there was irrefutable proof his wife had planned a rally that exploded into a full-scale riot. An ugly free-for-all where men destroyed government property and everyone's reputations.

Albigence pulled a handkerchief from his pocket to daub at the sweat on his hairline. The cloth was the one Josephine had given him, right after they reconciled after so many weeks apart. The kerchief was soaked in a matter of seconds.

Why is it always so blessedly hot in this office?

Unlike the rest of camp, where every cabin turned bitterly cold in the wintertime, the major general's office was as hot as the inside of a potbellied stove.

Albigence furiously dabbed at the sweat, and then positioned the kerchief in front of him, lest he need it again.

The same woman who gave him such a wonderful gift had doomed him to this moment. He was here on account of her and no one else. A woman too naïve, or too optimistic, to foresee what could happen. Why didn't she see? She was smart. She came from a fine family in upstate New York that prized books above almost everything else. Surely some of those books talked about the clans and gangs that plagued other countries.

No, it wasn't for lack of knowledge. If anything, Albigence blamed the disaster on her optimistic nature. She must've assumed no one at the camp would ever fight with anyone else. Not when there was learning to be had.

Such a naïve opinion. Just last week, a Sicilian corporal shot off the ear of a private from Northern Italy during target practice. The corporal blamed the mishap on a faulty gunsight, but everyone knew politics was to blame.

Or, what about the time a Catholic doctor from Ireland left a dirty surgical sponge in the chest of a Protestant? No one could prove the man's death was intentional, although the doctor disappeared shortly after the mishap.

One more dab with the moist handkerchief, then Albigence leaned forward to brace himself against the commander's desk. He should've warned Josephine she was playing with fire. Just once, he should've forced her to look at every angle. Even the unimaginable ones. Especially the unimaginable ones.

But he didn't. For that, he'd always be sorry.

"Well, Doctor?" the major general snarled.

"I'm ... I'm sorry," Albigence sputtered. "Did you say something?"

An irritated eyeroll. "Yes, Doctor. I did. Try to pay attention."

Now, Frank moved forward. He'd been standing in Albigence's shadow, but he pushed his way to the forefront.

"Answer the man, you idiot," he hissed in Albigence's ear.

This was just one more insult in a whole night of insults. First, Frank hauled him out of the canteen when the fighting started, over his objections, and pinned him to the ground, so he couldn't try to intervene. Then, when it became obvious the battle was over, and the men might trample them to death, Frank yanked him up and roughly shoved him toward the major general's office. Hauled him into the room and the place where they now stood.

He wanted to stay behind and help Josephine in the canteen. Set the place to rights again. From what he could hear, the fighting had destroyed everything in the hall not nailed down. The men, no doubt, left nothing behind but excruciating memories and a mountain of debris.

Either way, he didn't have a choice. When Frank grabbed him by the collar and dragged him halfway across the camp, he was done for. Now, here he stood, moments away from his fate.

"If I may say something, sir?" Frank took the lead, as always. "I'm afraid there's been a terrible mishap in the canteen tonight. A melee, as it were, in the mess hall."

"You don't say." The major general's voice dripped sarcasm. "Go on."

"Well, sir, as you know, my associate here staged a program and invited several hundred men. At my count, exactly two-hundred and forty-three men."

Albigence blinked. So, Frank had been counting noses during the event. Maybe he expected trouble all along.

"Anyway," Frank continued, "A fight broke out and the men destroyed the mess hall. I'm surprised we don't have a legion of fatalities."

Leave it to Frank to overplay his hand. Then again, Albigence couldn't blame him for the dramatics. He'd given Frank enough ammunition to destroy his career ten times over. Something the man had been dying to do since the day they met.

Crack. The commander slapped his desk angrily. "Get to the point, Dr. Beauchamp. I know exactly what happened in the canteen tonight. I have spies, of course. Apparently, the men fought like savages."

The commander rounded on Albigence. "What were you thinking, Doctor? Putting those groups together?"

"Well, everything began when one of the men—"

Whack. "That was a rhetorical question," he snapped. "I know exactly what happened out there tonight, and who was responsible. There's a reason we separate the men when they get to Camp Travis. No one from Northern Italy is ever seated next to a Sicilian. Not even in the latrine, if I can help it. If someone arrives here who once belonged to the White Hand Gang, we'd never bunk them with someone from the Black Hand Gang. Never! I thought you knew better, Doctor. What did they teach you at that fine university of yours? Obviously, not the basics of human nature."

"Bu—"

Again, the question must've been rhetorical, because the commander didn't wait for an answer.

Whack!

"I've heard just about enough out of you tonight. I'll let Dr. Beauchamp here help me decide on a proper punishment."

He turned to Frank. "So, what do you think is a fitting punishment for tonight's offense?"

"Well, sir. I've given it considerable thought."

I'll bet you have, Albigence whispered under his breath. *I'll bet you have.*

"Yes, I've pondered the matter at great length, sir. I think our only option is to issue a general court-martial for Dr. Pembrooke. As a civilian, his wife isn't subject to the same military laws, so she can't receive the same punishment. But he can, and it would serve as an excellent warning to other miscreants." He smirked. "I'd issue such a court-martial posthaste."

Albigence froze. If the major general agreed to the plan, he'd be handcuffed and hauled off to the military jail without further ado. As Frank said, "posthaste." And, he'd remain there until the commanding officer convened a tribunal.

He knew what the Official Manual for Court-Martials had to say on the subject. In fact, he'd memorized the manual, along with his other reading material, while at the officers' training camp.

And, not surprisingly, the commander suddenly perked up.

"Hmm. You're advocating I make this man a placeholder for his wife. Am I correct? Such a court-martial would separate Dr. Pembrooke from the rest of the camp. Which reminds me of another Inuit tradition."

Albigence weakly swayed, since he had no idea where the conversation was heading.

"Yes, quite so," the commanding officer continued. "The Inuit too banished any offender to the hinterlands for the good of the whole community. They'd send the guilty party packing with nothing but a knapsack and a pint of whiskey. Otherwise, the Inuit feared the wrongdoer would infect the entire village."

"Brilliant comparison, sir," Frank said, smugly. "Since the accused is a commissioned officer, he'd have to relinquish his certificate of eligibility for promotion. And, his future pay, if I recall correctly."

Of course. While Frank tried to sound nonchalant about his memory of the manual, he'd obviously read it from cover to cover too.

All of which was to say, the man desperately wanted Albigence to be thrown in jail. Denied future promotions. Denied his pay, even.

Think ... think ... think.

"Uh, hmm," Albigence coughed, since he knew he must say something—anything—in response. "May I propose a—um—compromise of sorts?" *That's it. A compromise.* A nice, benign word.

"Compromise?" The major general looked askance. "What sort of compromise do you have in mind?"

"Well, sir, I believe we can reach a compromise that will satisfy the army's need for retribution and still uphold your reputation in the process."

"Now ... now, see here," Frank sputtered. "The guilty party can't suggest his own punishment. It's not done. It's simply not done."

"Let the man speak, Doctor."

He'd obviously piqued the commander's enormous ego, which was something Albigence had counted on.

"Well ... what would happen if I were to leave the tribe?" Albigence said, "I mean, er, the Medical Officers' Corps. I could travel to one of the army's other outposts." *Think, think, think.* "Yes, quite so. One of the other outposts. A place far away from the tribe here."

So far, so good.

"You see," he continued, "there's this new psychological tool I've been reading about. It's used to combat something called, er, shellshock. Yes, shellshock."

No need to use correct terminology. No one here cares about the proper term, least of all the commander.

"Anyway," Albigence continued, desperately, "it affects soldiers who fight in the trenches. The noise of the battle alone is enough to drive some of them insane."

"Go on." His commander looked extremely curious now.

"Well, sir, there are many new treatments, some quite interesting, which are said to repair the men's nerve damage, and allow them to recover. Instead of banishing me to the hinterlands—er, from the military—I could be of some use to you."

"Huh. You don't say."

"Yes, sir. I'd face such horrible conditions near the battlefields, it'd be worse than any punishment here. Filthy conditions, deadly diseases, no food, minimal medical care ... the problems go on and on."

I could talk all night, if need be. For a hundred nights or a thousand. I could be like Scheherazade and regale the commander with story after story for as long as it takes.

"Conditions there are far worse than anything I'd face here," he concluded.

"Oh, for heaven's sake," Frank moaned. "You're not going to let this man decide his own fate, are you? Please, sir. He's trying to pull the wool over your eyes."

"Nonsense." Once more, the commander couldn't resist a fancy new psychological term. A word he couldn't wait to try out on his tongue. "Shellshock, you say. What an interesting concept. Tell me more about this disorder, Doctor."

"Certainly, sir. The disorder causes some of the men to tremble as soon as the fighting stops. Other times, the constant bombardment leaves them comatose."

The malarky just keeps coming. Thank heavens for those military manuals and the long, lonely nights in the infirmary.

"However," Albigence continued, his former trepidation long forgotten, "there are some innovative treatments on the horizon. Cold baths, electric shock therapy. Hypnosis, even."

"Hypnosis?" The commander's eyes widened even more. "You don't say. You do seem to bring up the most interesting ideas, Doctor. Go on."

"Well, sir, I've read that the Germans, those dastardly devils, are employing new trench mortars in France. The Germanic name is *minenwarfers—*" Maybe a little showing off couldn't hurt. "—which causes shaking, muteness, all manner of insanity, really, for the victims. Which renders the soldiers quite useless for future battles."

"So, you're proposing I deploy you overseas to help these men?"

"Yes, sir. I could travel to, er, France perhaps. Use my knowledge to help our soldiers in the trenches. I would be of service to you and be apart from the camp. Banished from the tribe, as it were."

"Brilliant!" *Whack.* Another fierce slap to the desk.

At this rate, the man would surely break his hand—or the furniture—due to his excitement.

"I think you've hit on the ideal solution, Dr. Pembrooke. Kudos to you for your inventiveness. Kudos."

"Thank you, sir."

"We'll draw up the paperwork tonight. You'll be held in the garrison until your steamer ship leaves tomorrow. The journey to the front takes roughly a fortnight. That'll be all."

"Oh. Thank you." Albigence faltered, since he hadn't realized his punishment would commence so soon. "Perhaps—"

"I said, that will be all."

"But, uh, what about my wife, sir? Surely, I could have a moment to tell her the plan?"

"I'm afraid not," the commander said. "If you want me to agree to this punishment of yours, it must begin immediately. Or perhaps you'd like me to change my mind—"

"Oh, no. No, sir. Not at all. I'm grateful for your consideration."

"Good. We're finished then. I'll sign the paperwork tonight."

Albigence couldn't quite make himself leave, though. "But if I could only find my wife, sir. I'd only need five minutes to tell her. Ten, at the most."

"Were you listening, Doctor? I just told you I'll agree to the overseas assignment. Even reinstate your pay. But I must insist you enter custody this evening. It's your choice. Either stay and face a general court-martial or give yourself up to the military policeman who's standing in the hall. I should think the answer would be obvious."

"But, my wife, sir," Albigence whimpered.

"You heard the man." Frank had been silent for so long, Albigence had forgotten he was in the room. "Your commanding officer obviously wants you to leave now."

The commander finally turned to Frank. "Why don't you deliver the news to Dr. Pembrooke's wife? Yes, that will work. I'm ordering you to explain the circumstances of this evening's proceedings to her as soon as possible."

"Yes, sir." Frank finally brightened a bit. "I'd be happy to. It'd be my honor. Nay, my privilege, to deliver the information."

No, no. no. Not Frank. He can't be trusted. If he does tell Josephine, it'll be convoluted. It'll sound all wrong.

"Good," the commander said. "Now, it's time for you both to leave. I haven't had my brandy tonight, and I'm quite thirsty."

He pushed a button on the side of the desk, and a lock popped. The door swung open and a military policeman marched in with handcuffs at the ready.

"Soldier, take Dr. Pembrooke into custody. He's to spend the night in the stockade before his steamer departs tomorrow. For the Western Front. See to it he's provided with enough uniforms and provisions to make the journey."

To Albigence, he added, "You're quite fortunate I'm giving you more than hardtack and whiskey. Don't let my magnanimity go to waste. Do your best with our soldiers at the front. That'll be all."

Albigence had no choice but to allow the military policeman to handcuff his wrists. Deep down, he knew he should feel relieved, since he'd avoided a military tribunal and inevitable court-martial, but his heart still splintered into a million pieces.

There was no telling what Frank would say to Josephine. Or, what he wouldn't.

CHAPTER SEVENTEEN

JOSEPHINE

CANTEEN, CAMP TRAVIS

LATE DECEMBER 1917

The scene before her was enough to chill anyone's blood. Broken picnic tables littered the floor like ruined doll's furniture, streaks of blood splattered the walls, injured men groaned miserably at her feet.

How did everything go so awry, so quickly? One moment, she was calling the meeting to order with a speaking trumpet, and the next, a roar of fistfights and angry shouts rained down.

Nothing made sense. Including the sight of Albigence leaving the hall with another man. How he deserted her. He should've stayed behind and helped her face whatever consequences arose, but he chose to leave when she needed him most.

The coward.

Weren't they supposed to be a team? Wasn't such unity the whole point of the marriage vows? They were supposed to take each other "for better or worse." Those were the words they uttered in front of a solemn minister on their wedding day. Sacred, immutable, words ... which she took to heart. Perhaps he didn't feel the same way.

Her memory of their elaborate wedding vanished when she felt a hand on her shoulder.

"Are you all right?"

Rebekkah stood beside her. The once-white apron she wore was twisted and stained.

"I really don't know," Jo whispered.

"You're not hurt, are you?"

"No, I'm not hurt. Not physically, anyway."

"Hallelujah. Thank goodness it's over. We're both fine. Everything will be fine now."

"How can you say that? Nothing will ever be fine again."

"Trust me. Whatever happens, please don't blame yourself for this. It's not your fault the men chose to fight. They were the ones who rioted, not you. So, don't take the blame for something you didn't do."

"I allowed everything to happen, though." Jo struck her forehead with an open palm. "Stupid ... stupid ... stupid! How could I have been so stupid?"

"You're not stupid, and I don't want to hear you say those words again. You didn't plan for this. There was no way you could."

"I should've known something could go wrong. I should've seen it coming. You don't even know the half of it."

"Wait ... there's more?"

"Albigence. I saw him leave the canteen with another man. He deserted me."

"What?" Rebekkah raked the hall with her gaze. "No, I don't believe it. He must be around here somewhere. He wouldn't desert you."

"You should've seen him. He couldn't get away fast enough. That's what bothers me most."

"Again … I don't believe it. Albigence wouldn't desert you like that."

"Look around. Where is he?"

"I don't know. Maybe he's outside."

"Hardly."

"Albigence," Rebekkah called out. "Where are you?"

No one responded, of course. Even the injured men who'd groaned at their feet had been taken away by comrades. The only noise left in the hall came from their own voices.

"Albigence," Rebekkah called, again. "Where are you?"

"Calling him won't help. He's not here. I saw him leave. You're wasting your time."

"Who's not here, eh?"

They both turned to find Euyon standing behind them.

"Albigence," Jo muttered. "He's gone."

"'Tis a pity. It's a right fine mess the boys made o' this place."

"You can say that again. They couldn't have done more damage if they'd tried." Jo suddenly remembered her manners. "But thank you for stopping them. I don't know what I would've done if you hadn't taken charge. Your idea to trick them into thinking the military police were coming was brilliant."

"Well, it was only a wee lie." He smiled slyly. "Not a big one a-tall. Who's to say the coppers wouldn't have shown up after a time?"

"I'm just grateful for your help," Jo said. "You're the reason the fight didn't get even worse."

"Ya mean, they didn't burn the place down? A pity, that. Would've meant a lot less work on our part."

"True enough." Rebekkah took a deep breath. "Well, you know what they say. Put one foot in front of the other, and don't stop until you get to the end."

With that, the three of them spent a final moment surveying the damage. Then, Jo wearily moved toward a bucket she'd spied near the lectern.

Armed with the bucket, a pile of linen napkins from the dessert table, and a grim determination, she set to work picking up pieces of broken pottery and shattered glass. By the time she knelt for the twelfth time, her back ached and her shoulders stooped, but she didn't stop.

She didn't pause until she'd removed every single piece of smashed pottery. Meanwhile, Euyon flipped over the upended picnic tables and ferried the broken wood out to a rubbish pile behind the hall.

For her part, Rebekkah went home to retrieve some supplies, and when she returned, she brought a broom, dustbin, and one very sleepy husband. Otto didn't even bother to change from his crinkled linen nightshirt. He merely tucked it into a pair of gabardines.

Jo's eyes widened. An emergency was one thing, but she never thought she'd see a pastor in his nightclothes. His blond hair stood on end too, as if his wife had awoken him from a deep sleep.

He whistled under his breath when he saw the carnage. "Dad-blame it all."

After that mild oath, he set to work with the rest of them.

Hour followed backbreaking hour, with no relief in sight. By midnight, Jo was ready to collapse. So tired she even forgot about Albigence's betrayal. There simply was too much work to be done and not enough time to do it.

At one point, she dropped to her hands and knees to scour the most stubborn stains. By the time she finished, lye soap soaked her dark hem, and sharp debris had torn her cuffs to shreds. All of which was a small enough price to pay, though, for the damage she'd caused.

Euyon handed her a whiskey flask a few hours before dawn. She was too tired to refuse and too grateful to say no. The acrid taste burned her throat and eyes, but it also brought some much-needed relief.

Sometime later, heaven only knows when, the sky outside finally lightened. She hadn't eaten anything since yesterday morning, and her stomach ached almost as much as her back.

"Rebekkah?" Jo called out. "Where are you?"

"Over here." Rebekkah emerged from the shadows, looking grim. "We cleaned the walls as best we could. Otto had to go home to prepare a sermon. But he gives his best. Said he'd be praying for you."

"Please thank him, and tell him how much I appreciated his help."

"Of course," she said. "He wanted to be here, no matter how it looked."

At that point, both women glanced at the doorway, half-expecting to find Euyon there. He'd been working to rebuild the transom, which the crowd had torn from the frame.

But he wasn't there. Instead, they spied a man wearing regulation army jodhpurs and a shiny waxed moustache.

Jo dragged herself across the hall.

"Weren't you with my husband last night?" she wearily asked.

"I was." Unlike the rest of them, he looked remarkably fresh. As if he'd enjoyed a full night's sleep, a hot shower, and a hearty breakfast. "He and I saw the whole thing from a spot over there."

He pointed to a place by the wall which had become much too familiar. It was the last place she'd seen Albigence, before he disappeared in a puff of smoke.

"Where is he?" she rasped.

"Didn't he tell you?" The stranger shook his head. "Tsk, tsk, tsk. Surely, he came back to explain why he had to go away."

"No, he didn't. I have no idea." It pained her to admit the truth. "I haven't seen him since last night. Do you know where he's gone?"

"Of course. The whole camp knows. I'm just surprised he didn't tell you first. Not very gentlemanly of him, was it?"

He tried to sound sincere, but she didn't believe him. For one thing, his smile didn't extend to his eyes, and his voice sounded too sweet to be real.

"Tell me where he's gone," she pleaded. "I need to know."

"Now, your question poses a certain conundrum. Yes, indeed. As a military officer, I'm not supposed to give the whereabouts of our forces. What to do?" Here, he tapped his chin as if deep in thought. "Whatever should I do?"

"Out with it," Jo finally demanded, when she couldn't take it anymore. She also grabbed his wrist firmly. "Once and for all, tell me where my husband went."

Her boldness shocked him. He wrenched his wrist free and took a step back. "Touch me again and I'll have you arrested. There's no reason to make a scene."

"A scene?" How could they possibly make a scene where they stood? "I need to know where my husband's gone. Please help me."

"That's better. Your husband volunteered to leave for Europe today. He couldn't resist the offer of a promotion, but I never expected him to leave without telling you. It's quite uncalled for."

Her resolve finally broke, and she slowly sank to the ground, numb with grief. "Is it true? He left for Europe? He volunteered?" Nothing about the statement made sense, and she struggled to understand. "What … what kind of promotion did they give him?"

"The major general offered him extra pay. Said he'd be working with soldiers who suffer from something called 'shellshock.' If you ask me, it's all a load of rubbish. Something created by cowards to get out of their military service."

He continued, "Your *husband*"—he overarticulated the word, as if Albigence hadn't earned the title—"told the major general he'd be honored to accept the position. I expect his steamship is somewhere in the mid-Atlantic by now."

After a beat, the man continued. "My dear, I can't imagine why he did this to you, but you need to pull yourself together. Just because he abandoned his duties at home—"

"No," she murmured. "I don't believe you." She lifted her gaze defiantly. She and Albigence had come too far for him to do something like this. No matter what anyone said.

"Dear me." The man shook his head again. "I worried this might happen." He calmly reached into his breast pocket and withdrew a piece of cloth. "Here you go. He asked me to give something to you. Said he wouldn't be needing it where he was going. I believe the handkerchief belongs to you?"

He dropped the cloth in her lap, as if it were a piece of rubbish. It was the same handkerchief she'd given to Albigence when they reconciled. The one she'd spent hours on, embroidering her new initials as a symbol of their love. Every elaborate stitch mocked her now.

The stranger droned on, unaware—or, more likely, unconcerned—with her distress.

"Some men have no respect for the institution of marriage," he tsked. "I've never been married myself, mind you, so I can't speak from personal experience. But your husband's actions seem rather cold, wouldn't you say?"

"What's this man telling you, Jo?"

She turned to find Rebekkah standing behind her.

"He ... he says Albigence left the camp." She limply lifted the handkerchief as proof. "My husband didn't want this anymore. He's in Europe now. With a promotion."

"Nonsense," Rebekkah said. "I don't believe that for a moment. You shouldn't either. Why, I ought to—"

"Dear me," the man said, as he made a big show out of checking his pocket watch. "It's getting so late. I really should be going. Good day, ladies. Good day."

He abruptly turned and left. He'd said his piece, apparently, and he didn't have the patience, or the wherewithal, to answer more of her questions.

He scurried to the exit like an exposed rat, and then disappeared.

"You don't believe him, do you?" Rebekkah said. "Please tell me you don't believe him."

Jo couldn't answer. She was too busy staring at the lace handkerchief in her lap. The edges tattered and dirtied now, like a piece of trash that'd been thrown away. Abandoned. Something no one needed, or wanted, anymore.

Much like her.

CHAPTER EIGHTEEN

ALBIGENCE

U.S.S. MADAWASKA, OFF THE COAST OF FRANCE

JANUARY 1918

Albigence leaned over the ship's rail again, sick to his stomach. He spewed what was left of his breakfast into the Atlantic and prayed it'd be the last time.

But it wasn't. It never was.

Every morning started the same way now. After a fitful night's sleep, he'd venture below deck for a breakfast of rubbery brown eggs and burnt toast. Then, he'd return to an upper deck to survey their position at sea. After only ten minutes or so, his throat would tighten again and sour acid would wash through his mouth.

The debacle had begun in Galveston Harbor. Most of the soldiers met up in New York Harbor at the start of their journey, but a once-in-a-century ice storm temporarily halted military operations up and down the Eastern seaboard. Had he been allowed to join his comrades in New York, he would've been assigned a different ship. Perhaps a smaller one with a better cook and fresher ingredients. The outcome could've looked much different.

The ultimate irony involved the ship's provenance. The German owners had christened the vessel *König Wilhelm II*, and then they left the vessel in the care of shipbuilders in New Jersey. Apparently, they expected the Americans to repair a broken propeller before the war broke out. Imagine their surprise when the United States officially entered the fray and promptly confiscated the vessel. The Yanks renamed it the *Madawaska* in tribute to a band of brave French-Canadian traders who'd come from a city of the same name. At three stories tall, with two smokestacks, the ship offered countless wraparound decks, which gave him privacy for the bouts of nausea when they afflicted him each morning. For that, Albigence was eternally grateful.

He didn't have such privacy in his own stateroom. The military had converted each single stateroom into sleeping quarters for six men. Six men! The smell alone was enough to drive a man insane. With so many men living in close quarters, the air constantly reeked of sweat, halitosis, and flatulence.

All of which was to say, he'd been miserable from the start of the journey some two weeks back and miserable he remained.

If only Josephine could see him now. She'd know what to do. She'd place a cool compress on his forehead and offer him a soft shoulder for his aching head. She might even wipe perspiration from his brow using one of her perfumed handkerchiefs, just like the kind she gave him when they reconciled. He never did find it after he left the major general's office. He'd turned his pockets inside out and searched everywhere, to no avail.

"Are you ill, sir?"

He turned his aching head to find a young soldier staring at him.

"What do you think?"

"You look mighty green to me. Just like one of those big ol' tree frogs we have back home." The boy smacked his lips appreciatively. "Um, um good. They're pretty tasty when you cook 'em in butter."

Albigence's stomach clenched, and he retched over the side of the ship for the umpteenth time that morning.

"Did I say somethin' wrong?" The boy looked surprised. "It's just tree frogs on the bayou are mighty green. And jumpy. Did ya know they can go from one side of a football pitch to the other in a single jump?"

"No, I didn't." Albigence wiped his mouth miserably on his cuff. He had no desire to engage the young man in conversation. In fact, he felt like leaping right off the deck, like one of those green tree frogs the boy kept jabbering on about.

"My name's Boone, by the way." The kid thrust out his hand, which left Albigence no choice but to reciprocate. "Like in Daniel Boone. The fella with the coonskin cap?"

"Yes, I know of him." He offered Boone the hand with the unsoiled sleeve, although he thought about using the other one.

"You don't look like all the other fellas in those funny pants. Whadda they call those pants, anyhow?"

"The technical term is jodhpurs." Albigence sighed wearily. "It's a type of riding pant. From India."

"India? Whoo-ee. Now, that's somethin'. Say, where do I get me a pair of those?"

"You can't. The army requisitions them. They're reserved for the Medical Officers' Corps."

The boy's eyes widened. "So sorry, sir. I didn't realize I was talkin' to an officer." He snapped off a crisp salute, as if embarrassed by his oversight.

"At ease, soldier. I'm not a commanding officer. I'm a psychologist, you see." Perhaps there was no way out of the conversation, after all. "I help men with their problems."

"You mean, like a priest or somethin'?"

"Not quite. I help people with mental issues. I also administer those intelligence tests the men take when they sign up for the army. The ones with numbers and such."

"You mean, the figurin' ones? Back home, we called that the pencil test. Took me a lot of ciphering to finish, I'll tell ya."

"Yes, that's the one. If you don't mind me asking, son ... how old are you?"

The boy looked much too young to be wearing an army uniform. His cheeks were too smooth and shiny, and his teeth were white as pearl buttons. He also wore an olive drab winter coat that hung on his skinny frame as if the coat belonged to someone else. His father, perhaps?

"I'll be fifteen next week," Boone said proudly.

"Then, what in the devil are you doing here? I thought the minimum age was sixteen."

"Well, they don't check or nuthin'. I told the man at the recruiting office I'd be sixteen soon enough. He said somethin' about fifteen bein' close enough for gov'ment work."

"I'll bet he did. Well, Boone, I enjoyed meeting you, but I'm afraid I'm rather ill. I think I'd better return to my bunk."

On cue, an enormous wave crashed against the ship's hull, which sent Albigence's stomach into a freefall.

"Wait a minute." The boy ignored a cold spray of seawater that splashed over them. "I got somethin' for that."

He reached into a coat pocket and, after a moment, thrust something in Albigence's general direction. It looked like a clump of dead leaves. Brown and brittle, no doubt due to the rigors of travel and time.

"Ever hear of somethin' called nightshade?" The boy offered up a wilted leaf. "Grows wild on the bayou, jus' like those tree frogs. So thick, you can hardly work your way 'round it sometimes. It'll settle your stomach right down."

"Really?" Albigence squinted at the boy's offering. At this point, he'd do anything to settle his stomach, even if it meant swallowing something brown and wilted.

"Where are you from?" Albigence asked, once he'd ingested a leaf. It seemed only right to repay the boy's kindness with a little conversation. "Your accent reminds me of the Southerners who lived at my training camp back in Texas."

"I was born in Louisiana, sir. Clear 'cross the state from N'awlins."

"Well, then. Why weren't you at Camp Travis? Don't all the Southerners train there?"

"Nah. They trained me up at place called Camp Pike in Little Rock. That's where I was livin' at the time. Where's your people from?"

"I don't have many 'people,' per se. My wife's back home at Camp Travis. No doubt wondering where I am."

"Sounds 'bout right. I 'spect we'll all be wondering what we signed up for when we get to the trenches."

"No, I'm going somewhere else." Albigence shook his head thoughtfully. "I'll probably be assigned to a military office in Brest."

"Yer lucky then. They told me my new home would be nuthin' but hardpacked mud and curly wire. No light to speak of. Sounds like yer getting' the better end of the deal."

Albigence silently considered it. While this youngster would spend his days and nights in a squalid trench, Albigence would be ensconced in a comfortable office building in Brest. The furthest thing from a filthy trench.

He'd seen photos in the newspaper. Lines of foxholes wound around the French countryside like one continuous scar, complete with barbed wire and sandbags stacked shoulder high. They'd become a breeding ground for head lice and something new called "trench foot."

"Do ya miss her?" Boone asked, which broke Albigence's reverie.

"I'm sorry?"

"Yer wife. You said you left one back home."

"Yes. Yes, I do." A heavy sigh. What could this lad know about leaving behind a woman like Josephine? He missed everything about her, all the time. If not for the seasickness, he'd think of nothing else.

"I guess it's too late to telegraph her now," the boy said.

"Telegraph?" Albigence started, despite the nausea. "What do you mean, telegraph?"

"You know, send her a ship-to-shore telegram."

Why, of course. A telegram. Why hadn't he thought of it? He could request one from the ship's captain. Perhaps he could even say it was an emergency. They'd have to deliver the missive to Josephine—they'd have no choice.

"So, I could send her a telegram." Albigence murmured. "Of course! Where do I go? What do I do?"

"Whoa, sir. Slow down." Boone frowned, for some reason. "It's too late now. We're too close to shore. They said so in muster anyway. The cap'n has to shut everything down 'fore we land. Didn't they tell you that in muster?"

"I ... I don't know. Probably. Maybe." There'd been so many instructions, and he was too sick to care. "I wasn't really listening, to be honest."

"Yeah, I'm 'fraid it's too late now. Maybe they'll let you send one when you get to that fancy headquarters yer goin' to."

"Maybe. We'll see."

"No chance of that for me, I guess. We don't git to stay in one place very long. We move around a lot. Kinda like those tree frogs jumpin' from one branch to the next." He grinned at his own cleverness.

Meanwhile, Albigence studied the approaching coastline, which was windswept and ghostly. The skeleton of an old fishing trawler lolled on the sand like a beached whale whose insides had been hollowed out by weather. Who knows what had become of the ship's captain?

And, the cliffs! A rock ledge towered over the beach like a fortress. A fortress made of sea salt and limestone.

"Will you look at that." He couldn't help but be amazed. "The coastline is so much longer than the one we have in New York."

Boone nodded. "Don't look like the Gulf, neither. We'll be there 'fore long."

"I'd say. Well, I guess I'll see you on shore, Boone." Fortunately, the Navy provided excellent cover for them in the port of Brest—their destination. Brest had a sheltering bay and nearby peninsula, which meant they wouldn't be fired upon. Very different from the acres of empty sand in Normandy.

In fact, he'd been told that Brest was strikingly similar to the bustling hamlets of upstate New York. People still walked the streets in Brest. No one covered their windows with newsprint, and even women and children felt safe enough to stroll outside.

Albigence carefully turned back to study the boy. He had something important to say, and he wanted to make sure he said it. He might never see this stranger again, and it didn't seem fair they'd drawn such different lots in the army.

"Take care of yourself out there, Boone," he said. "Watch your back. We all want you to come back home in one piece."

"'Course, sir." The boy chuckled, as if he expected nothing less. "Got to get home for next year's Mardi Gras, now don' I?"

The lad obviously wasn't acquainted with trench warfare. He hadn't read the same newspapers as Albigence, and he hadn't seen the same photos. He didn't know his safety was far from guaranteed.

CHAPTER NINETEEN

JOSEPHINE

PARSONAGE, CAMP TRAVIS

LATE JANUARY 1918

A fat wedge of sunlight warmed her cheeks as Jo gradually wakened. The bed was next to an East-facing window, which allowed the full strength of the sun to wash over her face.

She gradually turned and spotted a shadowy figure at the footrail.

"Hello, sleepy head," Rebekkah said.

"Where am I?"

Nothing about the room looked, or felt, familiar. Unlike her own bedroom, this one had yellow paper on the wall that flowered like a crop of sunny daises on the prairie.

"You're in the parsonage, silly. Though I don't suppose you've seen this room before."

No, she hadn't. She'd spent countless afternoons on Rebekkah's front porch, reading books, or at the kitchen table, drinking ginger soda, or on the Chesterfield in the front parlor, knitting socks for servicemen. But she'd never gotten this far inside the cabin before. It just wasn't done.

"We have two bedrooms," Rebekkah explained. "The building used to be a grain dispensary, so there was plenty of room."

Only then did Jo notice the musky scent in the air. Barley, perhaps? She'd always assumed the woodworkers had built Rebekkah's cabin like hers, with a bedroom, front parlor, and kitchen. But then she remembered some of the cabins started life with a different purpose altogether.

Like the schoolhouse, which served as a storeroom before the army converted it. She sat bolt upright.

"The children. Oh, my goodness! I completely forgot—"

"Relax. It's Sunday. You don't have to worry about the children today."

"Which means—"

"You slept through Saturday. Though no one could blame you. Not after our horrible night in the canteen."

Her words called forth the memories ... none of them good. She remembered a weasely man with a shiny waxed moustache, his oily smile so disingenuous. Holding a handkerchief—her handkerchief—which she'd given to Albigence. The man had flaunted it, as if he was ecstatic at her misfortune.

"Wasn't there a stranger with a waxed moustache?" she asked. "He told me Albigence was gone. Said he took a promotion or something overseas." She chose her words carefully, because she still couldn't decide whether she'd dreamt the conversation, or whether she'd actually lived through it.

"Euyon told me the same thing," Rebekkah said. "Apparently, Albigence left on a steamer ship. But I doubt he wanted to go."

"If they gave him a promotion, like the man said, why wouldn't he? He's always wanted one. He'd told me more than once."

"I still don't believe it. Your husband would never leave you."

"But it all makes sense now. Albigence wanted to be the chief medical officer."

"Yes, but think about it. He idolized you. He'd never do anything to jeopardize your marriage."

"But what if they promised him a *lot* more money—"

"Nonsense. If, for some reason, they made him leave Camp Travis, you have to believe he didn't want to go without you."

Jo raked her fingers through her matted hair. "This is all so confusing. I don't know what to believe anymore."

"Look ... he treasured you above all else. He wouldn't have left if he could avoid it. I truly believe he's coming back again."

"I wish I had your faith."

"Hmm." Rebekkah studied her. "There's a story in the Bible similar to your situation. Have you ever heard of a woman named Rahab?"

"I think so. Wasn't she a prostitute?"

"Yes, she was. But she also had a lot of faith. She hid the spies who were fighting for Israel, even though she could've been killed for doing it."

Rebekkah continued, "The spies told her to drape a red cord out her window, so they'd know which house was hers when they returned. Sure enough, when they came back to destroy Jericho, they saw the cord and spared Rahab and her family."

"But what does that have to do with me?" Although she didn't mean to sound selfish, Jo couldn't make the connection.

"Think about it. Rahab had so much faith, she believed the spies would do exactly what they said they'd do. So, she patiently waited for their return. I hope you'll do the same with Albigence. Patiently wait for his return. As a matter of fact ..."

She arose from the bed to retrieve something from the dresser. Something that looked like a rusty canning jar filled with buttons, threads, and whatnot. She rummaged through the jar until she found what she was looking for, which she brought to the bed.

"Here. I meant to use this on a pillow one day, but I want you to have it." She pressed something into Jo's hands. The circle was a mother-of-pearl button with a scarlet thread wound through the openings. "This button will remind you to have faith in Albigence. I believe he's coming back again. I want you to believe it too."

Jo cautiously took the offering. Although small, the bright red thread was unmistakable.

"If you say so."

Now, if she could just find out what they'd done to her husband and what they might do to her. Then, perhaps, she could have Rebekkah's confidence.

★★★

The days turned to weeks, but no one offered any news about her husband's disappearance. Once Jo finished at the schoolhouse each afternoon, she'd rush to the major general's headquarters to plead for information, to no avail.

After several weeks of this, it was time for another meeting of the Ladies' Benevolent Society. While she hated to put her search on hold, the pause might provide a few hours' distraction and give her something else to think about for a change. She'd also come to realize the group's members might be able to help her with her search.

Granted, some of the women had been downright rude to her when Jo asked them to volunteer for the rally. But others had been exceedingly generous. She'd also found that nothing made people more charitable than watching someone, like her, suffer a great downfall.

She might even ask the group's president for help.

That's it!

She could ask Mrs. Benedict to introduce her to officials at the War Department in Washington. She'd read about the department's American Expeditionary Forces, which was the new name given to soldiers who served in France. If Mrs. Benedict could help her find out where Albigence had been stationed, perhaps she could reach him by post or telegram.

She quickly threw the brocade shawl over her shoulders and dashed from the cabin.

Rebekkah was waiting for her on the footpath. Since the "incident" a fortnight ago, some of the camp's residents had taken a perverse pride in shunning her, so Rebekkah liked to escort her around the grounds.

She couldn't be everywhere, though. Just yesterday, Jo was walking by herself when a stranger approached from behind. She deliberately clipped Jo's heel with her boot, which pitched Jo forward. If not for a railing that broke her fall, she would've sprawled face-first onto the path.

Rebekkah greeted her with an encouraging smile, which softened the harsh memory.

"You look lovely," her friend said. "New blouse?"

"Yes. I've been saving it for a special occasion."

"Well, the color suits you." Rebekkah squeezed her arm. "Do keep your chin up. There's no telling what the others will say about us when we get there."

"Us? You're very kind to include yourself in my mess. We all know the riot was my fault, not yours. Just yesterday—"

Jo was about to tell Rebekkah about the incident on the footpath when someone tapped her shoulder. She turned to see Genevieve Johnson, the shopkeeper's wife, who had rushed up behind them.

"You have some nerve," the woman hissed. "It's a miracle they still let you teach at the schoolhouse. Shame on you. Shame on you!"

She'd stunned Jo into silence. Where was the amiable woman who liked nothing more than sweets and gossip?

"Stop it, Genevieve." Fortunately, Rebekkah had no trouble finding her voice. "Josephine was only trying to help the soldiers. She should be praised for what she did, not punished."

"Praised?" Mrs. Benedict scowled. "For your information, those filthy men bring all sorts of diseases with them. Everyone knows they're unclean. You, in particular. Why, I've seen how you herd them to the back of the chapel whenever we have a Sunday service."

"I do no such thing!" Now, it was Rebekkah's turn to look horrified. "People sit wherever they wish to in the chapel. Otto and I would never tell them where to sit." She paused to collect herself. "But, you're right. I'll make it a point to invite our newcomers to come closer to the altar next time. Thank you for reminding me."

"That's not what I meant, and you know it," the woman snarled. "I'd rather see less of those heathens—not more of them."

Now, Jo felt compelled to speak. "Mrs. Johnson, if you're so smallminded you can't even be nice to our brave soldiers, then I feel sorry for you. Let's go, Rebekkah."

She pulled her friend away, since she couldn't imagine

spending one ... more ... moment in such a horrible woman's presence, listening to her spew garbage about the newcomers.

Why did people have to be so hateful? She couldn't imagine hating a whole group of people simply because they wore different clothes or ate unusual foods or spoke with an accent.

Jo tried to shake off the conversation as they walked to the meeting. She paused on the threshold of the canteen. "Rebekkah? Do you think everyone else thinks the same way?"

"I honestly don't know. I do remember how hard you worked to get these women to volunteer for the rally, though. They didn't exactly embrace the idea. Maybe you should prepare yourself for anything tonight."

Jo nervously followed her inside. The move felt like stepping back in time. To the days before the riot, when picnic tables neatly ringed the podium. When U. S. Army posters hung from the rafters, crisp and colorful. When a table laden with sugary sweets welcomed people, the plates and cups still intact and beautiful.

As always, the board of directors commandeered the head table, which they'd placed near the front of the hall. Only one chair sat empty there. It was hers. The spot reserved for the group's sergeant-at-arms.

She calmly said goodbye to Rebekkah and slowly approached the waiting chair. Whispers, which she tried to ignore, floated on the air behind her as she walked.

Little by little, the voices fell silent. Apparently, everyone was waiting to see what she would do next. Would she take her rightful place at the head table, or would she slink off to a corner, like a criminal caught doing something wrong?

Well, if it's a show they want, I can't disappointment them, can I?

Jo steeled herself against the stares and marched

straight to the head table. Her steps wobbled, but she knew she had to take control of the situation.

"I'd like to say something." She spoke over the heads of the audience, so she wouldn't have to look anyone in the eye. "I'm sure you've all heard—"

Something sharp pinched her shoulder just then.

"Ouch!"

"Sit down." A woman's fingernails bit into her skin like icepicks.

"Stop it! You're hurting me."

"Good."

She turned to see Mrs. Benedict, the group's president, who finally released her grip.

"Sit down, Josephine," the matron said. "We'll deal with you later."

Jo faltered. On the one hand, she needed this woman's help if she hoped to find Albigence soon. On the other, she wanted everyone to know her side of the story and set the record straight. Explain to them what really happened during the rally, apart from the gossip and innuendo swirling through camp.

She couldn't do both. So, she held her tongue as she slunk back to the head table. Finding Albigence was more important than anything else at the moment. Even her wounded pride.

The president briskly called the meeting to order as if nothing had happened. Once she made the routine announcements, she sought out Jo again.

"Would Mrs. Josephine Pembrooke approach the lectern?"

It wasn't a question, and Jo knew it. So, she slowly rose, but as she did so, something in her pocket tapped against the edge of the table. The noise was the *clink* of the mother-of-pearl-button Rebekkah had given her, threaded as it was with a red silk cord.

She reached into her pocket and withdrew the treasure. The red thread was a symbol of faith. A symbol that meant everything was going to be all right, as long as Jo didn't lose hope. She grasped the button tightly and moved to where the group's president stood.

"You've left us no choice," Mrs. Benedict announced, "but to relieve you of your duties as sergeant-at-arms. As well as your membership in the Ladies' Benevolent Society. *If* you had read the charter's covenants, you'd know why." She cleared her throat and began to read.

> Any member who brings dishonor upon the Ladies' Benevolent Society, Camp Travis chapter, shall be summarily dismissed. Our goal is to maintain the utmost propriety at all times. Anything less will be grounds for termination and—

"Prop ... propriety?" Jo interrupted. "Is that what you call this? I'd call it small-mindedness. Prejudice, even."

Jo took a deep breath. Even though she wanted to find Albigence with all her heart, this was too much.

"They say war is hell," she continued, her voice shaking, "but sometimes the home front is no better. I'll gladly relinquish my position, but I'll never stop working for the soldiers here. The ones who come from far away. The ones who count on us to welcome them. Because they deserve it. Shame on you for not realizing that."

She stepped away from the lectern, and then, she immediately heard a swish of petticoats as someone joined her in the aisle.

Together, she and Rebekkah moved under the transom, which Euyon—a "dirty" Irishman—had so lovingly repaired.

She couldn't wait to escape the canteen now and breathe

fresh air again. Shake off the heat from the hundreds of eyes boring into her back.

She didn't stop walking until they stood outside.

"I'm so sorry, Rebekkah."

"Sorry? Whatever for? I'm proud of you."

"How can you be proud of me? I ruined any chance I might've had for Mrs. Benedict to help me find Albigence. Or to help the foreign soldiers here. I let my pride get in the way."

"It's all right."

"I doubt she'll ever help me now."

"You still have me, don't you? We'll figure it out. We don't need her."

Rebekkah sounded so confident. Much more confident than Jo felt. Although she'd tried to sound brave during the meeting, a wash of doubts crashed over her now.

How were two women ever going to help a whole camp full of foreign-born soldiers when no one else cared? How could they possibly find Albigence among the thousands of soldiers fighting overseas?

To do either would take a miracle, and she wasn't sure a miracle was on its way.

CHAPTER TWENTY

ALBIGENCE

CAMP PONTANEZEN, NEAR BREST, FRANCE

FEBRUARY 1918

A thin rain washed the gangplank of the *U.S.S. Madawaska* as Albigence disembarked. After two weeks at sea, he could've kissed the dirt beneath his feet when he finally stepped onto the ground.

He carried only a lightweight duffel, which the MP had packed for him, along with his military orders. Meanwhile, hordes of soldiers all around him struggled to maneuver down the gangplank with their arms laden with heavy gear.

The supplies were enough to make any soldier think twice about his deployment—gas masks, respirators, anti-gas capes. If someone hadn't worried about the deployment before, he *would* worry once he received such things. Who wouldn't think twice about deployment when the enemy was chlorine, which attacked the lungs, or mustard gas, which charred the skin, or bromide, which led to blindness? They were enough to make anyone afraid.

As if to compensate, the requisitions officer casually handed each man a metal helmet as he disembarked. As if a thin layer of steel could somehow protect the soldier from the power of a German howitzer. The helmet was arbitrary, and they all knew it.

Albigence carefully picked his way through the chaos and stepped aboard a troop transport bound for Camp Pontanezen. Although he'd originally been told he was headed for Brest, he soon learned his orders were for an army camp located three miles to the south. The camp was the first stop for fresh troops who arrived on the continent, and the last stop for men too injured to fight anymore.

The truck rumbled over wood planks placed end-to-end, which covered the muddy roads to protect the tires and axles. With each bump and bounce, soldiers sitting on the floorboards groaned as they rearranged the heavy equipment on their knees.

Soon enough, a dull, gray camp appeared. The army had conscripted an old French garrison as headquarters, which the natives ironically called "Napoleon's Camp." Since the Little General suffered such an ignoble defeat at Waterloo, the name did *not* bode well for the newcomers, but no one seemed to notice when they rumbled past the signpost.

The truck next careened through a set of iron gates and then stopped in front of the barracks. Much like Camp Travis, the officers here enjoyed actual cabins, which were made of wood and canvas. Meanwhile, privates and specialists had to make do with simple tents, not unlike the khaki tents back home.

Six stone buildings, a holdover from the camp's days as a garrison, stood among barracks and tents. The crumbling stone structures sagged into the earth, as if they wanted to disappear beneath the mud and muck.

Albigence headed for a building with a large red cross painted on its side. Once there, he stepped over a broken transom to enter a hall which was as gloomy and damp as the weather outside.

The first floor had no windows, which meant most of the light came from tin lanterns nailed to the rafters. He managed to find his way into the main hall, which was separated from the rest of the building by an enormous muslin curtain.

He assumed the curtain blocked off a recovery area of some sort, because low murmurs and soft moans could be heard on the other side of it. Every once in a while, an elbow poked the fabric and made it ruffle back and forth, like a coarse sailcloth in a breeze.

He finally spotted a bored orderly leaning against one of the walls.

"Hullo," he said, as he reached the man. "Can you tell me who's running the show here?"

"I'd say the Germans are at this point," he replied, drolly. "But whaddya need?"

"To find my office. I'll be working with the men in recovery. I'm a psychologist, you see."

The man shook his head. "I'm sorry to hear that."

"What do you mean? I just want to find the psychologists' offices. Do you know the way or not?" No matter the orderly's opinion of the place, he didn't have the right to be rude.

"It's just down the hall," the stranger said. "First door on your left. Good luck to you."

"Thank you. I appreciate it." Albigence hoisted the duffel and turned to leave.

At that moment, a loud scream tore through the space.

"Aiiiyyyaaa!"

"What in the blazes was that?" Albigence asked. The sound was inhuman. Horrific. The noise cut right through him.

"I tried to warn you, Doctor." The orderly chuckled now. "That's one of your patients."

Albigence shut his eyes against the noise. He had no desire to see what was on the other side of the curtain. There'd be time enough to wander the halls and meet his new patients later.

As he moved away from the orderly, though, curiosity got the best of him. Albigence let down his guard long enough to glance to his right. There, behind a gap in the curtain, sat a man on a gurney. The patient was young—no more than a boy, really—and he had the strangest look on his face.

He didn't seem to be physically injured—he wore no bandages—but something was terribly wrong nonetheless. Something about the boy's smile. So eerie and unhinged.

Albigence recognized the look.

He'd seen it more than two decades ago, when he was just a child. After he'd endured a fistfight on the playground, his mother took one look at his tear-stained face and announced they were going to the circus.

He'd never been to a circus before. He excitedly boarded a trolley with his mother, which brought them to a dusty field near Brighton Beach and a circle of tents that swallowed the sand dunes whole. He followed his mother into a certain one, the largest one, his eyes wide with wonder. A tightrope walker right above his head! And over there ... an acrobat on stilts! The angry roar of a tiger, somewhere in the wings.

Mother marched him down the dimly lit aisle toward a

banner over the stage imprinted with the name of an act called The Great Lester.

"Hold my hand, Albigence," she whispered as they moved along.

Although it was Friday, a typical workday, several men sat with their families. Most of the fathers wore suspenders and shirtsleeves, unlike his own father, who would never be seen in public without a coat and tie. At least that was true from the little he remembered of him.

Unlike several of the men here, who happily slung their arms around their excited children, his father would never touch him in public, either. Such an outright show of affection was unmanly, his father would insist, and completely unnecessary.

Even when his father left the family's house for good, he hopped into his Oldsmobile without a single hug goodbye. Not so much as a handshake.

After staring at the other fathers in the audience, Albigence had returned his attention to the stage, where a pretty assistant in tights pranced across the floorboards with a placard to start the show. That cued a tall, handsome man waiting in the wings.

The ventriloquist, for that's what the man was called, wore a shiny black tuxedo, replete with white spats and slick top hat, and he held a doll in his arms. A wood doll dressed just like him, down to a pair of tiny spats and a miniature tuxedo jacket.

But the face ... that was different. Whereas the Great Lester laughed and joked, the doll sat in his arms immobile. Unseeing. As unresponsive as a plank of lumber. What unnerved Albigence most, though, was the doll's eerie, malevolent grin.

He remembered the doll's grin for weeks. Never one to

experience nightmares before, he suffered through a month of them after his visit to the circus.

He shuddered now, and the memory vanished. Albigence instinctively knew what would happen if he waved his hand in front of the patient on the gurney. Nothing. No blink, no flinch, no acknowledgement of any kind. This was a classic case of battle fatigue. The soldier obviously had endured too much stress in the trenches, which his mind couldn't process. Instead, his brain shut down, stuck somewhere between the past and present with only an eerie smile to indicate his insanity.

So, this was to be Albigence's lot for the foreseeable future. To treat soldiers who could neither function nor think. Able-bodied men on the outside, whose minds were frozen on the inside.

Some of his associates derided shellshock as a made-up disorder for cowards and connivers, but Albigence knew better. No one could give such a smile on purpose. No one would feign a look that ghastly. There was nothing behind this patient's eyes—nothing beneath his unhinged smile.

What, exactly, had Albigence gotten himself into? Maybe the orderly was right. Maybe he had every right to feel sorry for himself.

Only time would tell.

CHAPTER TWENTY-ONE

JOSEPHINE

SCHOOLHOUSE, CAMP TRAVIS

FEBRUARY 1918

The next morning, Jo dressed in her warmest shirtwaist, several heavy petticoats, and a thick wool skirt. A late-winter storm had blown through camp the night before and frosted the windowpanes with ice.

Jo ducked her head as she walked to the schoolhouse. She didn't even stop to admire the bell in the schoolyard because she was too cold to think about anything but getting warm again.

The drafty classroom offered little relief. She shed her cloak anyway and set about stoking a fire in the potbellied stove. The only way to coax the iron contraption to life was to add copious amounts of kindling, char paper, and a newspaper or two.

She wanted the room to be toasty when the children came. They always hurried through the door with red, raw cheeks and watery eyes, reluctant to part with their mufflers or coats.

The children. Had they been told about what had happened in the canteen? Had their parents filled their heads with gossip about the incident? If so, she could only imagine what her students thought about their schoolteacher now.

Only time would tell. She finished with the potbelly stove and moved to her desk to wait for the children. Moments later, the classroom door flew open, followed by a thunder of rubber soles on hard floorboards.

"Children!" She immediately regretted the harsh tone. The children weren't responsible for the weather outside or for the terrible weekend she'd endured.

"Let's close the door, shall we?" she said, softening her tone. "Please go to your seats, and tuck your jackets and lunch pails away. We have a lot of work to do and not a moment to spare."

The children did as they were told, thankfully, and the room fell silent once more. Normally, it was nearly impossible to restore order on a Monday morning, when high-pitched squeals and laughter drowned out her voice. But, today, the children seemed too cold to do anything other than listen.

"Good morning, children," she said, more amicably this time. "All right, Cecil. Please fetch the flag."

She'd given Cecil the honor of holding the American flag this week when they recited their pledge, even though this was the same boy who'd insisted everyone from Ireland was either dirty or ignorant.

He seemed to have learned his lesson. He calmly and obediently fetched the flag from its iron holder and joined the other students in reciting the new pledge.

I pledge allegiance to my Flag, and the Republic for which it stands; one nation, indivisible, with liberty and justice for all.

The fledgling pledge was the brainchild of Francis Bellamy, a writer who worked for a magazine called *Youth's Companion*. Bellamy thought the nation's children owed it to their country to salute the American flag, since America paid for their education.

Of course, the ploy benefitted the magazine, as well, since each new subscriber received a crisp American flag in the post when he signed up.

"Now, class," Jo said, "we're going to work on our mathematics this morning. For some of you, that will involve your first times-table. For others, you'll be doing long division. I've written several equations on the blackboard for the older children to solve."

The entire class turned to their attention to the board, which was full of long-division problems. While everyone else at the camp was enjoying their supper last night, Jo had painstakingly chalked a series of mathematical equations on the blackboard in her classroom. Truth be told, she didn't mind. The exercise had given her something other than Albigence to think about—how much she missed him and longed for his return.

A tiny voice interrupted her thoughts.

"What happens," the girl asked, "if we don't know our figures yet?"

The speaker was little Imogene Morgenstern, who sat in the front row. The child looked mortified. On the verge of tears.

"What do you mean, Ginny?"

"How can I do my times-table," the child stammered, "if I don't know my numbers yet?"

"It's all right, dear. No one expects you to know *all* your numbers yet. Remember how I taught you to count to twenty? I promise we won't go past twenty. The chalkboard is only for the older children."

Jo studied the board again, this time from Ginny's perspective. Perhaps the figures were a bit intimidating, since she'd drawn a half-dozen divisors, quotients, and remainders. The numbers must look like hieroglyphics to someone as young as Ginny. No wonder the little girl looked ready to cry.

Her gaze swept the classroom. *Think, think, think.* She needed something less intimidating to use with the younger children. A way to present a basic times-table without frightening them or making them dread mathematics. To make learning fun, if possible.

Her gaze finally settled on the bookcase. There, on the bottom shelf, tucked away, sat a galvanized metal tub full of wood blocks. Each block was marked with a different letter of the alphabet, for a total of twenty-six blocks altogether.

Eureka!

Jo rushed to the bookcase and grabbed two of the blocks. Nothing said she couldn't use them for a different purpose, or for a whole different subject matter, if she wanted.

She worked her way to the front of the room again, careful not to disturb the older children, who were already working on their equations.

"Now, students," she said once she reached her desk again. She focused her attention on the first row, where Ginny and the other kindergarteners sat. "You see these blocks, right? How many sides do they have?"

"Four," the children replied, in unison.

"Actually, they have six sides." Here, she lifted a block to show them the top and bottom. "Now, what if I add another block to it?" She placed one block beside the other. "Now, how many sides are there?"

188

Nothing but silence. Obviously, the children were too intimidated to reply.

"Take your time," she urged. "There's no hurry."

Finally, one of the children worked up enough courage to hazard a guess.

"Eight?" he said.

"You'd think so, wouldn't you? But we can't forget about those sneaky tops and bottoms. Remember, each block has six sides. So, if we take two blocks, and each of them have six sides, that means together they have twelve sides. Two times six equals twelve. The right answer is twelve."

Unfortunately, the children looked more confused than ever.

"Okay, let's try this again," Jo said. "Why don't you wiggle out of your snow shoes and we'll try this a different way."

The children exchanged delighted glances at this sudden turn of events. No child ever went barefoot in the classroom. At least, not in wintertime.

Jo waited for the giggling to subside as the children kicked off their snow boots and loafers. "Okay, here we go."

She counted to twelve with the children, who used both their fingers and toes to arrive at the right number, and then she gave them her most encouraging smile.

"Very good, class. If you take one set of six, and then you add it to another set of six, you get twelve. So, if I take one block and add it to another, how many sides do I have?"

"Twelve," the children replied, since she'd already given them the answer.

"Yes. That's the basics of multiplication. Nothing more and nothing less. Two times six equals twelve."

Ginny, in particular, looked overjoyed at their accomplishment. She squealed as loudly as if she'd unlocked the secret to a new language or discovered an ancient pyramid in Giza.

All because of a simple math problem.

Suddenly, Jo remembered something else. Something that'd happened a week ago. She'd been dusting Albigence's desk in their cabin when she came across an old test paper. The first question on the intelligence test involved multiplication. But the instructions for solving it came with a long string of words that must look like hieroglyphics to someone who couldn't read them.

She'd immediately realized the problem. If someone couldn't read the paragraph, how would he ever arrive at the correct answer? That would be like asking her young students to solve a multiplication problem when the numbers meant nothing to them at this point.

She toyed with one of the blocks before the memory faded. The cubes were a wonderful way to figure out a multiplication problem. Given their six sides, they could be used to illustrate how to combine numbers exponentially. Without a need for words.

Aha!

Her mouth dropped open. What would happen if she rewrote the intelligence exam using drawings to illustrate the questions, instead of words? Simple drawings. Nothing fancy.

Everything would change.

By the time she remembered where she was, she noticed several of the older students had already finished their work. She quickly moved to the back of the room and whispered into one of the teenager's ears.

The girl immediately left to help the younger children up front. Jo returned to her desk and scribbled something on a piece of parchment before the slip of an idea could dissolve, like fog on a riverbank.

The rest of the day passed uneventfully. Once she dismissed the children for the night, she locked the schoolroom door behind her and headed for a certain cabin—one where she knew she'd find a supportive listener.

A few moments later, she banged her fist heartily against the door of the parsonage.

"Hello," Rebekkah said, once the door swung open. "My goodness. Is something wrong?"

"Quite the contrary." Jo swept into the front parlor, doing her best to hide the slight bulge beneath her cloak.

"What do you have there?"

"This ..." she said, as she let the blocks tumble to the ground ..."is the answer we've been looking for."

"Children's blocks?" Rebekkah pursed her lips. "I don't understand."

"You will soon enough. I finally realized how we can change the army's intelligence test so it makes sense to people who can't read English."

"I still don't understand. Have you forgotten about the fight in the canteen? How can you still be worried about the intelligence test?"

"Because nothing's changed. Men are still failing that blasted thing and still suffering the consequences."

"What does any of that have to do with children's blocks?"

"Only everything." She pointed to one of the blocks, her heart racing. "You see, I was trying to teach my younger students their times-table today. But they had no idea how to multiply numbers. None."

"So, you used wood blocks?"

Jo nodded. "I taught them to take one block and count the sides, and then I held another block beside it. Then, I had them count the total number of sides, including the ones they couldn't see."

"Which allowed them to arrive at the answer?"

"Exactly. We've been asking soldiers to perform math on an intelligence exam, only we've been using words to explain what we want, which they can't read, of course. What would happen if we gave them visual cues? Showed them what to do through drawings? *Viola!* They'd finally have a chance."

"Oh, my goodness. You're right." Rebekkah's eyes widened. "I understand. They wouldn't need words."

"Yes. Do you see why I'm so excited?"

"I think I do. Oh, Jo. You're brilliant!"

"Well, I wouldn't say that." Jo's cheeks warmed at the compliment. "I can't take all the credit. The children helped me. One girl was horrified at the prospect of not knowing her numbers. I just happened to have a tub of blocks handy."

"Now, you know we can't keep this idea a secret. You have to go to the major general and tell him about it. The sooner, the better."

"Not yet. The cubes will only help with a few questions. What about the other ones on the test? We still have a lot more work to do."

"We?" Rebekkah looked at her askance.

"Yes, 'we.' I seem to recall you promised to help me."

"I did?"

"You did, and tonight, I'm holding you to it. No matter how long it takes. You might as well put on some coffee, because it's going to be a long night."

CHAPTER TWENTY-TWO

ALBIGENCE

CAMP PONTANEZEN, NEAR BREST, FRANCE

MARCH 1918

Albigence studied his new office, if one could call it an office. The space reminded him of the dreary supply closet in the medical infirmary at Camp Travis.

As with the closet, the office provided only one source of light—a dingy yellow bulb suspended from a frazzled cord. Along with the bare lightbulb, the room offered a battered partner's desk, although he had no partner. There was also an armchair upholstered in knubby checkered felt and a hardback chair that didn't look nearly as comfortable as the soft armchair.

This was the room where he would interview his new patients in the coming days, and this was where he'd make diagnoses, which could change their lives forever.

The layout won't do. It won't do at all.

Albigence moved the more comfortable chair to the other side of the desk and took the hardbacked seat for himself. After studying the psychology manuals at Camp

Greenleaf, he'd become convinced of the benefits of talking about one's problems. This meant his patients needed to feel comfortable enough to sit for long periods of time.

Then, since he had no reason to stay, he wandered down the dreary hall and peered into the first room he came across. Apparently, he'd discovered one of the treatment rooms.

Again ... if one could call it a treatment room. An enormous steel machine took up most of it. Taller than a man and twice as wide, the medieval-looking contraption featured a flat console covered with knobs, along with a pair of sinister-looking paddles attached by rubber straps. The apparatus looked like something Dr. Frankenstein would affix to his monster. Albigence shuddered.

He had read about such contraptions before. The ominous-looking paddles, once affixed to a patient's skin, were supposed to deliver electric jolts to different parts of the body. To "wake them up," as it were. But, what difference did it make if a patient's legs were energized when his mind still reeled from the constant nightmares?

While electricity could jolt a patient from his stupor, it couldn't cure the sleeplessness. The treatment was akin to offering an aspirin to someone with a terminal disease.

He cautiously approached the machine. A chair next to it featured a trio of thick black straps designed to restrain a patient while electricity burnt his body. He bent lower, to study the straps, and saw deep gashes imbedded in the rubber. They were teeth marks. Someone had tried to chew right through the straps.

Another shudder.

After a moment, the bored orderly he'd spotted before in the recovery area sauntered into the room.

"I didn't realize this room was taken," the man said by way of apology. His muslin smock had several suspicious stains on it.

"It wasn't being used," Albigence said, "so I thought I'd look around. This contraption is absolutely medieval. Why do you still have it here?"

"You mean the magneto-electric machine?"

"Is that what you call it? I've only read about them in textbooks."

"Ah, yes. You're the new doctor." Like before, the orderly immediately threw him a pitying look. "I suppose you'll need to get up to speed on the machinery."

"How often do you use it?"

"Quite a lot. It's probably one of our most-used treatments."

"I wouldn't exactly call it a treatment. Not at all. Now, dare I ask what other machines are around here?"

"I could give you a tour, if you'd like."

"Definitely. Thank you, Mr.—"

"Olsen. Nice to meet you, Doc."

"Likewise. But, do call me Albigence. Now, about those machines ..."

"Follow me."

Albigence followed the man into the hall. This time, though, his guide turned left, which led them to a series of closed metal doors. Even with an outer layer of galvanized steel, the sounds of anguished wailing escaped from the first room. The second door was no better. Someone there screamed like a banshee.

"My goodness. Do patients always make such a commotion?" Albigence asked. "I can barely hear myself think."

"Always," his companion said. "Can't be helped. Some of the treatments are quite painful. Here we go."

They finally approached a room with an open door. This one featured a claw-foot bathtub with well-worn enamel sides. Inside the tub sat several large blocks of ice, most of them half-melted by now.

"The men are made to sit in there?" Albigence asked, horrified.

"Actually, no."

"Oh, thank goodness." To dunk someone in freezing water in the middle of winter was a sure recipe for pneumonia.

"Patients are made to lie in it. Sometimes for hours. All depending on the patient, of course."

"Doesn't that create other problems? Pneumonia, frostbite—"

"Well, they don't stay in one position for long. We move them around. We always take them out once their fingers turn blue."

"I should say so. Still—"

"Doctor," the orderly interrupted. "I can tell you don't approve of our methods. But it's all we have to work with. We have too many patients and not enough staff or equipment. We try to be grateful for the little we have."

Albigence fell silent.

I have no right to criticize the hospital so soon.

The army didn't consider the camp a high priority. How else could one explain the chipped tiles, peeling paint, and rusted metal? The facilities were obviously antiquated and overused.

"I don't mean to criticize," Albigence said. "As you know, I've only just arrived. But I never expected to see such old-fashioned machinery. Back in the States, we'd consider these things relics. Way past their prime."

The man shrugged. "You're not in the States anymore. You should remember that when you're working here. Otherwise, you'll never last. A lot of your kind don't."

"My kind?"

"Physicians. Psychologists. Whatever. People trained to work in sterile conditions. There's nothing sterile about trench warfare, Doctor. Not physically or otherwise."

A quick gulp. "I hesitate to ask, but are there any more machines?"

"You might be interested in what's next door."

Albigence thought about the man's choice of words as he followed him. Truth be told, his interest had turned to horror by now. There was nothing interesting about medieval machines that didn't work.

This is no way to treat the broken.

He followed the orderly into the next room. Here, he spied a nearly naked patient who ran on a conveyor belt. The young man's wrists were bound to a metal pole fastened in front of him. He had no choice but to grip the pole lengthwise. His knuckles were pale from exertion. Every once in a while, the young man flinched in pain.

"Now, what in the devil is that?" Albigence whispered, aghast.

"Something we use to make the men exercise." The orderly sounded blasé about the process, although the patient looked ready to faint. "Doctors say vigorous exercise can cure some of the side effects of war. So, we make them exercise. Whether they want to or not."

"It's inhumane. Why is he convulsing?"

"The pole delivers an electric charge. See? The nurse ramps up the voltage whenever she feels he's not trying hard enough."

Albigence's gaze traveled to the nurse in question. She looked ready to faint herself. Every once in a while, she moved a knob on the console—as if in a trance. As if she didn't care one way or another what was happening to the patient right in front of her.

"How does she determine what's 'enough?'"

"I think she makes it up as she goes along. I've never seen a number written down anywhere. They trust the nurses to act in the patient's best interest."

"So, the nurses spend a lot of time with their patients, then?"

"Excuse me?"

"The nurses. They must spend a lot of time with their patients to know what they need."

"No, I don't think so. I doubt they have time for it."

"Then, how can she possibly know what her patient is capable of?"

Finally, the soldier before them slumped onto the bar, unable to stand upright anymore.

"Now, see here." Albigence moved to intervene, but the orderly stopped him.

"I wouldn't interfere if I were you, Doctor. Not so soon. She'll only report you to her supervisor, and what good would that do?"

"But the patient. The boy—"

Thankfully, the nurse had turned off the horrible contraption by now, which allowed the patient to stop seizing.

Albigence cautiously moved to the lad's side and began to untie his wrists. Then, he gently helped him from the machine.

Not for the first time, Albigence wondered what in the world he'd gotten himself into. What type of facility would subject its soldiers to even more pain, all in the name of "treatment?"

The time had come to change how things were done around here. Ready or not, he'd find a way. He couldn't live with himself otherwise.

CHAPTER TWENTY-THREE

JOSEPHINE

PARSONAGE, CAMP TRAVIS

APRIL 1918

Jo was frazzled beyond belief when she returned from yet another long day at the schoolhouse. She'd been interrupted by a sharp rap on the schoolhouse door midafternoon—which rarely, if ever, happened.

She'd cracked open the door to find an army officer standing there, dressed in his full military regalia. She nearly swooned at the sight, because she assumed something horrible had happened to Albigence.

The colonel moved to put her at ease, though.

"Good afternoon, ma'am. I trust I'm not disturbing you?"

"We're doing our lessons, Officer. May I help you?" She didn't invite him into the classroom, because the last thing she needed was to expose her students to the sight of a military officer in full dress blues. The interruption would ruin their concentration, slim as it was, and make them impossible to teach for the rest of the day.

"I've come to inform you about a certain medical outbreak making people sick at our military camps." By now, his smile had thinned.

"Oh? What might that be?"

"A virus doctors are calling influenza. We believe the strain originated at an army base in Kansas. There's no need to panic, but we want everyone to take extra precautions given the circumstances."

"Extra precautions?" A beat passed while she processed the news. "What might those precautions be?"

"We're telling everyone to wash their hands more often than usual. This includes children, of course. We're also asking people to stay away from large groups for now. You don't have any large gatherings planned for the near future, do you?"

"Well ... we do have a matriculation ceremony at the end of the term. I planned to invite parents, siblings. Everyone, really."

"I'm afraid you'll have to cancel it." As if to underscore the serious nature of his visit, he lowered his voice. "We can't make any exceptions. I'm sure you understand."

"Of course. I'll cancel the ceremony."

"Good. We'll let you know when there's more news. For now, encourage your students to pay particular attention to their hygiene. Oh, and tell them to avoid playing in large groups. Even out of doors."

"But, I ..." Jo was about to tell him his request was impossible—she could no more tell children not to gather than she could tell wild horses not to run in a herd. He didn't seem the type to welcome a challenge. "Yes, sir. Of course. I'll do my best."

A brisk nod and he disappeared, leaving her to break the news to her students.

"We have some bad news, children," she said, as she closed the door again. "Apparently, there's been an outbreak of something called 'influenza.' Now, I don't want you to panic—"

Which, of course, they immediately did. The younger ones started to whimper for their mothers, while the older ones peppered her with enough questions to make her head spin. She'd been left with a roomful of anxious children and nothing much to tell them.

Jo finally dismissed them a few minutes early when she couldn't take it any longer.

Now, here she was, standing at the door to the parsonage, exhausted beyond measure.

Rebekkah was waiting for her when she knocked.

"Come in, come in," her friend said, quickly, as she ushered her inside. "Otto just left for a deacons' meeting. We only have a few hours to ourselves."

"What a day I've had." Jo wearily dropped onto the velvet Chesterfield. "Did you hear about the influenza outbreak?"

"Of course. Apparently, a hundred men fell ill at a place called Camp Funston. They don't know what to make of it."

"I know. My students had a million questions—none of which I could answer. Needless to say, we did *not* get our lessons done today."

"I'm sorry. Maybe we can salvage the evening, at least." She held out her hand to Jo and helped her rise from the Chesterfield. Together, they moved to the kitchen, where a jug of ginger soda waited. "In between visitors today, I had a chance to think about the other questions on the intelligence test."

"I'm glad." Jo took one of the chairs by the kitchen table. "I've been thinking about the test too. I can't seem to get one of the questions out of my mind. The one about cigars, of all things."

"Cigars? Oh, I know the one you mean." Rebekkah retrieved a copy of the test from the sideboard and leafed through the pages until she found the right one.

"Here we are." She began to read, "Mike bought twelve expensive cigars. He bought two more and then smoked seven. How many cigars did he have left?"

Both women rolled their eyes at the end.

"Who cares about cigars at a time like this?" Jo said. "Cigars have nothing to do with what happens on a battlefield. I understand the question is about adding and subtracting, but why don't we ask them something of actual importance?"

"Agreed. They say women are frivolous. No wonder so many men—even ones who *can* speak English—complain about the test. The questions don't apply to them at all. Let me show you something."

She quickly moved to another spot, where she found a copy of the *San Antonio Evening News*. She pointed to something on its front page.

"Look."

A grainy black-and-white photo showed a jagged trench. The photo had been taken high above a battlefield in France—no doubt by an Air Force pilot. The picture showed a birds-eye view of the twists and turns slithering through the field.

Jo knew enough about war to understand a soldier would position himself at the top of the trench to fight the enemy. However, this photo showed a battalion weaving its way through the belly of the trough, following a zigzag pattern. The muddy walls provided some cover, but it still looked challenging.

"Have you seen this?" Rebekkah asked.

"Not that particular photo."

"The story talks about the movement of American troops through France. All the men have for protection are mud trenches and barbed wire. The regiments go from one trench to the other to reach a battlefield."

"I'm sure it's terrifying, but how does that relate to the intelligence test?"

"Think about it. You once told me you have a certain way of teaching your students how to improve their motor skills. You'd draw a maze on the blackboard, and then, you'd ask them to figure out the best way to get through it."

"I would."

"You said they're quite good at it by the time the schoolyear ends."

Recognition slowly dawned. "You're right. Finding their way through the maze was about teaching them to see the big picture. I always draw different versions of the maze to help them practice. By the way, you have an excellent memory."

"Thank you." By now, Rebekkah's eyes were shining. "I think we should include a maze on the IQ test. While it'll only be a fraction of the size of a real trench, it'll still show whether they can think on their feet. Whether they can get from point 'A' to point 'B' in the shortest time possible."

"That's perfect. Who cares about the number of cigars someone has when a soldier really needs to know how to work his way through a trench? He has every reason to worry about finding his way." She beamed at her friend. "I could kiss you right now."

"Please don't," Rebekkah laughed. "We have too much work to do. We still need to figure out other ways to improve the test."

For the rest of the night, the women worked side-by-side. Although they placed their chairs next to each other, they sketched in complete silence. The only sound came from a clock on the mantlepiece, which methodically ticked off the seconds from one hour to the next.

Fortunately, one of the deacons stopped by at midnight to tell Rebekkah about Otto's delay at a deacons' meeting, which meant he wouldn't return for several more hours. One of the collection plates had gone missing.

After yet another hour, when Jo was too tired to think straight anymore, she finally yawned. "I think we've done enough for one night."

"I agree. But, please don't yawn. You're making me sleepy."

"Can't be helped. Anyway, there's something else I wanted to talk to you about before I leave. I've been thinking about what's going to happen to the test once we've finished it."

"What do you mean ... what's going to happen? You're going to make an appointment with the major general, and he's going to think you're brilliant. End of story."

"Not quite. The man hates me now. Don't give me that look ... you know it's true. He won't listen to anything I have to say. Not after what happened in the canteen."

"He's just misguided. He has to blame someone for the riot, and it's safer to blame a civilian, like you. Not to mention, a woman."

"Regardless, I don't think he'll let me into his office."

"So, you're not even going to try? You're going to give up?"

"I didn't say I wanted to give up." Jo gave her a sly look. "I think there might be another way."

CHAPTER TWENTY-FOUR

ALBIGENCE

FIELD HOSPITAL, CAMP PONTANEZEN

APRIL 1918

My Dearest Josephine,

I pray to God this letter finds you well. I've finally come across a patient who trained at Camp Travis and hails from San Antonio. He promised to deliver this letter to you upon his return to the States, and I seized on his offer. This is the first chance I've had to commit my thoughts to paper since I've been here. My time has been a whirlwind. Or … a nightmare. I'll leave you to decide which.

First of all, I never had the opportunity to explain why I left Camp Travis so suddenly. They never gave me the chance, my dear. After the men rioted—you were not to blame, so please don't judge yourself harshly—I was hauled before the major general by one of my associates. The man is as ridiculous as the waxed mustache he wears. If you ever have the misfortune of meeting a psychologist by the name of Frank Beauchamp, I pray you run the other way. He's not to be trusted, so don't let him fool you with his smooth manners and false modesty.

Anyway, I'm serving here at Camp Pontanezen in Brest. We're not near the Western Front, so please don't worry for my physical safety. But I still serve in a war, of sorts.

You see, they have me stationed at a hospital here, as you can tell by the return post. They really could use a hundred more psychologists, because the facility is overflowing with men who need help but too few professionals to treat them.

The noise is quite deafening. I'm thankful you live a whole ocean away. Again, please don't fear for my safety, because the patients are quite harmless. At least, to others. To themselves, they pose a great threat, because they can't think rationally anymore. They can't even communicate. Their minds have been broken by trench warfare. The constant noise of battle, combined with knowing their next breath might be their last. They sink into a world of their own making. I desperately want to find a way to bring them back.

I have a request to make of you, darling. Could you please send the treatment manuals, which I left on the desk in the parlor, by steamer ship? I'm afraid the policeman who packed my duffel didn't think I'd need the manuals. They'll help me treat these wretched souls in a more humane and compassionate way than what they've received.

I also long to hear your thoughts on the subject. When you have a child who is beside himself and can't think straight, how do you soothe him, to put him back together again? What do you say to bring him back from the crisis? I know children are experts at working themselves into a frenzy, so you must have ample experience in bringing them out of it.

I could tell you more about the horrific things I've seen and heard, but I won't. I don't want to place those images in your mind—images I can't erase. Living with such dreadful thoughts wouldn't be good for either of us.

I long to spend the rest of my life with you, learning how to forget those thoughts myself.

In the meantime, please take care. Every night, before I retire, I pray for your safety. How comforting to know you're in a classroom, tucked away from the evils of this war. I know the schoolhouse is your refuge—where nothing ever changes, and time stands still.

Something I'll always treasure. For now, please know I long for the warmth of your company.

Your husband,
Albigence

CHAPTER TWENTY-FIVE

JOSEPHINE

OFFICE OF MAJOR GENERAL HENRY ALLEN, CAMP TRAVIS

MAY 1918

Spring had arrived by the time Jo and Rebekkah finished rewriting the intelligence test. The mercury in Josephine's grand Edwardian thermometer inched up to fifty ... sixty ... seventy degrees.

Normally, such warm temperatures would be reflected in people's moods around the camp. Residents would venture outdoors again, happy to be free of their thick coats and bulky gloves. Neighbors once more talked to neighbors, and the children ran free.

The influenza outbreak changed all that.

Now, people scurried past each other, their faces half covered by gauze. They didn't want to expose themselves to a mysterious virus whose origin was suspect and whose symptoms offered few treatments. Better to separate oneself and remain safe.

What bothered Jo most of all, though, was seeing the effect the virus had on the children. While Jo longed to hear their bright laughter in the schoolyard, now all she heard were dark whispers and hushed conversations. The chief concern seemed to be a rumor which had been circulating for days—the American Red Cross would start conscripting the camp's mothers to serve as nurses. All the trained nurses were busy treating soldiers, which left no one to care for the influenza patients.

Day by day, rumors swirled around the camp. People said streetsweepers in cities like New York were forced to dig gravesites, rather than trash piles. Judges held court in open-air spaces, such as parks and yards, which allowed criminals to escape with alarming frequency. Once the epidemic jumped the ocean to infect Europe, the news got even worse.

Most of the reporting came from Spain. That country didn't impose a blackout on foreign reporting, so people took to calling the virus the "Spanish flu," even though Spaniards had nothing to do with it.

Jo wished she could discuss everything with Albigence. Now that she knew he was in France and relatively safe, she longed to hear more from him. Each day, she stopped by the post exchange on her way home from the schoolhouse to see if they'd received another letter. Even though he'd sent one early on, and she'd shipped him the manuals he requested, she hadn't heard anything from him since.

She told herself Albigence simply was too busy to write more. She imagined him working in a large field hospital, surrounded by gleaming equipment, crates of medicine, and well-trained staff. Once the war ended, Albigence would come home to her with a headful of new ideas and interesting new ways to help soldiers recover from the horrors of war.

The thought soothed her. Albigence was feeling useful and fulfilled overseas, since he couldn't help the soldiers at Camp Travis anymore.

But, enough of that. She had other things to worry about tonight.

This was the night she and Rebekkah planned to visit the major general. They'd already agreed Jo would hide in the shadows, while Rebekkah did all the talking—the only way they could hope to see him.

Once she collected Rebekkah from the parsonage, the women traveled in silence to the major general's office. All the while, Rebekkah clutched a leather concertina folder to her chest, which held the test papers. The requisitions officer was so busy ordering antibiotics and morphine, he didn't even ask her why she'd need it.

Darkness engulfed them. Everyone knew the commanding officer would still be at work, since a lamp glowed in his window. What better time to speak with him than when everyone else was fast asleep?

Once they reached the man's office, Jo ducked into a stairwell, while Rebekkah lightly knocked on his door. After a moment, a military policeman—his rifle held at the ready—opened the door.

"Yes? Who's out there?"

"It's Rebekkah Schmidt, sir. The chaplain's wife. I've come to see the major general."

"Oh, hello. I'm afraid he's very busy."

She held out the folder. "But I need to give him this."

"What is it?"

"Something he'll find very interesting. It's about the testing program here. The intelligence test, in particular."

"I see." The policeman left, but soon returned. "I'm afraid he's too busy to see anyone right now. Unless your visit is about the influenza outbreak, he can't speak with you."

"But ... but this is important."

"I'm sorry."

Jo watched from the shadows as Rebekkah tried to hand him the folder again, which he refused to accept.

"He's only seeing medical personnel now," the policeman said. "Given that influenza is his number one priority. But he said to give you his regards."

Rebekkah moved to reply, but the man slammed the door shut before she could. She glumly returned to Jo's side, clearly shaken by the encounter.

"I tried, Jo. He wouldn't even meet with me."

"I know. I heard everything."

"Apparently, he's only interested in the epidemic now. Nothing else matters."

"Why now? We've known about the virus since February. Three whole months ago."

"I know, but more people are dying now. Civilians too. Maybe he's getting desperate."

While she didn't doubt Rebekkah was right, Jo still felt like barging into the man's office and insisting he read the papers. He'd realize how the new test would help him, because more men would pass the darn thing and join the army. The test would make his job easier, not harder, if he'd only listen.

There had to be another way. But, how?

A few days later, Jo and Rebekkah sat on a faded quilt in front of the chapel, listening to Otto deliver one of his sermons. Since no one could meet inside anymore, the only alternative was to gather on the lawn.

Fortunately, the true start of summer was still several weeks away, and the temperature was mild enough for cotton shirtwaists. Along with the ever-present gauze masks, of course.

"We've hit a wall," Jo whispered to Rebekkah, as soon as the congregation started to sing. "The virus is only getting worse. No one knows when it'll end."

"I agree."

"In the meantime, more men will get kicked out of the camp, like Glyn." She hadn't said his name for quite a while, and it felt strange on her tongue.

"Maybe you're right." Rebekkah shrugged. "Maybe we need to stop waiting for the perfect moment."

As if on cue, the hymn ended, and the crowd rose to its feet. The camp's residents still separated themselves into groups, and Jo spied the Welshmen standing across the way. Derwyn slouched against a post, clearly exhausted.

He'd changed from a surgical smock into a faded work shirt, with the collar open at the neck. Like most men nowadays, he'd stopped wearing neckties to save on soap and water.

They rarely saw each other anymore. Derwyn's heavy surgery schedule and her busy teaching duties didn't allow for it. How he managed to find time to attend church at all was a minor miracle.

Jo poked Rebekkah in the ribs.

"Ouch. What was that for?"

"Look over there," she whispered. "It's Derwyn, with his friends."

"So? They always come. They're very faithful."

"I know. But Derwyn's a surgeon."

"Of course, he is. What's wrong with you?"

"You'll see," Jo said.

When the congregation finally dispersed, Jo walked to where Derwyn stood with his friends, with Rebekkah on her heels.

"Hello," she said.

"Aye, ladies." He gave a courtly bow. Although he looked exhausted—deep wrinkles creased his forehead— his eyes still twinkled. "To what do I owe the pleasure o' your company on this lovely day?"

"We need to speak with you," Jo said. "Alone."

"We do?" Rebekkah sounded confused.

"Yes, we do."

"Truth be told, I'd like nothing better," Derwyn said. "But best be quick. I'll be needed in the operatin' theatre soon. No rest for the weary, eh?"

"I'll be fast. I promise."

Jo led them to the biggest prickly pear cactus she could find, which she ducked behind.

"Now, what's all this about?" Rebekkah asked, once they were all together again.

"We need to let Derwyn know what's going on. You see ..." She turned to him. "... we have some papers for the major general. Important papers, but we can't get into his office to show him. He only cares about the influenza epidemic right now."

"Justly so," he said. "It's a beast. Who could foresee such a terrible t'ing?"

"He'll only meet with medical personnel," she continued. "If you get my drift."

"Ah." His eyes widened. "An' that's where I come in?"

"That's where you come in. We need you to present the papers to him under the guise of discussing the flu epidemic."

"'Tis an interesting proposition. A wee bit o' deception." His amusement deepened the crinkles around his eyes.

"Which doesn't bother me a'tall. The old man has short-staffed me enough times ta wish him the worst."

"So, you'll do it?"

"Be my pleasure."

"Now, Derwyn, don't agree so quickly," Rebekkah cautioned. "If the commander finds out what you're up to, he could be furious. Either he'll let you speak your piece—"

"Or he'll toss me out on me ear," he finished for her. "'T'wasn't so long ago you two ladies helped me. 'Tis time ta return the favor."

"Thank you." Jo took his hand. "We'll show you what we have in mind. I think you'll be very interested in it too."

"Leave the papers for me at the infirmary. I'll get them there. G'day, ladies."

Finally, they emerged from their hiding place. The rest of the congregation had already dispersed, anxious to return to their own cabins, safe and sound.

Jo lingered, though. If everything went according to plan, Derwyn could present their idea to the commander as soon as tomorrow.

What would happen during the meeting was anyone's guess.

CHAPTER TWENTY-SIX

ALBIGENCE

FIELD HOSPITAL, CAMP PONTANEZEN

MAY 1918

When Albigence stepped outside the hospital, the first thing he noticed was the changing landscape. The soil had finally reawakened after a long winter slumber, and tender shoots of grass valiantly pushed toward the sun.

He felt the same way. As if he was awakening after a long winter slumber. He'd been so busy at the hospital that he had rarely ventured outside. His schedule wouldn't allow for it. He only had time to work and sleep. Work and sleep. Over and over again. So many soldiers passed through his office, all of them presenting with the same vacant stares and fixed smiles, his days and nights all ran together.

Albigence had vowed to improve things for the hospital's patients when he first arrived, which turned out to be an uphill battle. Too many nurses and orderlies stood in his way. They all watched his every move, as if they wanted to catch him doing something wrong. They'd grown so accustomed to their barbaric ways they had no desire to change them. Maybe if they caught Albigence making a mistake, they reasoned, they could report him to the commander-in-chief and get him reassigned. His transfer would allow them to exert at least a little control over an uncontrollable situation.

He continued to try, though. As often as possible, he lowered the charge of electricity on the blasted machines, until his patients felt only a twinge—and not a jolt—of pain.

Other times, he rescued his patients from the freezing baths the moment the nurses turned their backs. He did his best to hide these small acts of treason behind closed doors and locked treatment rooms.

Mostly, he allowed his patients to sit and talk to him. For hours and hours, sometimes. About whatever was on their mind, which was all they wanted, really. To have someone listen to them, without making judgments. And if battle fatigue left a patient mute? He'd sit with the boy in silence until the tremors passed. Knowing one day, the soldier might be ready.

Most of his patients were young enough to be students in Josephine's classroom. Mere boys, really. Not men at all. Too young to have such deeply lined faces and snowy white hair.

He learned early on to speak to them in a whisper, so he wouldn't traumatize them further. And he always ended their sessions with a comforting word. Albigence wanted to thaw their resistance to the outside world, little by little, as he gently lured them back from the dead. To show them not everyone was a monster. Not everyone wanted to see them killed.

He'd even hold their hands sometimes. Especially if a boy's trembling was over the top, and his arms fluttered about like birds' wings. His worst case involved a boy who continually jerked his left hand up and down, up and down, as if reloading the chamber of a rifle. He did this even while he slept.

During his own sleep, Albigence focused on Josephine. Except for receiving the manuals, he hadn't heard from her since his departure, although he'd sent her a half-dozen letters by now. He didn't expect her to respond to every one, of course, but he longed to know what she thought of them. What she thought of *him*.

Either she was too busy with her students—which he prayed was the case—or she'd never received the letters in the first place. Since he didn't want to believe that, he chose to believe her students kept her too busy to respond.

Even so, he thought about her constantly. The memory of her beautiful smile sustained him through long days in the infirmary. The sweet sound of her voice pulled him back from the nightmares which plagued his sleep. Only memories of her kept his hopelessness at bay.

Enough of all that. For a few hours, at least, he felt sunlight, however weak, on the top of his head, and a whiff of sea salt reached him. He'd been given a precious day pass to spend as he liked in the port of Brest. For a few hours, at least, he could wander through the village without looking over his shoulder.

His senses slowly reawakened. The air was so much fresher than the usual stench of the infirmary—sweat and urine, dried blood, and fresh iodine. He carefully hopped from one ancient cobblestone to the next, mindful of gaps on the path designed to trap his bootheel and send him tumbling.

The wharf in Brest was ancient by American standards. Locals called it the Battery, he'd been told, in reference to the hundreds of ocean battles sailors had fought there over time.

At the tip of the wharf ran a line of shops, all of which catered to soldiers now. He passed near a boulangerie, where the doughy scent of fresh-baked bread tickled his nose, and then a bistro, where laughter ruffled the morning air. A scattering of metal tables stood outside the front door of the bistro, all of them occupied by Moroccan soldiers in colorful turbans and khaki coats.

He barely noticed them, though. His goal was the *bureau de poste*, where he hoped to ask the postmaster about his missing letters. Was he doing something wrong? Perhaps the gentleman—or gentlewoman—could tell him how to circumvent the army and get a letter to his sweet Josephine. Best yet, how to get one of hers, since their current method of exchange obviously wasn't working.

However, first he had to find the building. Along with crumbling cobblestones, he faced a labyrinth of crooked streets with no clear pattern. One road seemingly ran into the next, which spawned a half-dozen more. He couldn't read the street signs, and he was hesitant to ask for directions with his sloppy French.

So, he wandered. Not altogether aimlessly, because he had a clear goal in mind. He knew he'd spot an American soldier somewhere along the way who could provide directions.

His wish was granted a short time later. Just past a flower stall fronted by giant sunflowers in brown tissue, he came upon an American regiment on its way home. A ragtag group of soldiers on the dock, all of them broken and bandaged in some way. He spied wooden canes, metal walkers, unused stretchers at the ready. Obviously, these men were returning to the States because trench warfare had broken their bodies beyond repair.

The only thing missing was a gauze face mask to protect each of them from the flu. They must've realized the virus was nothing compared to the horrors of war, so why bother? Not one person on the dock wore one, which he found oddly refreshing. So much so, he removed his own mask, which he shoved in his pocket.

He cautiously approached a clutch of American soldiers. One boy looked well enough to provide Albigence with directions. The boy toted his own duffel, for one thing, which was rare, given his comrades all wore slings around their shoulders.

Albigence cautiously approached the stranger with the duffel.

"I say ..." he said, as he lightly touched the boy's sleeve, "but do you know where I can find the post office?"

When the boy turned, Albigence froze.

The stranger was Boone. Or, what was left of him, anyway. Half the youth's face was missing, no doubt blown off by mortar fire. Instead of his usual nose, a field surgeon had hastily sewn skin from another part of his body to his cheek. If not for the oversized khaki coat Albigence now recognized, he might never have identified the boy at all.

"That bad, huh?" Boone asked, when Albigence automatically shuddered.

Albigence had seen terrible injuries before, when men lost their limbs, or their minds, but nothing like this. Everything about the boy's face was wrong. The horrific damage caused by gunpowder was made worse by a rushed surgery in an ill-equipped field hospital.

"Well, Doc?" the boy insisted.

Even if Boone's scars healed—which was a big assumption—his face would never look normal again. How could it?

"Hello," Albigence said, once he found his voice. "What a coincidence to see you here."

"So, whaddya think?" the boy persisted. "Do ya think my Ma will recognize me?"

Albigence struggled to come up with a response. He wanted to say something—anything—to encourage the young man. "Well, um. I'm sure she'll be happy to have you at home, no matter what. You have some beautiful weather for your voyage too. A westward breeze, a bit of clouds. Soon enough, you'll be home."

"Sure thing. Umm, Doc ... do ya got anything shiny on ya? They took away my canteen, so I couldn't look at it. Because, you know."

He didn't finish the sentence. But, then again, he didn't have to.

"Shiny? No, I'm afraid not. Not a thing. The only thing in my pocket is a day pass." Which was a terrible lie, since he also carried a smooth silver comb that would make a fine mirror. But Albigence knew the lie was for the boy's own good.

"All right," Boone said. "Whaddya need to know? Somethin' 'bout a post office?"

"No, no. Really. Don't worry about it. I'm sure it's right around the corner. I've never been to town before, so I'm a little lost."

"Well, you gotta try the bakery. People tell me the bread smells good."

"I'll do that. Yes, quite so. Well, take care of yourself, Boone. Godspeed, and all that."

"You too, Doc."

All this time, without realizing it, Albigence had been inching further and further away from the lad. Repelled by the sight and smell of him. Not just the horror of the boy's injuries, but the smell of his breath, as well. His breath reeked of something sour, like vinegar, which no doubt came from the copious amounts of morphine he'd been given. Albigence wouldn't be surprised if the boy carried an entire liter of the stuff in his duffel. He only hoped it helped him.

"Hey, Doc?"

"Yes?" Although he was desperate to finish the conversation, he didn't want to be rude. Boone deserved better. After all, he was the one who'd lost half his face on the battlefield. Not Albigence.

"I'm glad ya got that desk job ya wanted. Guess I shoulda' done the same."

"Desk? Oh, yes. Desk. Well, I don't really use a desk at the hospital, to be honest. I tend to walk around or visit my patients at their bedside."

"Ya know what I meant."

"I think I do."

With that, Albigence finally turned, horribly ashamed. While Boone had made the ultimate sacrifice to serve his country, Albigence was free to walk around the streets— unencumbered. To glance into a mirror, if he so desired, or come upon a shiny glass window and peruse his reflection. Nothing in his life had changed much, while everything in Boone's had.

He felt like a fraud. A terrible fraud. Like someone who cleaned up messes caused by others, but never actually participated in the mess-making. Someone who showed up after everyone else already had done their job. A weak substitute for the actual warriors.

Somehow, he'd lost his desire to find the post office now. He could never tell Josephine what he'd just seen or what he'd heard. No, he should keep such things to himself.

Maybe it was better if he stopped writing her letters altogether. Whether she even received them was doubtful, since she hadn't responded. Since he didn't want to tell her the truth, and he didn't have the heart to tell her lies anymore, what was the point?

"Are you looking for something?"

A strange voice broke through his thoughts.

"Pardon me?"

"You look lost. Are you looking for something?"

The speaker was an American soldier in full-dress uniform. Albigence apparently had strolled all the way to the end of the pier, without even meaning to.

"No, no. I'm quite all right."

"If you say so."

The stranger stood near a metal card table, close to which he'd placed several chairs.

"You see, I just bumped into someone I know," Albigence hurriedly said. For some reason, he felt the need to explain his distracted response. "A boy I met on the trip over here. He was terribly injured. Horribly so."

"He'll get a pension from the government," the stranger said with a shrug. "And more medical care if he needs it."

"Yes, but I'm afraid it won't help much. Not when he's already been stitched up like a rag doll. His features are quite set now."

"But the doctors will try, nonetheless."

"I suppose." Albigence didn't want to argue with the man, but he knew the truth. "I just wish I could counsel him before he goes back to his home and family."

"You're a doctor, eh? I figured as much. Knew right away you didn't come from the trenches."

"You did? How so? Could you tell by my clothes?"

"More than that. Your hands. They're too clean. You've never held a rifle, have you?"

Albigence froze. Although the man was right, he didn't realize it was so obvious. He quickly thrust his hands into his pockets.

Why was he even here? He didn't belong on this pier. He belonged back in his office, amidst a pile of dusty old books and dry papers. Not out here, in the real world.

"I suppose you're right," Albigence said. "We don't get much rifle fire in the medical infirmary."

"I didn't mean to insult you. I'm sure what you're doing is very important, and you'll get to go home in one piece. Something you can't take for granted."

"But it's not all fun and games," Albigence insisted. "Most of my patients are quite sick by the time they reach me. Sick in the head. There's nothing worse than trying to talk to someone who can't talk back. I don't recommend it."

"Point taken."

"It's downright impossible, sometimes," Albigence added, as if to convince both of them.

"I'm sure what you're doing is vitally important, Doctor."

"To be honest, though, sometimes I wonder. Especially late at night. Am I doing any good? Does what I do matter at all? The boys are usually so far gone by the time they reach me."

"Only you know for sure." The stranger pointed to the card table. "Have you ever thought about moving closer to the front? The army needs men—all different kinds—at Chaumont."

"The Western Front?" For the first time, Albigence really studied the man's card table. The soldier had placed some official-looking forms next to a cupful of fountain pens. "Are you a military recruiter?"

"Yes, as a matter of fact, I am. I'm looking for men who want to move inland, to another base."

"Oh, no. I couldn't." Albigence started to back away, shocked at his own ignorance. He didn't realize what was happening before. The man wanted to recruit him for the Western Front. A notorious place he'd only heard about until now. A barbaric place, which caused the kind of horrific injuries he'd just seen with Boone.

"Why? Why couldn't you do it?" the recruiter said. "You told me you don't feel useful here. I'm giving you an opportunity to change things."

"But ... the front?" Albigence paused a moment to consider it. "So, what is this place called Chaumont like?"

"It's the temporary headquarters for the American Expeditionary Forces under the command of General Pershing. And it's closer to the fighting, which sounds like what you really want."

"You could sign me up? Today?"

"I don't see why not. They're desperate for men, you see. The soldiers you meet there will be fresh from their time in the trenches. You'd be making a real difference."

"Well, what would I need to do?"

"Nothing. I'd arrange everything. It's easy to move about now since the Central Powers are winning. The American generals are desperate."

Albigence stared at his companion. Given he'd seen the horrific price paid by real soldiers, like Boone, how could he return to the safety of Camp Pontanezen? How could he sleep at night, on a real horsehair mattress, knowing boys like Boone had nothing but slop and mud to rest their heads against? How could he go on living in a comfortable shelter, when the real war was being fought in a place called Chaumont?

He desperately wished he could ask Josephine for her thoughts. Consider her opinion, since hers was the only opinion that mattered. But since he couldn't, he'd have to rely on his own instincts. His own instincts told him he couldn't live with himself if he said no. If he spent the rest of the war hiding out in the medical infirmary at Camp Pontanezen. Far away from the fighting, and a lifetime away from the physical suffering.

He quickly gestured for a pen—before he could change his mind.

"You won't be sorry," the recruiter said, as he watched Albigence apply his signature. "You'll see."

The pen shook as Albigence finished. He didn't know how, and he didn't know when, but his life was about to change.

CHAPTER TWENTY-SEVEN

JOSEPHINE

OFFICE OF MAJOR GENERAL HENRY ALLEN, CAMP TRAVIS

LATE MAY 1918

Jo and Rebekkah arrived at the administrative offices close to midnight when the building was shrouded in shadow and fog. Once more, they'd waited until very late when no one except the commander would be awake.

Fortunately, Derwyn was a man of his word. He waited for them in the shadows, still dressed in a surgical smock. Thankfully, the dim light made it impossible to see whatever new stains he'd acquired in the operating theatre.

"Evenin,' ladies," he said, as he stepped into the light. "What brings ye out on this fair night?"

"Very funny," Jo said. "By the way, did you read the papers we gave you?"

"I did. They're right smart. Never imagined you two could put yer heads together and come up with such a t'ing."

"That's because men never give women enough credit. We're good for a lot more than needlework and dusting, you know."

"Now, Jo," Rebekkah said, "calm down. Derwyn is trying to help us. We should be grateful for his help."

Jo gulped. "Of course. Thank you for helping us, Derwyn."

"O' course. Like I said, 'tis right smart. I think it'll spare a lot o' the men. And, it's better late than never." Fortunately, he didn't elaborate. "Now, exactly what do I say to me commander?"

"Tell him you've noticed too many immigrants are failing the test. Too many of them are harming themselves afterward."

"'Tis true enough. We found another one hanging in the supply closet last week. Couldn't speak a word o' English, but the boy knew how to tie a fisherman's knot 'round his neck well enuff."

"That's horrible! Did he survive?"

"'Fraid not. The poor bugger got sent home in a casket. But it'll make a fine illustration for me point, eh? 'Tis a shame to lose even one man like that."

"That's what we thought. There's an empty office on the second floor, right next to the commander's office. Albigence told me about the office once before he left. Said he couldn't believe they'd let an entire room go to waste. Rebekkah and I will hide in that room while you speak to your commander."

Thank goodness, Albigence also said that despite the fancy woodwork on the building's exterior, the interior walls were terribly thin. They'd be able to hear every single word spoken through the paper-thin walls.

"All right, then," Derwyn said. "Looks like me time is up."

One tug at his muslin smock, and Derwyn disappeared. Jo and Rebekkah followed him through the doorway, doing their best to remain in the shadows.

They only parted when they arrived at the second floor.

While Derwyn made his way to the commander's office, Jo pointed to another office nearby.

"We'll go over there," she whispered to Rebekkah. "Follow me."

She inched along the dark corridor, her back to the wall, until she reached the room in question. Once she slid around its doorframe, she found the space was empty, save for a lone desk with a large wall map pinned above it.

She hurried to the furthest wall. Next to the baseboards, she spied a cast-iron heat register cut into the floorboards. Soft voices rose from slits in the register.

"Come in," someone said from the other side of the wall.

"You have a guest, sir. A medical doctor. Someone by the name of Derwyn MacDonald."

"Doctor, eh? Send him right in."

A moment of silence while the military policeman fetched Derwyn. Although Jo couldn't see anything, she could imagine everything.

"Good evening, Doctor." The major general's normal speaking voice was loud, thankfully. "I assume you're here on account of this blasted flu epidemic."

"Aye," the Welshman said. "Found out something today, er, unusual. Another death, it was. Aye, another death. Hoped you could spare me a moment o' your time."

"What's he saying?" Rebekkah whispered, since she couldn't hear anything from her spot behind Jo. Her voice sounded ragged now, no doubt due to the late hour.

"He's inside the office," Jo said. "Told the general he wanted to talk to him about the flu epidemic, just like we asked him to."

"Like *you* asked him to," Rebekkah said. "I never agreed to lie. You know I don't approve of it."

"Fine. I should be ashamed of myself. Yet, somehow, I'm not. But can we please discuss my character flaws later?"

"Of course. I only—"

"Shhh!"

"What do you have there, Doctor?" the commander continued from the other side of the wall.

Heavy footsteps sounded, which meant Derwyn was drawing near to the man's desk.

"Somethin' to make your life easier, sir," Derwyn said.

"Unless you have a cure for influenza, I doubt that's possible. But, here. Hand it over."

Jo breathed a sigh of relief, as the general accepted the papers.

"What's all this?"

"It's a new way ta test the foreigners who came here from abroad. A way ta test their minds. Nearly failed the wretched t'ing me-self when I took it, since me English wasn't so good."

"But what in the devil does a test have to do with the epidemic?" The commander sounded irritated now.

"Well, I could barely pass the t'ing me-self, as I said. Which set me to thinking. Derwyn, I said to me-self, we have us a problem, we do. If men can't read the test—which they can't—then 'tis impossible to do well. But ... what if they saw pictures, instead o' words? That'd solve the problem right quick. You've lost too many men to this epidemic. Can't afford to lose any more because o' a simple test."

"Huh. You have a point. Go on."

The pages ruffled again, the sound moving through the register, but this time they moved faster.

Please, Lord, Jo silently prayed. *Please help the commander understand.*

"Like I said," Derwyn continued, "you're losing perfectly good soldiers to the flu. You don't need to lose them to a bloody test too. Would be a right shame."

The rustling abruptly stopped.

"You're quite right, Doctor. Please have a seat, while I read through these again."

Jo heard the legs of a chair *squeak* against the floorboards, and she imagined the two men facing each other now. What she couldn't imagine was how Derwyn felt. Was he nervous? Afraid? Did he fiddle with the hem of his smock, knowing the man in front of him could have him court-martialed at any time? While he normally sounded so confident, Derwyn wasn't half as gutsy as the camp's commander. No one was.

Just when Jo thought she couldn't wait another second, a loud slap rang out.

Whack!

"This is brilliant, Doctor. The idea seems so simple, doesn't it? But it's just what we need. Why didn't anyone think of it sooner?"

"Don' know, sir."

"Yes, indeed. The War Department will be very interested in what you've done here. Very interested, indeed."

"Thank ye. But I must confess, I can't take all the credit. Not a'tall. Two others helped."

"Of course, of course. Please, tell me their names, so I can thank them, as well."

"'Twas Mrs. Josephine Pembrooke, the psychologist's wife, along with the pastor's wife, Rebekkah Schmidt. They're the ones ye'd do well to thank."

"Excuse me?"

"Yes, 'twas the women folk who first thought it up. Bloody brilliant too."

"Now see here, Doctor." Suddenly, the man's tone changed. Hardened. Gone was the affable manner Jo had detected earlier.

Oh, no. Don't do it, Derwyn. Take it back! Say you didn't mean it.

After a beat or two of silence—a pregnant pause when everything hung in the balance—the commander finally laughed. A deep, hearty guffaw, which rumbled like thunder through the iron register at Jo's feet.

"Ha, ha! Good one, Doctor. Quite the kidder you are. You really had me going there."

"'Scuse me, sir?"

"Such a comedian. I thought you were serious for a moment. Two women working together. Ha! You and I both know Washington won't buy it. Oh, that's rich."

"But—"

"But nothing, Doctor. Everyone knows two women can't work together. They're territorial ... like cats. Working together is the perfect recipe for a catfight. Women weren't really created to think for themselves. It's not in their nature. By the way, Doctor, did I ever tell you about the time I lived with the Innuits in Alaska? Their women were quite feisty too. One time ..."

Jo finally stepped away from the iron grate. From what Albigence had said, the major general could talk about his time up north for hours. There was no telling how long he'd make Derwyn listen to his stories, since he had a captive audience now.

"Let's get out of here," she whispered to Rebekkah.

Her friend gave a ragged cough in response.

"Hey ... are you all right? You don't look well."

Rebekkah's eyes had turned glassy and her cheeks were red.

"What's wrong with you?" Jo whispered.

"Nothing. I'm fine. Don't worry about me."

"But you don't look fine." She raised her palm to Rebekkah's forehead to check, but her friend sidestepped her.

"I said, I'm fine. A little warm, maybe. The building's furnace must've switched on."

"I don't think so. I'm actually quite cold in here."

"Who cares? We have to focus. Let's go."

"Hmm." Jo reached forward again, and this time, she moved too quickly for Rebekkah to duck. "I knew it. You're burning up. All right. Let's get you out of here."

She took hold of Rebekkah's shoulders and gently guided her to the stairs. As expected, the door to the commander's office remained closed, and would probably remain so until morning.

Bless Derwyn for his patience. And, bless him for trying to give credit where credit was due, even if the commander scoffed at the idea.

For now, the commander's slight was the least of her worries.

★★★

Jo finally let down her guard after she'd tucked Rebekkah into the wrought-iron bed at the parsonage.

It wasn't like her friend to get sick. Rebekkah was the one who generally took care of everyone else, and not the other way around.

Not only that, but she was far too hot for Jo's liking. She'd had enough experience at the schoolhouse to know the difference between an everyday illness and a serious one.

Thank goodness, they'd found Otto fast asleep in the parlor when they arrived at the parsonage. He'd dozed off with an open book in his lap and his spectacles still on. She didn't have the energy, nor the desire, to chat with him tonight. Or with anyone else for that matter.

She arranged Rebekkah under a muslin sheet in the bed, and then she wearily sank into a nearby chair. She curled her own legs beneath her and allowed her eyes to close.

The sound of Rebekkah's quiet breathing soothed Jo. She remembered standing in the empty room next to the commander's office, her ear trained toward the heat register in the floor.

Her mind snagged on a certain phrase. The commander had told Derwyn women weren't created to think for themselves. She'd been shocked by that. Because she'd heard those words before. Many years ago, and somewhere far away, but the sentiment was the same.

She was twelve years old the first time it happened. A schoolgirl in petticoats, who stood next to a massive oak desk as wide as a barn door.

"But why, Papa?" she'd asked, as she stood in its shadow.

"Because women weren't created to think for themselves," her father had replied. "It's not in their nature."

The only reason she found herself in her father's office to begin with was because of his desk. With its enormous kneehole, it created the perfect hiding place during a rousing game of hide-and-go-seek with her brother.

Teddy would never look for her there. In fact, he avoided their father's study at all costs. He said he didn't like the

236

smell of the musty leather-bound books, and the stale tobacco smoke that clung to the velvet curtains.

She used to drag one of their father's thick law books into the kneehole for company whenever Teddy pretended to look for her outside. It was her favorite one, and she loved to study a picture on its back side. In it, a dignified man in a long black robe stood before a galley full of curious spectators. He seemed to mesmerize them with his performance—like an actor in a stage play.

Little by little, the picture piqued her curiosity enough for her to crack open the pages, where she spied interesting new words like "jurisprudence," "acquittal," and "indictment." Long words, which told incredible stories of drama and intrigue, right and wrong, confinement or freedom.

She always knew she was safe under her father's desk, reading from the heavy law book, because her brother would never search for her there.

One night, she crept to the edge of the massive desk after dinner and waited for her father to notice her. When he finally did, she moved closer.

"Hello, Papa."

"There's my girl," he said, as he patted her head.

"Can I tell you something?" she'd asked.

"Of course. You can tell me anything."

The broad smile encouraged her to share her secret. Even so, she had to screw up her courage to force the words out.

"I want to be a lawyer, Papa. Just like you."

"A lawyer?" The smile faltered, for some reason. "Where on earth did you get that idea?"

"Be ... because I want to work with you."

"I see." That wiped the grin clean off his face. "I'm

afraid that's impossible, sweetheart. I always intended to ask your brother to join me in the practice."

"Teddy?"

"Do you have another brother I don't know about?" Though he added a chuckle, there was nothing funny about their conversation by now.

"Teddy hates all this." Papa might as well have said he wanted to bring one of the hunting dogs into the law practice.

"That doesn't matter, my dear. Now, are you sure you don't want to *marry* an attorney? You'd get all the benefits of the profession without doing the hard work."

"No—"

"Think about it. Your mother enjoys the fruits of my profession—just look around you at this beautiful home— but she doesn't have to worry herself with pesky details, like appearing in court. Doesn't that sound more fun for a girl like you?"

She'd sucked in her lower lip then, unable to speak. What good was the money when you didn't get to do the actual work?

Her vision turned watery when she could no longer hold back the tears.

"Won't you even th-think about it?"

"Oh, child. You do say the funniest things. Run along now and play. I have to work on a deposition tonight."

"Deposition," she'd blurted out, her voice trembling with the effort, "means to take an oral account from a witness who's under oath."

"How on earth did you know that?"

"I've been reading your books, Papa. I don't understand everything, but I've learned a lot."

"You've been reading my books?" For some reason, he

sounded angry now. "Do you mean to tell me you've been coming into my office when I'm not at home?"

Oh, no.

"Well, sometimes," she mumbled. "You see—"

"Now, Josephine. I don't want you in here. My papers are highly confidential. I thought you knew that. I suppose I'll have to put a lock on the door now."

"But, Papa—"

"No 'buts.' This isn't a place for play. There are serious documents in here meant for my eyes only. About things you wouldn't understand."

By the time he finished, tears flowed freely down her cheeks. Not only did her father hate the idea she'd proposed, but now he'd banished her from his office—the one place she felt comfortable in their drafty mansion. The one place where she learned interesting new words and found endless opportunities.

The memory vanished when Rebekkah suddenly called out in her sleep.

"Josephine!"

Jo snapped awake, and then she tumbled to the bedside. "I'm here, Rebekkah. What's wrong?"

"Water," her friend moaned. "I'm so thirsty."

Rebekkah's cheeks flamed with fever and sweat drenched her hairline.

"Of course," Jo said. "I'll be right back."

She started to move away, until she realized something and froze. Rebekkah's sickness was obvious. Undeniably obvious.

Her best friend had contracted the Spanish flu.

CHAPTER TWENTY-EIGHT

ALBIGENCE

AMERICAN EXPEDITIONARY FORCES HEADQUARTERS, CHAUMONT, FRANCE

JUNE 1918

My dearest Josephine,
I told myself I wouldn't write you another letter,
because I doubted that you'd ever received the
others. But, the most amazing thing happened
yesterday, and I can't get it out of my mind.

Albigence balanced the notepad on his knee, as the truck rumbled along the road to Chaumont. The conversations inside the truck made concentration difficult, but he vowed to try his best.

You see, I met the most amazing boy on the voyage
over to France. We have nothing in common—he's
quite the "outdoors" type. I prefer the natural
wonders of a well-stocked library, as you well know.
The lad struck up a conversation, and he also gave
me the most wonderous cure for seasickness.
As an aside ... I know you would've been appalled

by the boy's grammar. Apparently, some people in Louisiana think nothing of chopping whole syllables off the ends of their words. They leave them hanging in midair, as if it's up to the listener to fill in the gaps.

Regardless, the boy told me all about his rural upbringing in a city near New Orleans. He sounded quite cheerful, even though he was bound for the Western Front. I would've thought the reason for the trip would've soured his mood, but no. I chalked his attitude up to his youth. The boy considered it a grand adventure to be sailing on such a wonderous ship. He found the journey fascinating. In that regard, he reminded me of your students. So enamored with the world around them. So naïve, but in the best possible way.

There's more. I came across him by accident yesterday while enjoying a rare outing in Brest. Such a lovely day, but that's not what I wanted to tell you about. I'll never forget what happened when I came across the boy—his name is Boone, by the way, as in Daniel Boone—with his regiment. The entire troop went home yesterday. They'd been too injured to continue and too traumatized to be useful anymore.

Josephine, the poor boy was missing half his face. I'll spare you the grisly details, but suffice it to say the gunpowder removed most of what God had put there.

I can't imagine what will happen to him when he returns home. I can't imagine what other people will say either. Or what they'll do. He'll have to find a whole new way to live. One without mirrors or shiny objects or storefronts with glass windows, since he has no idea what's happened to his face. Can you imagine such a thing?

Although I fell in love with you because of your mind, I was not oblivious to your lovely face. Will people ever take time to see beneath Boone's wounds? To get to know him as a man, for he's grown into one now, without the benefit of a face? Such questions kept me awake all night.

I don't want to be a hypocrite. I was quite appalled when I first saw his injuries. I hope I'm getting better at seeing beyond a person's outward appearance and glimpsing the soul inside. I've sat beside many a soldier now whose face was perfectly fine, but whose soul was black as night. I've sat beside other soldiers who've lost an ear, an arm, or their ability to form full sentences, but their souls glow from within.

How could that be? I don't have all the answers yet, but I'm working on it. As I mentioned, I don't want to burden you with my troubling war stories, but I wanted to share what's been happening in my life. How the war has changed me. I don't want to come home without being changed. I want to be better than that. With your help, and the good Lord's, I'm trying to be better.

As always, I pray this letter finds you healthy and happy. Your happiness is what I long for, above all else.

Your husband,

Albigence

He hurriedly tucked the letter in his pocket as the truck arrived at the gates of Chaumont.

CHAPTER TWENTY-NINE

JOSEPHINE

PARSONAGE, CAMP TRAVIS

JUNE 1918

Night turned to day, and still Jo remained at Rebekkah's bedside. Over a span of forty-eight hours, she changed the bedsheets no less than eight times, drenched as they were with Rebekkah's perspiration and spittle.

How Rebekkah contracted the influenza virus was anyone's guess. Perhaps she caught the bug when someone knocked at the door to the parsonage in search of food. Or when a mother dropped off an infant in a mad dash to get medicine for another child.

Regardless, so many people tromped through the parsonage on any given day, the virus could've entered the home in a thousand different ways.

When the third morning dawned, and Rebekkah still seemed as sick as ever, Jo knew she couldn't wait anymore. If she didn't find medicine for her friend, Rebekkah's lungs never would heal.

Once she made up her mind, Jo leaned over the bedrail to whisper in Rebekkah's ear. She had to try, although she didn't know what she'd find at the post exchange, given the scarcity of medicine and the incredible need for it. Even if it meant she'd have to deal with Mr. Johnson and his equally awful wife again.

"Hey, there," she whispered, in the off chance Rebekkah still could hear her. "You need real medicine now. I'm going to find some ... or at least try."

She softly kissed Rebekkah's cheek, and then she hurried through the kitchen, where Otto sat at the breakfast table. He looked exhausted, with his head in his hands and his shoulders slumped, but she didn't stop to comfort him. She had to focus on first things first.

Lately, it was all anyone could do to focus on the sick, let alone the well. There wasn't time to worry about both.

Jo strode down the path to the post exchange, ducking her head to avoid any possible conversations. She needn't have worried. Everyone skirted the perimeter of buildings and pathways nowadays. They were too afraid to speak with strangers face-to-face.

She lifted her head only once on the journey, and that was to spy someone who briskly approached her on the path. The woman pumped her skinny arms furiously back and forth, as if she couldn't wait to reach Jo's side.

"You, there," she screeched, as she came to a stop a respectable distance away.

Jo felt as if she'd awakened from a deep sleep. Her manners went by the wayside. "What? Me?"

"How dare you!" The woman thrust something at Jo. Something that resembled a slip of paper, about the size of a playing card.

"What's this?" Jo asked, as she narrowed her eyes.

"You have no right to endanger everyone else around you. Are you mad?"

Jo blinked. She had no idea what the woman was talking about. And since she wore an enormous gauze mask, there was no way Jo could recognize her.

Her mouth fell open when she realized something.

The facemask. Of course.

In her hurry to leave the parsonage, she'd forgotten to grab a facemask from a pile by the front door.

"I forgot my mask. I'm so sorry," Jo squeaked.

"Sorry doesn't save lives, now does it?" The stranger waved the card at her aggressively, as if she held a loaded gun and not a slip of paper.

Jo timidly took the offering. Sure enough, it was a ticket of some kind, printed with two, stark sentences.

> **You are in violation of the country's Sanitary Code.**
> **A fine of $5 is payable immediately.**

Jo stared at the ticket, momentarily confused.

"You can settle the bill at the post exchange," the stranger said.

"Surely, you're not serious."

"Of course, I'm serious. We have to abide by the rules."

"I don't have money to pay for this."

"You should have thought of that before you broke the law."

Jo palmed the silver dollar in her pocket. One of the last she had. She'd already worked through her savings, since Albigence's paycheck was being sent overseas, and she wouldn't receive her teacher's salary for another three months.

"I'm on my way to get medicine, you see," Jo insisted, hoping the stranger would take pity on her. "My friend's very sick."

"Sick?" The woman blanched. "All the more reason for you to wear a facemask. For shame. For shame!"

The lady spun on her heel after saying her piece, no doubt in search of another victim to terrorize.

Whatever had happened to common decency and good manners?

For some reason, people acted as if the epidemic gave them permission to be awful to each other. As if the virus trumped the normal rules of society.

Perhaps that was the real sickness. People had forgotten how to be cordial. Or maybe they never were, and the epidemic merely exposed their true natures.

But Jo couldn't entertain such a depressing thought, given she had enough depressing things to worry about. Like the bare shelves she expected to find when she got to the post exchange.

She thrust the card into her pocket and soon reached the exchange. At the last moment, she untied the cotton sash from around her waist to use as a facemask, tying the ends behind her head. While the substitute didn't work nearly as well as a regular one, it would have to do.

The shopkeeper glanced up when she hurried into the exchange.

"Oh. It's you." His voice was frosty. "Hello."

"Hello. I need to buy some medicine. Quickly. What do you have?" She didn't have to say what the medicine was for. At this point, everyone knew.

"'Fraid you're too late."

"What do you mean—too late? Surely, you have something in here," she said, as she gazed hopefully around the tent.

He casually moved over a foot or two. "I'm plum out of aspirin. So sorry." He tried to sound empathetic, but he couldn't quite pull it off. He was lying to her.

"You mean to tell me you don't have any medicine at all? Not one aspirin?"

"Not one."

He shrugged, and that's when she noticed a small glass cabinet behind him. He seemed to be guarding it, as if he didn't want her to know what was inside.

"You're lying," Jo said.

"That's a right fine thing to say to someone. Why don' you check with the infirmary? Ya might have better luck there."

"You and I both know doctors there need every bit of medicine they have."

He'd left her no choice. Jo impulsively moved forward and grabbed the lip of a large whiskey barrel stuffed with dry goods. She heaved the barrel over with a grunt, and then she watched the contents spew every-which-way. Spools of thread rolled sideways, paper packets full of buttons launched into the air, and a few skeins of soft gray yarn tumbled to the ground.

"Now see here," the shopkeeper yelled, as he jumped forward to stop the puddle of merchandise from spreading.

The hullabaloo left the cabinet behind his back wide open. On the third shelf, Jo spied a priceless treasure—a small yellow and brown tin of Bayer aspirin. She instantly recognized the brown writing on its lid.

While the merchant scrabbled to collect the supplies, Jo lunged for the aspirin.

Once she grabbed it, she slapped the silver dollar on the counter. Never let it be said she was a thief.

She rushed from the tent without looking back.

By the time she reached the parsonage, she couldn't breathe. Worse than that, though, was a niggling thought she couldn't ignore. She'd just broken a commandment—

Thou shalt not steal—and she did so willing. Her only excuse was that she didn't have a choice. She *did* pay for the medicine afterward.

She was a fine one to talk about civility. To talk about manners and morals in the middle of an epidemic. Perhaps she was no better than anyone else.

With such a sobering thought in mind, she returned to Rebekkah's bedside, and not a moment too soon. Her friend was fading fast.

CHAPTER THIRTY

ALBIGENCE

AMERICAN EXPEDITIONARY FORCES HEADQUARTERS, CHAUMONT, FRANCE

JUNE 1918

The troop transport finally reached its destination at twilight. Albigence was relieved to find buildings made of granite and iron here, unlike the flimsy plywood structures at Camp Pontanezen.

He grabbed his duffel and pitched himself over the tailgate as soon as the engine stalled. He'd become quite athletic over the past few months, if he did say so himself. He had no trouble at all leapfrogging over other passengers to reach an empty spot in the road.

His short time at Camp Pontanezen had changed him in so many ways, including physically. Every day, all day long, he'd hoisted patients off the machines before they could do themselves any real harm. Other times, he'd retrieved heavy boxes from the rafters of the infirmary. He'd even carried crates up and down the stairs which led to a cellar.

Now, whenever he went to lift a book or tie a shoe or slide a straight razor across his chin, an actual muscle moved on his arm. The first time he noticed the movement, it'd taken him by surprise. He'd never had an actual bicep on his arm before. What a strange, and welcome, change.

Albigence hurried to a building he assumed was an infirmary, given a crude red cross painted on its side.

"Excuse me," he asked a nurse by its entrance, "but where do I sign in?"

"Sign in?" The exhausted matron rolled her eyes. "No one 'signs in' here. This is not a country club, if you haven't noticed."

"I realize that. I just meant—"

"Over there. Go over there. They'll help you."

She nodded to a desk inside, which was manned by another nurse. Unlike the first one, though, this woman was quite beautiful, with dark hair and amber eyes. She reminded him of Josephine, which made his heart flutter.

"May I help you?" the girl asked, when he finally worked up the courage to approach.

"Uh, yes. Please." He dropped his duffel with a *thump*. "I'm a psychologist, you see. I'm supposed to have an office here."

"We've been expecting you."

"You have?"

"Yes, of course. They told us we were due to get an actual psychologist any day now. And here you are."

"Yes, here I am." He tried to return her smile, but the enthusiasm unnerved him. "Don't you have other psychologists here?"

"Goodness, no. They've only just decided to give us one. We've had far too many cases of battle fatigue and not a soul to treat them until now."

Ah, she called the disorder by its actual name.

"Good for you," Albigence said, forgetting his shyness when he realized he was in the company of a kindred spirit. "You knew the correct name for the disorder."

"Of course, I did. Why wouldn't I?"

"Most people call it 'shell shock.' Which is quite disrespectful to the doctors who named the disorder, if you ask me."

"I agree. The patients here aren't just shocked. They're downright exhausted when we see them. Mentally, that is. Sometimes, they're physically fine."

"I'm delighted to meet you, Miss ..."

"Wheatley. But, please, call me Sarah. I already know your name, Doctor Pembrooke. Follow me."

When she arose from the desk, he noticed she wore a brown fan skirt, which was quite out of place amidst the white ones he'd grown accustomed to seeing.

"So, you're not a nurse then?"

"No. I'm a field director with the American Red Cross. I'm in charge of staffing the wards here."

"Hmm. I didn't realize they were letting women do such things nowadays." No need to be coy about it. He honestly didn't know. "I thought women only worked as nurses, cooks, or perhaps volunteers for the army."

"Not anymore, Doctor. The war's changed a lot of things. Some for the better."

"I agree. My wife is a schoolteacher back home in the States. I never thought I'd grow accustomed to seeing a woman work outside the home. But, as you say, things change."

"War has a way of speeding change too. Anyway, I've set aside an office for you. I know it's not much, but it's the best I could offer given the accommodations here."

They'd reached a miniscule room, no larger than a supply closet. Luckily, he was accustomed to tiny spaces. Next to the window, Albigence spied a pit latrine, along with a metal washstand. On the opposite wall was an iron cot with a thin, bluetick mattress. The only other furniture in the room was a heavy oak bookcase that leaned precariously against one of the walls.

"I see. So, I'll be working and sleeping in the same room, then?"

"Yes. I hope you don't mind. We all have the same arrangement here. Easier to find each other when the shelling starts."

"Shelling?"

"Yes, when the shelling starts."

"I see." Interesting choice of words. "I noticed you said 'when,' and not 'if.' Does it happen a lot? The shelling, I mean."

"Unfortunately, yes. We're very close to the fighting, you know."

"I do now."

To be honest, he didn't mind the living quarters, the pit toilet notwithstanding, although he didn't relish the thought of hearing bombs going off overhead.

His stomach growled, which jerked him back to the present. "Listen, Sarah. I haven't eaten anything today, and I'm quite hungry. Famished, truth be told. Since I've seen my quarters, could you please show me to the canteen?"

"Of course, Doctor. Follow me."

They walked in silence through the infirmary. Unlike the hospital at Camp Pontanezen, no one here wailed uncontrollably or thrashed about or clawed at his face. These men's injuries were far too serious for movement. The majority wore thick bandages around their skulls and yellow tubes that tethered their wrists to silver poles. The tubes reminded him of amber snakes that slithered from the bedframes to the infusion bags.

Surprisingly, a few men clutched Teddy bears to their chests. The toy had become quite popular back in the States, once pictures of Teddy Roosevelt emerged of the president freeing a black cub from a hunter's trap.

"You look surprised." She'd followed his gaze to a nearby gurney. A patient there cradled a chestnut toy to his chest, as if the toy was a newborn. "We find a stuffed animal can comfort the men, especially those who are about to have a salt bath. The salt cleans out mustard gas, but it's incredibly painful."

"No doubt. Now, how will I know when a man is ready to speak to me?"

"Oh, you'll know, Doctor. At some point, they get strong enough to sit up in their beds. A few never do, unfortunately, but you shouldn't worry about them. You'll be able to help the ones who slowly come around."

"I'm sure it takes time to break through to them."

"Yes. They're completely disoriented when they wake up here. They expect to be back in a trench, waist-high in mud and slop, and here they are. With crisp sheets, soft pillows, and nothing but silence. Sometimes, they get dizzy. More than one has thought he'd already gone to heaven when he awoke in his bed."

"I can see why. I've also noticed there are no clocks on the walls. Was that intentional?"

"So, you noticed. We don't want to surprise the men when they wake up. It's important for their internal clocks to reset on their own. There's no night or day at the Front, so there shouldn't be here, either."

"Fascinating. I do wish I could hear more about your operations, but I'm afraid my stomach won't wait. If you don't mind ..."

"Not at all. You'll have time enough to work with the men once you've had something to eat and drink."

Sarah walked to a door that opened to the outside, where workers had constructed a temporary canteen amongst the trees. They'd scattered several iron tables and chairs about, none of which were occupied at the moment.

"Here you go. Do have a good evening, Doctor."

"You too, Sarah. Thank you."

After a quick meal of cold lentil soup and stale bread, both of which a surly cook slapped on a tray, Albigence crossed his arms on the tabletop and laid his head down. Just for a moment, to collect his thoughts. The noises around him gradually faded, until the *crunch* of a broken branch jerked him awake again.

He immediately straightened. A clump of soldiers had crashed through a hedge across the way. They seemed to rotate around an older gentleman with a hangdog expression and four shiny gold stars on the shoulder of his jacket.

Albigence straightened even more.

"Enough," the general barked at his men. Obviously, he hadn't noticed Albigence yet. "Go get something to eat—all of you—and leave me alone. I need to think, and you're ruining my concentration. You're dismissed."

The group immediately disbanded. Once they were gone, the general wearily drew his hand across his eyes.

Albigence couldn't believe it. Given he was fully awake now, he realized the man standing across from him was none other than John Pershing, commander of the American Expeditionary Forces. The general looked exactly as one would expect. Dignified. Rumpled, yet elegant. Piecing blue eyes that surveyed the scene like a hawk.

Those eyes finally cut across the empty space to land on Albigence.

"You, there," the man barked, "shouldn't you be back in your quarters, getting ready for muster?"

Albigence gulped. "But—but I'm not a soldier, sir. I'm a psychologist, you see—"

"Ah." The commander crossed the void in three long strides. When he reached Albigence's side, his expression softened. "Thank goodness for that. I'll lose my mind if I have to inspect one more soldier."

He sank into an empty chair without waiting for an invitation. This didn't concern Albigence at all. If anything, it made the day seem even more surreal. Who would've thought he'd meet General John Pershing at the edge of the Western Front on his very first day?

"How long have you been here, son?" the man muttered.

"Just arrived, sir. Came from Brest. I heard they needed psychologists closer to the Front, so I volunteered."

"Good for you. Most men try to leave this place, not the other way around." The general extended his hand. "I'm John Pershing."

"I know who you are, sir." The man's humility spoke to his greatness. "I've seen your picture in the newspaper many times. I'm Albigence Pembrooke."

A heavy sigh. "You said you're a psychologist. You must try to repair the men once we've broken 'em, eh?"

"Something like that, sir. I'll be working in the hospital here. Mostly with men who suffer from battle fatigue. You know, shell shock."

Far be it from Albigence to assume the general would know the exact term.

"Such a terrible thing," the commander said. "I've seen it all up and down the line. So many men suffer from nightmares because of what they've seen in the trenches. All that tragedy."

His choice of words triggered a certain memory that had stalled in the back of Albigence's mind. Something about the general and a personal tragedy. One that involved a house fire, wasn't it?

Albigence had read all about the fire in the newspaper. Apparently, the culprit was a spark from a fireplace, which skittered across a waxed floorboard and quickly engulfed the house in flames. Killing a woman and three young children. All while the man of the house was leading his troops in battle at the southern border.

"I was so sorry to read about your wife and children, sir," Albigence said. "I don't know what I'd do if something similar happened to me."

The general's face fell, and Albigence worried he might've crossed the line. Especially since the story mentioned how the general refused to talk about what happened afterward.

Oh, dear me.

"Forgive my impertinence," Albigence rushed to say. "I've been traveling, and I'm not quite myself today."

"At ease." The general wearily waved the comment away. "I'm not offended. I expect most people know about what happened."

"I can only imagine, but I had no right to bring up something so personal. Like I said, I'm not myself today."

"All of three of my daughters died, you know."

"Sir?"

"Only my son survived." He lowered his gaze to study the tabletop. "They never stood a chance."

"That's what the story ..." Albigence's voice trailed off. He purposefully bit his lip, then, to keep himself from saying more. If the general wanted to talk, he shouldn't interrupt the man. Psychologists were supposed to listen, after all.

"They still haunt my dreams," the general confessed. "I was supposed to be their protector. I was too busy protecting America's interests instead. Such an irony, eh?"

He glanced at Albigence as if waiting for his response.

"Um ... you can't blame yourself, sir. You couldn't have foreseen such a horrific accident."

"The army trusts me to look into the future and predict how a battle will play out. Why in the world couldn't I predict my own family's fate?"

"Because you were distracted, I imagine. As we all are. I've come to the conclusion military life will swallow you whole, if you let it."

The general shook his head. "That's no excuse, and no doubt why I work twenty-four hours a day now. I'd rather work than see them in my sleep."

"I'm sure your family wouldn't blame you, if they were here." Albigence struggled to think of something—anything—comforting to say. "The disaster could just as easily have happened to someone else."

"You really believe so, son?" the general said.

"I do. Sometimes our actions lead to great tragedies, but sometimes we can't avoid them."

"I suppose that's easier to believe when it's not your family—or your tragedy," the general said. "I still blame myself. I vowed I'd never again become so distracted I'd lose sight of what's really important."

"I understand. I was supposed to run a testing program at my last post, but I got carried away. I'm afraid my actions hurt a lot of people. It's taken me a long time to reconcile what I did with what I should've done."

"Sounds like we're both living with regret, Doctor."

The conversation lagged, and Albigence placed his hands in his lap. Hands that had once belonged to an academic, soft and uncalloused. Now, thick scars capped his knuckles and crisscrossed his palms. They looked like hands of a working man. Hands he could be proud of.

"I do believe we learn from our mistakes," he finally said. "And, we're supposed to use what we learn to help others."

The general grunted. "I suppose so. Is that what they say in those psychology textbooks of yours?"

"No, sir. That's what they teach in the Bible."

"Ah." The general nodded and slowly rose. "Perhaps it's time I cracked open the Good Book myself. Past time. At ease, Doctor. At ease."

Albigence watched the man amble away, his back stooped under the weight of all those medals. Despite them, or maybe because of them, he bore the weight of a thousand "what ifs."

Albigence didn't envy him. Not in the least. He had enough demons to battle, and he wouldn't wish for any more.

★★★

By the time the general disappeared through the hedge again, Albigence was ready to retire for the night.

Once he reached his new quarters, he teetered through the doorway and collapsed onto the cot, fully clothed. For better or worse, this was to be his home for the foreseeable future.

He immediately fell into a deep, dark sleep. Before long, his dreams took him back to the cabin at Camp Travis, where he sat across the dinner table from his lovely Josephine.

She looked radiant, as always. Her auburn hair glowed with lamplight, and her delicate features grew animated when she told him a story about the schoolhouse. Something funny about a black bear, of all things, which had escaped the circus and arrived at her classroom.

My, how she laughed and laughed!

He joined her in the laughter, so happy to be with her again. Then, for some reason, her laughter turned to song. She began to sing to him. Softly, at first, but then the notes grew louder and louder.

Such a lilting tune. A hymn, perhaps? Regardless, it sounded so real. The warm cabin, the glow on his wife's cheeks, a soprano song that poured from her mouth. He prayed it would never end.

But her song did end. It turned into a wail, which screeched high above his head, like a rocket's launch.

K-Boom!

His eyes flew open. Somehow, the ceiling in his office had caught fire, and bright sparks rained down on him.

He rolled off the cot and bellycrawled to the doorway, trapped behind a wall of heat and smoke. He reached for the door handle, but metal singed his thumb, so he made his way to the washstand instead. Once he grabbed a washcloth, he doused it in cold water, and then he wrapped the cloth around his hand.

He'd almost reached the door again, when the heavy bookcase by the cot began to wobble. The next thing he knew, the massive case fell over and drove him to the ground.

That was the last thing he saw—or heard. Only the crack of wood against his skull, followed by a cloud of darkness. No more fire or heat. Only black behind his eyelids and utter silence.

Is this how it feels to be dead?

CHAPTER THIRTY-ONE

JOSEPHINE

MEDICAL INFIRMARY, CAMP TRAVIS

LATE JUNE 1918

Jo tiptoed to the bed, hesitant to rouse Rebekkah. But, if she didn't take some medicine soon, her friend wouldn't get strong enough to fight the infection.

Jo lifted a water glass to her lips and softly called her name.

"Rebekkah. Wake up."

"Yes? What ... what's wrong?" her friend mumbled, in a voice that was barely audible.

"I've brought you something." Jo removed the yellow and brown tin from her pocket.

"Hmm?"

"Medicine. I got you some medicine from the post exchange. You need to take it. Here. I also brought water."

Rebekkah clamped her lips stubbornly.

"C'mon now," Jo said. "You *have* to take the aspirin."

"I don't need it. Find someone who's worse off."

"Nonsense." Jo lifted her friend's head from the wet pillow and placed a pill on her tongue. "Here. Take a drink."

She hated to admit it, but things had gotten even worse in her absence. Instead of thrashing about on the bed, Rebekkah seemed much too calm now. Placid. As if she'd accepted her fate and was too tired to fight anymore.

"Rebekkah? Can you hear me?"

"Hmm?"

"Please don't give up. You *must* get better. And you will. You'll get better soon."

What was worse ... the way the lie rolled right off her tongue or the way Rebekkah wouldn't even challenge her? They both knew what would happen next. First, patients struggled against the virus, their lungs straining for air, their bodies all instinct and fight. Later, when their systems grew accustomed to a lack of oxygen, the muscles began to relax, too weak to fight anymore.

Which meant the end was near.

"Please don't give up on me," she whispered in Rebekkah's ear. "We've worked way too hard for you to laze around in bed like this. Please. I need you."

Rebekkah tried to smile, but all she could manage was a pained grimace.

"Oh, Jo. You don't need me anymore."

"That's where you're wrong," Jo said.

Rebekkah weakly shook her head. "You're stronger than you know. Just promise me one thing—you won't give up on Albigence."

"What are you talking about? You'll be right there with me when his ship comes in. We'll go to the pier together and wave like crazy. You'll see."

Rebekkah finally managed a smile. "You really think so?"

"Of course," Jo said. "We'll wave like fools, and he'll be so happy to be home again."

"Come here." Rebekkah motioned for Jo to move even closer. "Promise me you'll also finish the work we started. You can do it. I have faith in you."

"I don't want to finish without you." Jo swallowed the panic rising in her throat. "You're going to walk out of this bedroom, Rebekkah Schmidt. With me. We're going to change how they do things around here. Together."

By now, a tear rolled down Jo's cheek. She wasn't ready to say goodbye. Not yet.

"The medicine will help you," Jo said, as she wiped it away. "Aspirin will bring your fever down. And once your fever's down, your lungs can heal again. You'll see."

"But I'm not afraid."

"I know. But I am."

With that, Jo closed her eyes. She couldn't listen anymore. Because if she didn't listen, she wouldn't have to face the truth. She could act as if everything was going to be all right.

"Jo?"

The sound of Rebekkah's voice forced her eyes to reopen.

"I lied before. I want you to promise me something else."

"Anything. You know I'd do anything for you."

"Look out for Otto. He's not used to being alone."

Jo nodded as another tear rolled down her cheek. How could she take care of Otto when she wasn't sure she could take care of herself?

★★★

By nightfall, Jo knew what she had to do. With Otto's permission, they brought Rebekkah to the medical infirmary, where she was assigned a number and a cot.

This way, Otto would never wonder if he should've done more.

Jo waited for her friend to fall asleep once they'd completed the move, which didn't take long. If not for the ragged rise and fall of Rebekkah's chest, there'd be little indication she was even alive.

The sound of Rebekkah's breathing, however soft, comforted Jo. She listened for a moment or two, thankful for its reminder, before she too nodded off to sleep.

She only awoke because a loud voice reached her from behind the curtain.

"'Tis all right now," a woman there said. "Don't worry ye-self 'bout nuthin' a'tall."

Jo smiled, despite herself. The woman sounded just like Derwyn. No doubt she'd come from Wales too.

"Got your papers today, Skye. Ye passed with flyin' colors. Didn't miss a one. Thank the good Lord for dem drawings."

"Hmm," a man's voice replied.

"Now, they say ye might hafta take it again. Dere's a man wants to change everythin' back to tha way it was. Says it's not fair. We'll see, though. We'll see, indeed."

Jo twisted her head toward the curtain. Was it possible? Did someone really want to change things back to the way they were? After all the time and effort which she and Rebekkah had spent on the test?

Jo longed to peek her head around the curtain and ask the woman by the next cot what she meant. But, then, she'd have to admit she was eavesdropping, which didn't seem right, given the circumstances.

"'Tis a pity," the woman continued. "Can't imagine such a t'ing. But I'll keep me ear to da ground, Skye. I'll let ye know soon enough."

Rebekkah murmured something in her sleep, which broke Jo's concentration. She reached for a cloth in her pocket and lightly dipped it in the water glass to cool her friend's forehead.

Jo willed the voice next door to continue. She couldn't imagine the commander would permit the test to go back to the way it was. Why should he? Regardless of who got credit, the test seemed to be working, which was the most important thing.

She lightly touched Rebekkah's face with the cloth. The voices next door had fallen silent, unfortunately, and she heard nothing but the sound of Rebekkah's ragged breathing.

Hopefully, the anonymous speaker was misinformed. Hopefully, she'd heard a rumor on the streets, which she'd mistakenly accepted as fact.

Jo didn't have the time, or energy, right now to fight for anything else.

CHAPTER THIRTY-TWO

ALBIGENCE

MEDICAL WARD, AMERICAN EXPEDITIONARY FORCES HEADQUARTERS, CHAUMONT, FRANCE

JUNE 1918

The first thing Albigence noticed upon awakening was the light. A soft glow pierced the darkness and urged his eyes open. The images were blurry, but he seemed to be inside a building, surrounded by shiny silver equipment and white linens. That much, he knew.

But, the pain. He didn't expect the pain when he tried to lift his head off the pillow.

Oof!

The stabbing pain drove his head back to the mattress.

When he finally dared look sideways, Albigence realized he was lying on a gurney, with a brownish tube that ran from his arm to a bagful of something or other.

Was this heaven? If so, where was the music? The streets of gold? He expected the sweet scent of jasmine, not the sterile odor of bottled bleach. Maybe he was nowhere near the Pearly Gates. More like a hospital of some sort.

"Ah. I see you've come back to us."

A woman's face floated above him. A round face with kind eyes behind a pair of spectacles.

"Do I know you?" he murmured. She didn't look dangerous, but one could never tell nowadays. He wouldn't be in this predicament if someone hadn't harmed him in some way.

"I'm your nurse. You've been out for some time, Doctor."

Doctor? I'm a doctor?

"What happened?" He didn't mean to sound stupid, but nothing about the conversation made sense. If he was a physician, like she'd said, why was he lying on a gurney? Shouldn't he be the one treating a patient, and not the other way around?

"You were struck in the head," the nurse explained. "Took quite a lump there, I'm afraid."

"Oh, I see. I got knocked in the head. Well, that makes sense."

He finally realized he'd curled his arm around something soft and squishy. He carefully shifted it into view.

"What's this?" Apparently, he'd received a stuffed toy at some point. One with a round snout and sweet smile.

"A new friend," the nurse said, smiling herself. "You can call him whatever you like. Some of the men like to name their bears."

"But, why do I have him?"

"For company." She sounded quite sure of herself, as if the answer should've been obvious.

"So, I'm not in heaven, then?"

"Heaven?" A soft chuckle. "Goodness, no. You're still at the Front, although you're due to be sent home soon. We wanted to wait until you woke up."

"Of course." Since she'd sounded so confident, the least he could do was follow along.

"Now, we've been giving you thirty milligrams of aspirin a day," she said, "but I need to ask you about the pain you are having. Would you say you have a lot of pain, a medium amount, or hardly any at all?"

"Seriously? Well, I'd say the highest."

"Hmm. That's what I was afraid of. You see, we've only just realized too much aspirin isn't good for our patients. They're calling it 'aspirin poisoning' now, which we're supposed to avoid at all costs. Let me see about getting you a morphine drip instead."

"I'd appreciate it. Thank you." He didn't quite remember this person, but he was grateful to anyone who wanted to ease the ache in his head. "Before you go ..."

"Yes?"

"Am I really a doctor?"

"Of course, you are. You're a psychologist. You help people who have problems."

"You mean, people like me?"

"Not quite." She chuckled again. "You have a different kind of problem. Your pain will go away at some point."

"Oh, well. That's good." He clutched the toy bear tighter, since he knew it was his.

"You'll be going home soon," she added.

"Home? Where *is* home?"

"Hmm. Maybe you're not as far along as I thought. Let me get your medicine first, so you can rest."

She backed away before he could ask anything else. He had a million questions, of course. *That's it!* A million is a huge number, so he should've told her that's how much pain he felt.

The good news was that he was going home. He didn't like it here, with the sharp scent of antiseptic everywhere and scratchy white sheets. Everything looked clean, of course, for which he was grateful, but he felt marooned in a sea of white. Surrounded by white sheets, whiter walls, and no clock of any kind.

He didn't know where "home" was, but it had to be better than this.

CHAPTER THIRTY-THREE

JOSEPHINE

MEDICAL INFIRMARY, CAMP TRAVIS

JUNE 1918

There wasn't an inch of room to spare in the medical infirmary when Jo worked her way down one of the aisles the next morning. Cot followed cot, with nothing to separate them but a chiffon sheet strung across a wire. The makeshift barrier was supposed to prevent germs from traveling around the room.

Which was ridiculous, of course. There was no way something so flimsy could stop a hellacious virus from circulating.

Jo gazed about sadly. Volunteers had thrown open the infirmary's windows, but the room still felt incredibly hot. Everyone—patients and visitors alike—looked miserable. Perspiration dripped down people's chins, sweat stains marred the starched bedding, and puddles of blankets piled on the ground where delirious patients had kicked them off. It was no wonder the sick looked so wretched. But, then again, so did the well.

Since she couldn't see around the partitions, Jo wandered from one aisle to the next until she found Rebekkah's cot. Her friend had fallen asleep again, and she still looked much too peaceful for Jo's liking.

Not only that, but a streak of dried blood scarred the woman's chin, which meant Rebekkah's nose had hemorrhaged at some point during the night.

"May I help you?"

Jo turned to see a volunteer in a starched white smock. No doubt she was someone's mother, given the housedress beneath it. Nowadays the camp's mothers replaced nurses in all but the most critical surgical areas, and everyone did the best she could.

"How's the patient doing?" Jo asked.

"No idea." The volunteer sounded depressingly nonchalant. "But, it's time for her medical treatment." She grabbed something from a pocket of her smock, which turned out to be a large amber bottle.

"What's in the bottle?" The jug looked suspiciously large. Definitely not a dose of morphine.

"Whiskey. A hundred proof. Helps with the phlegm." She twisted off the cap and poured some into a spoon she found in another pocket.

"Oh, no. My friend doesn't drink."

"She will now. Whiskey is all we have left."

When something moved behind her, Jo whirled around. Derwyn stood behind her, praise the Lord.

"Oh, Derwyn. I'm so glad you're here. I hate to bother you ... but can you help? This woman is trying to give Rebekkah whiskey. Whiskey!"

"She's only doing her job." His voice was weary. "Eh, it'll help somewhat. I can administer the dose me-self if you'd like."

"Thank you, but whiskey won't solve anything. Can't you give her something else? A real medicine?"

He sighed. "'Tis not so simple. There's none left. Most o' what we have goes to the Front nowadays."

"I understand, but you must have something in the pharmacy. Please."

Derwyn quickly scanned a clipboard he found lying at the end of Rebekkah's cot.

"Well, she's already had a dose o' laxative today. Can't give her too much o' the laxative for the charcoal. The real problem is her polio, you see. The lass's system was compromised from the start. No goin' back and fixin' that."

"What about more aspirin? Would that help?"

"I'm savin' me aspirin for surgery now." He returned the chart to the footboard. "I do have a bit o' camphorated oil in the back, though. 'Tis under lock an' key."

"Could she have that? I could fetch it. They obviously can't spare you out here."

The infirmary seemed to be staffed mostly by volunteers and family members now, with only a few doctors in the mix.

"Aye, then. Here's the key to the medicine locker. 'Tis hidden in the back."

He handed her a skeleton key, which dangled from an old shoestring. How depressing that something as simple as camphor oil had to be locked away for safekeeping.

"Mind yerself when you're back there," he warned. "Can't be too careful nowadays."

"Thank you, my friend."

Jo moved to the other side of the hall, clutching the key. This side of the room looked just as packed as the other. How heartbreaking to see so many people she knew stuffed into the infirmary. Everyone from newborns to elderly, parents to children, both males and females. All with sheets pulled taut under their chins and faces as pale as the bleached linens.

Once she reached the back of the hall, a stranger in a crisp linen dress shirt caught her eye. Obviously not a doctor, since his clothes looked far too clean and pressed for that, he nodded when she approached.

"Hello," he said.

"Hello. I'm looking for the hospital's pharmacy. Do you happen to know where it is?"

"Are you authorized to go there?"

"Yes. I have the key." She held out the key as proof. The man's voice sounded oddly familiar, although she couldn't quite place it. Identifying people now was almost impossible, given the enormous facemasks. "I need to fetch a bottle of medicine for one of the doctors."

"I see. Well, then. Follow me. It's next to my office."

He strode away without waiting for her. She followed behind, wondering where she'd heard that voice before.

"Here you go." He'd stopped in front of a room fronted by a large wood door. The word PHARMACY appeared in a pebbled green glass window. "If you need to break open a box, there are scissors on my desk. Make sure you return them when you're done, though."

"I will. Thank you, sir."

Fortunately, he left her alone after that, because he made her feel uncomfortable. He was much too slick for an army camp, and the way he eyed the front of her shirtwaist made her skin crawl.

She shivered, and the moment passed. Once she opened the pharmacy and slipped inside, she faced a large enamel cabinet with four deep shelves, most of which were empty.

An opaque brown bottle sat on the third shelf, though. One that held the camphorated oil, according to a label on its side. Next to the bottle was a yellow tin of Bayer aspirin and an unopened box of cotton balls.

Since Derwyn would need a cotton ball to apply the oil, Jo grabbed the box too. Then, she quickly left the room and locked the door, glancing over her shoulder to make sure no one was following her.

She moved on to the next room, where she'd apparently find a pair of scissors to pry open a flap on the box.

The stranger must've been an administrator of some sort, because his office held a multitude of technical manuals and textbooks. One of those was titled *Introduction to Psychoanalysis,* by the famous Austrian doctor, Freud, so maybe he was a psychologist, just like Albigence.

Aha!

The stranger who provided directions was the same one who'd lured Albigence away from the canteen the night of the riot. The one who'd happily informed her that Albigence had left for the Western Front, as if Jo's great loss was his personal gain.

Regardless, she had too much to do to worry about him, so she quickly moved to the desk and grabbed a pair of scissors in the corner. As she turned, she accidently knocked over a pile of papers which perched on the edge. Brittle as rice paper, they fluttered to the ground like snow.

She bent to retrieve them, but the first one stopped her cold. It was letter of some sort. Not just any letter, but one addressed to *her,* in care of the post exchange at Camp Travis. The crimped C looked like it'd been written in Albigence's hand. She'd seen his handwriting often enough to know, since he'd written her so many letters from Cornell.

Everything else fell away as she scooped the papers off the floor. What in the world was this man doing with a stack of letters from Albigence? Each one had "par avion" stamped in the corner, which meant the letters had come all the way from France.

She started to open the first one, until she remembered where she was. The office's rightful owner could return at any moment and catch her in the act. No, this wasn't the time, nor the place, to read what she'd found. So, she slipped the bundle into her pocket and reached for the scissors instead.

With shaking hands, she managed to slice open the box of cotton balls and fumble a few of them into her pocket. Then, she returned everything to its proper place, careful to lock the pharmacy one last time. She even jiggled the handle for good measure before she left.

Nothing had changed in the infirmary when she returned, of course, but everything felt different now. Off-kilter. As if she moved a step or two behind everyone else.

Albigence had sent her letters. From the Front. At least a dozen of them, at first glance. He was trying to reach her, after all.

She rounded the corner before Rebekkah's cot and paused. There was no telling if Derwyn remained, or if he'd been pulled away to help another patient.

Thankfully, he'd stayed, and he leaned over the cot to check Rebekkah's heartbeat with a stethoscope.

He gently moved the instrument from one spot to the next. Once, twice, three times. As if he didn't like what he'd heard the other times.

"Well, what do you think?" Jo asked, as she moved next to him.

"I won't lie to you," he said. "It doesn't sound good. Not good a-tall."

Once again, the world stopped as she struggled to take in his words.

"What do you mean—not good at all?"

"'Tis true, my dear." He gazed at her sadly. "She's got the pleurisy. Nothing more to be done about it, I'm 'fraid."

"She's lasted this long. Maybe—"

He silently shook his head, which told her everything she needed to know.

"Stop it, Derwyn. You're scaring me. Tell me she's going to be all right."

She couldn't help herself. Maybe if she forced him to say it, the words would come true. She could somehow convince herself Rebekkah was only sleeping, and she'd wake up soon enough. She refused to believe Rebekkah was caught somewhere between life and death, heaven and earth, with only a weak heartbeat to tether her to this life.

"'Tis no use," Derwyn repeated. "'Tis only a matter of time now."

He didn't mean to be cruel—she understood—but the words sliced right through her heart.

"I ... I don't know what to do, Derwyn. Tell me what to do."

"You could always take her home. 'Tis not usually done, though."

"No, I can't do that," she said, more forcefully than she'd intended. "It's not fair to Otto. I don't want him to ever wonder if he should've let her stay here. To blame himself for whatever happens next."

Plus, the longer Rebekkah remained in the infirmary, Jo thought, the longer she could pretend her friend still had a chance.

"All right, then," Derwyn said. "I'll let her stay here."

"Thank you."

Whether it did any good, his kindness meant the world to her, and she hugged him tightly.

She'd forgotten what it was like for someone to be kind.

CHAPTER THIRTY-FOUR

ALBIGENCE

U.S.S. MADAWASKA, MIDWAY THROUGH THE ATLANTIC OCEAN

JULY 1918

The salty air stung Albigence's cheeks and made his eyes water, but he felt wonderful as he stood outside again. He'd spent far too much time below deck in his stuffy stateroom.

They'd assigned him to a single stateroom, no doubt because of the seriousness of his injuries. His room included a lone cot, a personal washbasin, and a miniature porthole, although too much salt and brine caked the window for it to be useful.

After sleeping through the first week of his journey, he finally awoke and decided to make a go of it. If he were ever to leave the ship, he must learn how to navigate the stairs himself and climb to one of the upper decks.

And now, here he stood. How strange to see the sun again and feel its warmth on his hair. Even with a thick gauze bandage wrapped around his temples, the breeze blew across the square of cotton and cooled his skin.

He leaned over the rail to appraise the waves. Huge whitecaps crashed against the ship's hull and rocked it to and fro. Fortunately, his stomach held fast. While other men turned quite green at the sight, he felt not a flutter or flop of his own. He even studied the whitecaps as they dispersed in sparkly bursts of mist, completely mesmerized by the sight and sound of it.

The water amazed him. When he finally shifted his gaze, he beheld a soldier standing next to him, who leaned over the rail miserably. The man looked quite green in the gills. He wanted to pat the soldier's arm, or at least divert his attention to the majestic ironworks all around them. The smokestack alone had to be three stories tall! Since the other chap was indisposed, Albigence studied the vertical structure for himself. There, on its side, was a particular name—the *U.S.S. Madawaska*. What a strange and curious name. He'd never come across such a name, but he imagined it belonged to someone famous. Someone important. Why else would they paint someone's name on a smokestack three stories tall if he wasn't important or famous?

He'd know more soon. A nice man at the dock explained to him that he was going home. And, according to the man, "home" was an army camp in a place called Texas. Which he'd never heard of, either, but he still looked forward to it. The gentleman had gone out of his way to describe purple mountains and amber waves of grain. Which all sounded heavenly. Afterward, Albigence thanked him profusely for the description.

He even had a wife there waiting for him. A woman by the name of Josephine. Such a lovely name. He only hoped she knew how to prepare his favorite meal of scrambled eggs and porridge. They'd get along fine, as long as she didn't try to pass off burnt eggs or leave lumps in his oatmeal.

One more deep breath before he turned away. He needed to return to his quarters. He'd sensed a dull ache at the base of his neck, which signaled the onslaught of another migraine. Headaches always began the same way ... a dull pain that gradually grew into a viselike grip on his skull. So strong, he'd grit his teeth in agony and try to shut out any noise.

Once the pain commenced, even medicine couldn't soothe him. The good Lord knew he'd been given a boatload of medicine since the shelling. They even gave him a liter of the stuff, which he'd been told was something called 'morphine,' to take home. He'd stashed the bottle in his duffel bag, where no one else could find it.

Better to nip the pain in the bud and gulp down medicine instead of allowing the pain to worsen.

He'd learned *that* lesson a few weeks ago, when he thought he might forgo the morphine by focusing his mind on something else. Anything else. The infirmary offered little in the way of entertainment, but he noticed a nurse had placed a black book next to his cot.

So, he opened the pages to see if maybe *that* would take his mind off the pain. The letters swam on the page, like an unruly school of minnows, so he returned the book to the nightstand and closed his eyes. Why should he read if it only made his headache worse?

That was the one, and only, time he tried to open a book. He'd just have to make do without books for the rest of his life, which shouldn't be a huge problem. Should it?

Surely, they'd find him a job at Camp Travis where he didn't have to read. If only he could remember what he'd done before. He obviously wasn't a real soldier, because he couldn't recall ever holding a gun. Was he an ambulance driver? A medic? If so, one would think the smell of disinfectant would trigger some sort of memories, which didn't happen.

Did he drive a lorry then, delivering supplies? *Now, that would be interesting.*

Someone had mentioned he was a doctor, but he couldn't remember who said it, or why.

Whatever his new job, he'd take it without complaining. Anything to get away from France. He never wanted to see the jagged French coastline again, or muck about in the mud and mire. While he hadn't experienced the trenches, like a lot of other men, he'd had enough rain and fog to last a lifetime.

Perhaps this "Texas" would be different. Drier. Warmer. He surely hoped so. Just one more week to go, and he'd find out.

He didn't know exactly where he was going, but anywhere had to be better than where he'd been.

CHAPTER THIRTY-FIVE

Josephine

Post Exchange, Camp Travis

July 1918

This time, Jo barely noticed the stifling heat as she strode toward the post exchange. Morning sun glinted off the dry, cracked path and nearly blinded her as she hurried toward the building.

She hadn't slept a wink the night before, and not just because her best friend in the whole world—her only friend, to be honest—was lying in a hospital bed, with no medicine to speak of. No, there was more to it. She'd also realized something around midnight, when she'd read and reread the first of Albigence's letters.

She'd been so wrong about him. About everything. She'd pictured him stationed at a fully functioning army hospital, with proper equipment, ample staff, and medicine that was so much better than what they had stateside. Everyone said the best medical supplies were sent overseas, to where the battles raged. Which was true enough, but it sounded as if the soldiers' injuries were so horrific even the best supplies didn't make any difference.

She knew her husband wanted to spare her the gory details, but she could read between the lines. When he mentioned being unable to recognize someone he'd met earlier, what was she supposed to think? Even with a gauze facemask, only horrific injuries could change a person's appearance so much they'd be unrecognizable.

Now, she stormed into the tent that served as the post exchange, propelled by the force of her anger.

"How dare you," she yelled, when she spied the shopkeeper behind the counter.

She waved her husband's letters high in the air, the delicate paper ripped and ragged now, after being read and reread so many times.

The shopkeeper froze. He'd been standing next to a customer, explaining the contents of something or other. The customer was Mrs. Benedict, the shrewish president of the Ladies' Benevolent Society.

"Beg pardon?" the merchant meekly asked.

Jo brushed past Mrs. Benedict to slap the letters on the counter. She didn't even bother to acknowledge the older woman, but launched right into her speech, which she'd practiced on the walk over.

"Correct me if I'm wrong, Mr. Johnson. Isn't it a federal crime to give someone's mail to another person?"

"I—I—"

"I'm not finished yet. Apparently, you felt justified to confiscate these letters my husband sent *to me*, and give them to someone else. Someone they didn't belong to. As far as I'm concerned, you're nothing but a thief. What do you think the major general will have to say about that?"

The man's face slowly reddened as he realized the truth.

"Now … now see here, Josephine," he sputtered.

"It's *Mrs. Pembrooke*. Mrs. Albigence Pembrooke. The same name found on *each and every one* of these letters."

"Keep your voice down," Mrs. Benedict hissed. "You're making a scene. Get ahold of yourself."

"I'm only making a scene because of what this man did. Stealing someone's mail is a crime. So, what do you have to say for yourself, Mr. Johnson?"

Jo stared straight at the merchant now, since her fight was with him and no one else.

"I—I can explain," he whispered, urgently. "When the letters got here, I planned to give them to you. I really did. But then that other psychologist—you know, the one with the big moustache—told me what'd happened. Said you were suffering from female hysteria. He called you 'unhinged.'" He drew out the word, as if the term explained everything. "He said he'd keep the letters safe for you until you got better."

"I was never ill to begin with." Jo's voice had iced over. "Not every woman who shows emotion is insane. I've always been fully aware of what's going on around me."

"Which I didn't know at the time."

She threw up her hands. "Stop. I don't want to hear another word. If this ever happens again, I will go straight to the attorney general's office at the United States Department of War. Don't think I won't."

With that, she scooped up the letters and marched away, too angry to say more.

She didn't stop walking until she reached the main road. By now, her fury had boiled over and had finally begun to cool, so she could breathe again. *Why does everything have to be so difficult?* The only reason she couldn't have

Albigence's letters was because some man didn't want her to have them—a man who had no stake in the affair.

Which wasn't right, and it was only the latest insult in a whole year of them.

Since she had no desire to return to an empty cabin, filled as the house was with memories and ghosts, she decided to head for the infirmary instead. Although Derwyn had warned her about Rebekkah's health yesterday, perhaps her friend would feel well enough to talk to her today.

She couldn't wait to tell her about the letters. Perhaps she'd even sit beside Rebekkah's cot and read them to her, one at a time. Only the good ones, of course, which didn't contain anything dark or troubling. Maybe they'd take Rebekkah's mind off her own suffering for a moment and give her something else to think about.

Today was a new day. Perhaps this was the day Rebekkah's health finally turned around. Even with Derwyn's dire prediction, anything was possible. Maybe after a good night's rest—what with the whiskey and camphorated oil—Rebekkah's body would rally. Perhaps the two "medicines" would offer the right combination to finally heal her lungs.

Once Jo reached the hospital, she automatically took the aisle that led to her friend's cot.

Which sat empty.

Oh, someone had pulled the sheets taut, but there was no patient beneath them. Where was Rebekka, tucked in tight, with an overworked volunteer at her side?

Confused, Jo retraced her steps. This time, she tried counting the cots as she walked. She expected to pass eleven beds in all. She'd need to get a good night's sleep tonight, because she obviously couldn't think straight. She couldn't even find a place she'd visited less than twelve hours before, for goodness' sake.

The result was the same. She stared at the empty cot until a voice broke through her thoughts.

"I'm so sorry," a man said.

She was about to turn around and face him, but found she couldn't move.

"Hello, Otto."

"She's—she's—"

"It's okay. You don't have to say it. Please don't say it."

She reached behind her to grasp his hand. Worried that if she didn't hold onto something firm, her legs would give way, and she'd crumble to the floor.

Rebekkah was gone. Taken in only a week's time.

★★★

The funeral was a dry, dusty affair held the next day.

Since the US Department of War still insisted people avoid large gatherings, so as not to spread the virus, only a handful of Rebekkah's closest friends and neighbors could come.

They formed a tight semicircle around the pine casket, as they all waited for the eulogy to begin.

Otto was too devastated to deliver it. The man who'd stood at the head of a hundred caskets—the one who'd held countless hands as people lay dying, someone who'd listened to innumerable last confessions—was too bereft to speak at his own wife's funeral.

So, he'd asked the major general to do the honors. The commander, who was never at a loss for words before, stood stiffly beside the casket, uncharacteristically tongue-tied.

"Um, so. Here we are. We're here to—to, uh, say goodbye to someone dear. A mighty fine woman. Yes, indeed. She wasn't the first person to die from this terrible disease, and she won't be the last."

Jo flinched. While what he said was true—the disease had claimed more than fifty people at the camp so far—it seemed deeply disrespectful to lump Rebekkah in with everyone else. Hers was a singular life and a singular death, and special in its own right.

Jo only wished Otto had asked *her* to deliver the eulogy. She'd find a better way to memorialize Rebekkah than someone who didn't know her as well.

The commander continued, "I should probably quote from the Bible at some point. Quite so. Well, I believe there's a passage that says nothing in life is promised. That's what I remember, anyway."

He cleared his throat before continuing, "Like I said, Rebekkah Schmidt was a fine woman. A helpmate to our pastor. She always supported him in his work here. Something every woman should aspire to."

Jo looked at him askance.

"Excuse me," she said, softly. "I'd like to say something."

She didn't wait for anyone to agree with her. Instead, she inched toward the casket as if automatically drawn there. While she knew Rebekkah wasn't really inside the box, she wanted to stand as close by as possible.

"There's more to be said," she began. Jo leveled her gaze at a far-off point to calm her thoughts. "You see, Rebekkah was not just one person among many. She was her own person. A light that helped so many of us during these dark times."

She heard Otto catch his breath.

"Yes," she continued, "the Bible says we can expect suffering, but we don't have to be devastated by it. We need to remember all the wonderful things about Rebekkah—the way she giggled when she thought something was funny, her gentle spirit when everyone else was harsh. She had the strongest sense of right and wrong I've ever known. I don't expect to meet another person like her this side of heaven."

If people were going to see the real Rebekkah, they needed to know her as an individual. Not just as one-half of a couple, but a whole person in her own right.

"Rebekkah led a singular life," Jo continued. "Her death leaves a terrible void. I, for one, will never be the same. I just hope I can be the kind of friend, neighbor—and yes, even wife—Rebekkah was."

At that point, the most amazing thing happened. Instead of chiding her for butting in where she wasn't wanted, Otto smiled. The edges of his facemask trembled with the effort, but it was beautiful to behold.

"Thank you, Josephine," he whispered. "Your words were perfect."

"Rebekkah heard them too," Jo said.

After they all recited the Lord's Prayer together, everyone quickly dispersed, since they'd all been warned not to mingle any more than necessary.

She slowly approached Otto. "Please let me know if you need anything. Anything at all."

"I will. She loved you, you know."

"I know."

Jo turned away from the casket, drained beyond measure. Only then did she spy Derwyn, who stood near the giant prickly pear cactus they'd once used for shelter. She wearily trudged through the dust to reach him.

"How're you doin' there, lass?" he asked, as she approached.

"Probably the same as you. I miss her already."

"'Tis a terrible shame. I only wish I coulda done more for her."

"It's not your fault. You did everything you could. We've given you doctors an impossible job, haven't we? You don't have enough medicine or help, so there's not much you can do."

He shrugged. "We can pray, I s'pouse. 'Tis the only t'ing keeps me going."

"Well, thank you for being such a good friend. And for helping us with the commander."

"Eh, what are friends for? Speaking o' which ... the old man jus' told me somethin.' I know it's scant comfort now, but the army wants your test to go everywhere. Not jus' our neck o' the woods."

"That's wonderful. But I heard he also wants to change it."

"Is that so?"

"Well, we can't let it happen."

"We?" He looked at her askance. "Oh, no. I'm afraid I need to bow out, darlin'. I've got nothin' more to give ye."

She wasn't surprised. Derwyn was stretched so thin by so many people, it was a wonder he hadn't lost his mind by now. "I understand. Thank you for everything you've already done."

"O' course. I've got to get back to the operatin' theatre. They'll have want of me in surgery."

"I understand. Thank you, again."

Jo watched him leave, her emotions seesawing between gratitude and despair. How could she fight this newest battle on her own? The new test was *their* project—hers and Rebekkah's. And every moment she worked on the test would only remind her of everything she'd lost. Of everyone she'd lost.

UNFIT TO SERVE

Perhaps it was time to throw in the towel. She wasn't sure she had anything left to give.

CHAPTER THIRTY-SIX

ALBIGENCE

CABIN P–79, CAMP TRAVIS

AUGUST 1918

Albigence walked into the army cabin and set his duffel lightly on the rag rug. He'd been told to come here, to a certain cabin, where a certain woman would be waiting for him.

Nothing looked familiar, but that didn't mean anything. A lot of things didn't look familiar to him anymore, including the young woman who suddenly appeared beside him.

"Albigence? You're home! You're finally home. I didn't expect you until six-thirty tonight."

"Uh, hullo."

"Hello, darling."

The woman threw her arms around him, which called up the scents of rosewater perfume and talcum powder. Lovely things, those, so he inhaled deeply.

"You must be Josephine," he said, when he pulled away again.

"Of course, I am," she said. "Who did you think I was?"

"Well, you're just as they described. How do you do?"

"Albigence," she said, "don't you know who I am?"

He glanced at her sideways. Then, he reached into his breast pocket and pulled out a notecard he'd been storing there. He'd worn the crease flat, since he'd opened and closed the paper so many times.

"Of course, I do. You are Josephine Pembrooke. We are married. You and I. Which means we get to live together."

She gasped. Apparently, he'd said something wrong.

"Wait, wait. Isn't that right? You don't have to live with me if you don't want to." He spoke quickly, since he'd obviously upset her.

"No, it's not that. Not at all. Of course, I want to live with you."

Relief washed over him. "Oh, good. I thought I said something wrong."

"No, darling. You've done absolutely nothing wrong."

Josephine led him to the kitchen and pulled out a chair. His wife was kind and beautiful. How did he manage to marry such a lovely woman?

"We don't have to live together," he insisted. He hadn't meant to upset her, and she still looked troubled.

"It's not that. Here, let me take your bag for you."

She reached for his duffel, which he'd carried into the kitchen, but he moved the bag out of her grasp.

"Please, don't. I'd rather keep it myself, if you don't mind. You see, it has my medicine. I don't go anywhere without my medicine."

"Of course. We'll put the bag away when you're ready. Are you hungry, darling?"

Albigence considered it. "No, I don't think I am. But thank you for asking."

He'd been working with a nice woman in France on his speaking skills. She was one of the first people he saw when he awoke in the infirmary. Initially, he thought she was an angel, until she corrected him and said something about being a "field director" with the American Red Cross. Which was strange, because they weren't in a field, and the only thing she directed was *him* when he tried to study the notecards she'd written. Cards full of simple words and phrases, which did seem to help.

Which reminded him of something else.

"They told me you're a schoolteacher. How wonderful."

"Yes, it is. I teach the officers' children. And you are—uh, were—a psychologist. Do you know what a psychologist is?"

"I think it means I help people. They talk to me, and I listen. Is that right?"

"Something like it. The first thing—"

Unfortunately, a sharp knock interrupted her. Albigence wished the visitor would go away, because he quite enjoyed talking to this beautiful woman.

"I'll get the door," she said. "You wait here."

He studied the kitchen as she rose to leave. He was going to like this place. The cabin smelled like warm bread and melted butter, and his companion seemed more than capable of preparing his favorite meal of eggs and porridge.

She returned a moment later.

"Albigence, there's someone here to see you."

A strange man in a military uniform appeared with Josephine in the doorway.

"Doctor Pembrooke? I've been ordered to escort you to the major general's office. Could you come with me, please?"

He looked to her for guidance.

"It's all right, Albigence. I'll go with you."

Well, if she agreed, who was he to argue? He arose from the table too and followed them both from the room.

The visitor stopped short, though, when he noticed something.

"You don't need your duffel, Doctor. You can leave it here."

But Josephine shook her head.

"It's okay," she whispered. "He takes the duffel with him everywhere. Let's get going, shall we?"

They traveled down the steps and onto a dirt path. Albigence had noticed the army tents all around him when he first arrived, but he hadn't realized there were so many. Row after row of them, one after another. At the end of each row, the soldiers had dug small firepits. Thank goodness none of them had been lit, because he never wanted to see another fire as long as he lived.

Maybe longer.

CHAPTER THIRTY-SEVEN

JOSEPHINE

PATH TO MAJ. GEN. HENRY ALLEN'S OFFICE, CAMP TRAVIS

AUGUST 1918

After the shock of watching Albigence read from a notecard to introduce himself, as if they were strangers, Jo had quickly put two and two together.

Albigence had returned to her a much different man. He could speak well enough, only now he relied on monosyllabic words and basic phrases to get his points across.

The major general had warned her to expect as much. He'd explained that military doctors at the Front did the best they could to repair Albigence's physical injuries—to fix the obvious, outward ones—but they couldn't repair his mind. Not yet. And not with the tools they'd been given and the limited time at their disposal.

Such a recovery would take months, if not years, of hard work.

The more Jo had listened to Albigence in the kitchen, the more she felt as if she was back in the classroom, addressing the youngest students in the front row.

She'd learned how to teach five-year-olds while at Bennett College. First, she'd lean over a child's desk and look directly into her eyes to boost her confidence. Then, she'd deliberately slow her speech and overenunciate her words, to make sure the child had time to absorb their meaning.

The child wasn't to blame if she couldn't understand anything more difficult. Her mind simply hadn't developed enough to process more complicated words and phrases. Such maturity would take time, study, and practice—all things Albigence would need as well, given his current state.

Yes, her conversation with Albigence had brought her right back to the classroom. She was grateful for the reminder, because it called up yet another memory that might prove even more useful in the end.

At the end of a recent school day, she'd stopped by the post exchange to retrieve her mail—what little she had of it, anyway. She'd found a strange postcard lurking amongst the letters. A colored postcard with an illustration on one side and a few sentences written in a crude hand on the back. All of it topped by a postmark from Baltimore, Maryland.

Baltimore? She didn't have any friends or family in Baltimore. Intrigued, Jo had brought the card home with her and studied the illustration for several minutes. The drawing, which showed a cluster of temporary buildings around an old brick fort, was labeled General Hospital No. 2 at Fort McHenry.

The drawing showed dozens of temporary wood buildings, each only inches from its neighbor, so the whole operation filled the isthmus to the brim.

What little handwriting there was on the card appeared on the other side:

They told me to rite and say somthin' to you. Much obliged for the lernin'.
—Sergeant Michael Hollingsworth

Michael Hollingsworth? Wasn't that the name of the brute she'd found pummeling a poor Mexican soldier in the ribs? The miscreant she'd berated until he'd finally stopped?

Apparently, this Michael Hollingsworth had enlisted in the army and ultimately wound up at a place called Fort McHenry in Baltimore.

At this point, Jo had more questions than answers, so she hurried to the infirmary, where she spied Derwyn standing outside the operating theatre.

"Look," she said, as she shoved the postcard under his nose.

"Hullo to you too." He'd peered at her over a pair of spectacles, since the poorly lit operating theatre had ruined the Welshman's eyesight.

"One of my former pupils sent it to me," she'd said. "What do you know about Fort McHenry in Baltimore?"

"Ah. 'Dat's what dat is." He'd clucked his tongue knowingly. "'Dey be doin' wonderful t'ings there. Takin' men and puttin' 'em back together again. Mentally, 'dat is."

"But how?" Jo remembered pressing Derwyn for details, because she'd been so intrigued by the concept. "How can they put men back together again?"

"Dey teach 'em skills." Derwyn had shrugged, as if it happened every day. "Carpentry, bookkeeping, dat sorta t'ing. He musta been made to work on his writin'."

"Interesting. How very interesting."

She'd tucked the postcard into her bedroom dresser and forgotten all about it. Until now.

Now, Jo hurried to catch up to the military policeman who escorted her and Albigence to the major general's office.

Jo couldn't wait to discuss the possibility of such a program for Albigence. Couldn't wait to hear the commanding officer's reaction. After all, the army owed her husband something for his pain and suffering. For all the struggles he'd endured.

Whether or not the commanding officer would feel the same way remained to be seen.

CHAPTER THIRTY-EIGHT

ALBIGENCE

OFFICE OF MAJ. GEN. HENRY ALLEN, CAMP TRAVIS

AUGUST 1918

After a few minutes' walk, the group arrived at a three-story building made of wood and glass. The building had fancy mahogany trim around the windows and real flower bushes by the front door.

Albigence followed Josephine and the policeman into the building and up some stairs, until they arrived at a certain destination.

"There he is!"

An older man with sharp features stepped around a desk to greet them. He clapped Albigence heartily on the back, as if they were old friends or something.

"Do I know you?" Albigence asked.

"Has it been that long?" the gentleman said, laughing. "You've been gone—what—four months or so? Of course, four months is an eternity on the Western Front. Sit down, my boy. Sit down."

Albigence did as he was told, since the man seemed to be important. The soldier who escorted them into the room watched the man's every move. One glance from him, and the younger one scuttled away.

Yes, he must be someone powerful if one look is enough to make people move.

"Now, first of all," the gentleman said, "I want to thank you for your sacrifice in France. I heard that you volunteered for the Western Front. Such bravery, my boy. Such bravery!"

He didn't pause, so Albigence couldn't interject. Apparently, the man was more used to talking than listening.

"You've made this camp quite proud," the gentleman continued. "Quite proud, indeed. I signed off on a Medal of Honor today, and I'm quite certain you'll receive it."

"That's wonderful," his newfound wife said. "Isn't it the highest award the army gives?"

"Quite so. What do have to say for yourself, Dr. Pembrooke?"

"Well, I'm grateful for the award," Albigence ventured. "Is that why you brought me here?"

"Isn't that reason enough?" The old man chuckled. "But since you asked, there's also the small matter of renumeration. The U.S. Army wants you to be compensated for your sacrifice. Quite handsomely, might I add."

"Okay." Albigence didn't really understand what the old man was talking about, but it seemed important enough.

"In fact, you could retire tomorrow," the commander continued. "The funds are more than enough to provide for you and your wife."

"That's wonderful news, sir," Josephine said. "I'd like to take Albigence away for treatment as soon as possible.

There's a certain hospital in Baltimore for people like him. I'm told they're doing amazing things there."

"Yes, indeed. I've heard about Fort McHenry too. They provide every patient with a job, don't they? Be it farming, carpentry, or whatnot. To help them recover and feel useful again."

Carpentry, hmm? Now, that might be interesting. Hadn't he known a carpenter once upon a time? Yes, a gentleman with a funny accent.

The memory was the first he'd recalled in a very long time. Briefly, but it felt real enough.

"Perhaps we could leave as early as next week," the pretty woman continued. "With your permission, sir."

"Granted. I'll discharge Dr. Pembrooke right away. It's the least we could do."

Albigence beamed happily. He'd never heard of this place called Baltimore, but he trusted the lovely woman sitting beside him.

Josephine rose. "Thank you, sir. We'll leave in the morning."

"You know, my dear, this quite reminds me of another brave soul." The commander leaned back as he mulled over a memory. "Yes, quite so. A man I met when I was in Alaska ..."

For some reason, the pretty woman gently pulled Albigence to his feet. The next thing he knew, they were hurrying toward the door, since she seemed determined to leave. He hated to be rude, but she seemed quite intent on making a hasty exit.

The older gentleman was still talking when they moved into the hall.

"He was speaking to us," Albigence protested. "You're not being very nice."

"Trust me, we got out of there just in time. Let's go home, darling. We'll have some tea to celebrate."

After a few paces, though, Albigence abruptly stopped.

"I don't quite understand what you said. Are we leaving the camp?"

"Yes. We're going to a place where they can help you," she said. "I hope you're not upset."

"Upset? With you? I could never be. But I *did* want to hear that man's story. He seemed to like to talk, didn't he?"

"You have no idea," she said, smiling. "But you'll remember soon enough."

Just as they were about to leave the building—would the old man even notice?—another man rushed into the hall and nearly knocked Josephine down.

"Careful, sir!" Albigence pulled her aside in the nick of time. "You'll have to slow down. You nearly knocked over my wife here."

"What? Sorry, old chap." The man whirled around to face him. "Why, it's you, Albie! You're back early, aren't you? I tried to keep tabs on your whereabouts in France, which wasn't easy."

"What're you doing here?" the woman demanded, her voice icy.

Albigence was shocked by the change in her demeanor. She'd gone from sunny to sour in an instant.

"I'm here to talk to the commander," the stranger said. "I just learned the most amazing thing."

The man had a funny-looking moustache, which wiggled under his facemask whenever he spoke. The wiggling was quite funny, only his wife didn't seem to notice.

"Get away from us," she said.

"Of course. I was just going to volunteer my services to the commander. Apparently, we're getting a new test to use with all foreign recruits. I'd like to review the thing and offer my suggestions."

"I'll bet you would." Again, she sounded bitter, for some reason. Not at all like the sweet woman who'd offered him tea earlier.

"Well, that simply makes sense, don't you think?" the other man said. "Since Albie wasn't here, they put me in charge of things. I don't mind stepping in and taking charge."

"I'll bet you don't."

By this time, the beautiful woman next to him was seething, so Albigence drew her close.

"Now, dear," he said. "Didn't you mention there's a nice cup of tea waiting for me in our cabin? I'd like to go there now. Please."

The man with the funny moustache squinted at him curiously.

"What's this?" he said. "Are you feeling all right, old chap?" He shot Josephine a funny look then. "He's not—"

"He's not anything," she snapped. "Leave him alone. I don't want you to speak to him ever again. To either of us."

"Now, now," Albigence said. She'd gone too far this time. "You're not being very polite, dear. Is that how we talk to our friends?"

"Friends?" Something sparked behind the man's eyes then. "Oh, I see what's going on. I'd heard something about an injury to his head. Oh, this is rich."

"Don't worry, he'll get treatment," Josephine snapped. "World-class treatment, which the army will pay for. So, don't count him out just yet."

"I only meant to say—"

"I *know* what you meant to say. Come to think of it, why don't we all go in and talk to the major general? Right now.

I'm sure he'd love to hear what you've been doing lately. You've been quite busy with letters and such."

"Letters?"

"I found them." She sounded oddly triumphant now. "A whole stack of them. Right there, on the edge of your desk."

"Uh, um. I have no idea what you're talking about."

"You know *exactly* what I'm talking about. I'm sure the commander would love to know about it too. I do believe it's a federal crime to steal another person's mail."

"Wait a minute." The stranger took a step back. "You wouldn't dare—"

"Try me," she said. "Because I would."

"Now, now," the man with the funny moustache said. "Don't be too hasty. I'm sure we can talk this through."

His wife moved so quickly she caught even Albigence by surprise. Jo grabbed the other man's arm and yanked him forward. Since he longed to help her, Albigence took hold of the man's other arm, and together they maneuvered him up the stairs.

While Albigence didn't understand what was going on, the woman seemed to think it was important for all of them to go back to the commander. The stranger put up quite a fuss, but he was no match for the two of them, and soon they arrived at the office again.

"You've come back," the major general said, once he glanced away from his paperwork. "Did you forget something, Dr. Pembrooke? Josephine?"

She shoved the stranger forward. "As a matter of fact, I did. There's something you need to know. All this time, my husband's associate here has been stealing my mail. I never received any of Albigence's letters. I had no idea if he was alive or dead."

The commander gasped. "What? Is that true, Dr. Beauchamp? Why in the world would you do such a bloody thing?"

"Well, I—I—"

"Silence!"

Crack.

The commander's hand snapped up from the desktop. "Stealing someone's mail is a federal crime. I knew there was something about you I didn't like. How dare you dishonor a war hero like that."

The man stuttered in protest, but the lady obviously had heard enough. She turned to Albigence and jerked her chin toward the door.

"Let's go," she said. "These two have a lot to talk about."

He practically ran from the drafty office and emerged into warm sunshine, where he waited for her. For some reason, the man with the funny moustache had upset his wife, which Albigence didn't appreciate at all.

He seemed to recall the man's name began with an F. Francis? No, that didn't sound correct. Frank?

Yes, that's right.

Funny how words had begun to make sense again. At first, he'd struggle to find a particular one, only to have the word pop into his head an hour later. Now, he could recall words in a matter of minutes, if not seconds.

How remarkable.

His brain reminded him of a giant puzzle on a card table. Every time he filled a slot with a new piece, he had an easier time filling the next one. And the next. Who knows where it'd all end?

CHAPTER THIRTY-NINE

JOSEPHINE

GENERAL HOSPITAL #2, FORT MCHENRY, BALTIMORE

SPRING, 1919

Jo leaned out the window of the railcar, hoping to catch a glimpse of Albigence before the train stopped. She'd sent him a letter last week to tell him about her plans to visit, and she hoped he'd received it in time.

She also hoped this visit would go better than their last.

During their last visit, Albigence had burst into tears when she told him she needed to leave. He'd cried and cried, unwilling to release her wrist, where he accidently left pink welts for days afterwards.

Which broke Jo's heart.

How she could leave Albigence with strangers, while she was free to come and go as she pleased? Everything about it felt wrong. She hated to walk away although she knew he belonged in the hospital at Fort McHenry.

His physician had tried to warn her. He'd told Jo that Albigence looked to her for all his memories now. He clung to her because she represented everything good in his past, and he didn't have the skills to anticipate a future yet. Ergo, the minute Jo disappeared from his life, he thought his life was over.

More than that, his injuries had affected Albigence in other, strange ways. He insisted on structure and symmetry in all aspects of his life now. He'd had neither of those at the Western Front.

First, he asked Jo to rearrange the furniture in his room to stand at precise ninety-degree angles to the door, which made no sense at all. Then, he insisted she rearrange his wardrobe so no two pieces of clothing touched. Finally, he begged her to create a schedule for him to chronicle every hour of every day until she returned.

In short, she'd been exhausted by the visit, not to mention heartbroken.

Jo shook her head now, and the memory vanished. She looked at the platform and spied Albigence standing next to a caregiver in a white apron. Her husband clutched a bouquet of blue delphiniums to his chest.

"Albigence," she cried, as soon as the door to the railcar burst open.

"Josephine. Finally." He offered her the flowers, along with an impish smile that recalled the Albigence of old.

"They're lovely, Albigence. Wherever did you get them?"

"I grew them." His smile broadened. "You didn't know I could garden, did you? Please say hello to Ida."

"Charmed," Josphine said, then took husband's elbow and gently guided him away from the caregiver. "I've missed you so."

"And I, you."

For some reason, Albigence stopped right then and there. He took her face in his hands and passionately kissed her on the lips, in full view of God and whoever happened to pass them on the platform. Afterward, her husband acted as if he kissed her like that all the time.

"Oh, my," Jo said, when she finally came up for air.

"I should have done that more often, my dear. I'm sorry I didn't."

"It's not too late. For now, I'd love to see the hospital. Love to see what you've been working on."

"Of course. Come along."

They threaded their way through the concourse and soon arrived at the fort, with the caregiver following behind at a discreet distance. Jo had learned more than a thousand men passed through these gates every month, and the army expected to treat twenty thousand by the war's end.

A receptionist welcomed the trio as soon as they stepped into a cavernous lobby.

"Dr. Pembrooke. I see your wife is back with you. So nice to see you again, dear."

"Thank you." Jo said.

"Would you be surprised to know your husband has made quite a name for himself here? Everyone knows him. Everyone."

"Really?" Jo looked askance at Albigence. Since when had her husband become the life of the party? He'd spent his whole life trying to blend in, not stand out.

"Indeed," the woman said. "So thoughtful. He grows armloads of flowers for us workers. Have you shown her the garden yet, Doctor?"

"Not yet. Josephine?"

He took her elbow then and led her away from the desk. But not before he tossed the receptionist a saucy wink.

"What's happened to you, Albigence?" Jo asked, as soon as they emerged into the brittle sunshine. "You're not acting like your usual self."

"I'm grateful, that's all. Happy to be alive. And happy to be with you."

He pointed the way to a small garden, where a few benches had been scattered about.

"Do you mind if we sit for a moment?" she asked.

"Not at all."

He gently took the flowers from her and placed them beside her on the marble bench.

"I've been thinking about something," she said, "and I wanted to get your opinion."

"Of course. I'll do my best."

"Yes, well," she said, as she took a deep breath. She'd steeled herself for this moment all day, but still she felt ill-prepared. She had no idea how he'd take this bit of news. "I might not be able to see you as often in the future."

"Oh?"

"Yes. I'm afraid I might not be able to visit you as much."

"I see. Well, it would make me sad, but I know you'll be back."

Josephine blinked. "I'm ... I'm sorry. What?"

"I know you'll come back for me. You shouldn't stop living on my account, Josephine."

"I'm so glad to hear you say that." Jo finally released the breath she hadn't realized she'd been holding, "I thought you'd be upset. You see, I've been toying with the idea of going back to school. Law school."

"Law school? You don't say. I think you'd be very good at law. You do like to argue."

His easy humor astonished her. Where was the Albigence of old? The one who over-analyzed everything she said? The man who parsed every word, always vigilant for hidden meanings?

The change in him was remarkable.

"Nothing's settled yet," she added. "I might not even be accepted into law school. But I wanted to talk to you before I tried."

"I think you should apply. They'll accept you, I'm sure. But don't get such a big head you forget to come back for me. I like this place, but I like being with you better."

"You don't have to worry about me not returning. And, like I said, all this talk of me going to law school might be for naught. I've wanted to be a lawyer ever since I was a little girl, but my father forbade it. It's just an idea at this point."

"Then, get to it. I can't be the only one in our union with a job, now, can I?"

"A job? So, you've decided to go back to psychology?"

"No, not that. Reading still makes my head hurt. I don't want to fix myself anymore, like I used to. I'd rather be outside. Doing something useful with my hands. Maybe I'll work with flowers."

"Flowers? What a marvelous idea."

"They help me forget, and the more I forget, the better I feel. Guess that's why they put me to work out here."

Jo gazed at him, putting all her love in her eyes.

"I promise I'll try to help you forget. For as long as I live, so help me God."

EPILOGUE

JOSEPHINE

ADMISSIONS OFFICE, ITHACA, NEW YORK

FALL 1919

Josephine gulped as she stepped over a threshold into a long, dark hall. Just as she'd feared, a gauntlet of formal portraits lined the walls, no doubt a record of the school's many deans. Each picture featured a somber looking man in a black robe, who looked nothing at all like her.

She clutched the papers against her chest as she passed under their watchful gazes. She kept her own gaze trained on a reception desk that loomed across the way.

"Excuse me," Josephine whispered, when she arrived. "I'm here for my interview."

The receptionist glanced sideways. "Um, I don't think so." She automatically returned her attention to a Remington typewriter on the desk.

"I have a two-thirty appointment," Jo insisted.

"Really? Are you sure you're not looking for the department of home economics? You'll find that one in Comstock Hall. This is Boardman."

"No." Josephine shook her head emphatically, although the receptionist wasn't watching her. She'd come too far to be turned away now. "I'm right where I'm supposed to be."

The woman sighed and moved away from the typewriter. "So, what is your name?"

"Josephine Pembrooke. I have an interview at two-thirty."

The woman referenced a calendar on the cluttered desk. She gave another sigh when she realized Josephine was right.

"Fine. The entry only says J. Pembrooke. I assumed it was a man. You can have a seat over there, ma'am."

A quick flick of the wrist, before she resumed typing.

"Thank you." Although the woman hadn't even apologized for her mistake, Jo refused to sink to her level and forget her manners.

Once Jo moved to the green leather armchair in question, she delicately perched on its cushion. After a long day's journey in a B & O railcar, she appreciated the relative silence of the foyer. Aside from a rhythmic *clack* of typewriter keys, nothing else sounded. No screeching train brakes, no frantic porter shouting instructions, and no other passengers to break her concentration.

She needed time to collect her thoughts.

Everything had happened so quickly. Once she'd made up her mind to apply to Cornell, the pieces automatically fell into place. Rather like that puzzle she'd set out for Albigence in his hospital room, which he'd worked with gusto.

Deciding on a university was the first piece. Applying to its law department was the second, which proved to be a bit more challenging, but not insurmountable. Since Cornell had been accepting women to its law department for thirty years, she didn't have to fight *that* battle.

"Ma'am?" the receptionist called, now using a warmer tone. "The dean's ready to see you."

Josephine stood and nervously smoothed the front of her peplum skirt. A deep breath for courage, and then, she walked stiffly to the man's office.

Anytime she felt overwhelmed, like now, she merely called up an image of Albigence in his gardener's smock. He'd spend hours at Fort McHenry working with flowers, knowing the work therapy program was part of his recovery. Everyone she met, from physicians to therapists, marveled at his progress.

He'd even whittled a wood pen for her in arts-and-crafts class, which he wanted her to use when writing her application to Cornell's law department. He told her he prayed over the pen while he worked the lathe.

Imagine that. Her Albigence offering up a prayer for her success, then telling her about it afterward. A man who was once so private, he never talked about his relationship with God. She was relieved to find he still had one, since she feared he might have lost his faith at the Western Front.

Quite the contrary. His months in France seemed only to have strengthened his faith. Although he came home horribly injured, he seemed grateful to be alive. So was she.

"Ahem." The memory vanished when the receptionist pointedly cleared her throat. "You should go in now."

"Oh."

The door to the man's office stood ajar, so she slipped inside and took her place before his desk. The mahogany behemoth reminded her of the desk in her father's study, lo those many years ago.

In fact, the whole room reminded her of her father's study. A massive bookcase stretched from floor to ceiling, and someone had oiled its leather volumes to a high sheen.

Meanwhile, the scents of parchment and Prince Albert pipe tobacco permeated the air.

"It's perfect," Jo muttered, under her breath.

"Hello, there." The dean gave her a curt nod and indicated an armchair beside his desk, which she gratefully accepted.

"Thank you."

"I understand you'd like to apply for the fall semester."

"Yes, sir." Jo automatically proffered the paperwork, which required leaning forward.

I wouldn't be surprised if there's a child-sized kneehole right under this desk.

"You're smiling," the dean said, as he accepted her paperwork. "I'm glad to see it. This office sometimes intimidates people." He indicated the opulent furnishings with a wave. "Not every law office looks like this, you know. I hope you're not one of those students who thinks a law degree will automatically assure you a hefty income."

"Not at all, sir. In fact, the paycheck is the least of my concerns."

"Good. It's all about the work, then."

"Even though someone once said the opposite to me. My father." For some reason, she trusted this man. Enough to divulge part of her past to him. "He thought I should marry an attorney and enjoy the privileges without doing the actual work."

"What an unfortunate opinion. But you didn't agree with him?"

"Not at all. I've always wanted the experience. Everything else is secondary."

"Well, that's good to hear." He began to read her file, and, after a moment, glanced up again. "I see you spent the bulk of the war at an army base in Texas. What was the base like?"

"Good and bad, to be honest. I served as the schoolmarm for the officers' children. Unfortunately, I saw a lot of hate directed at people who were different from the Americans there. I even rewrote one of the examinations the army uses to make it more fair for men coming from abroad."

"Yes, I see that." He looked at her curiously. "You don't strike me as the type to butt heads with the military. That must've surprised them."

"They *were* surprised. But I had a good reason. I saw what was happening with the men who failed the test. My heart broke for them. I knew if I didn't stand up for them, no one would."

"Go on."

"They had a primary test, but the wording was too difficult for foreign recruits. Every man had to take it, even if he couldn't read English. That was the first time I saw how the army does things. The army way is to keep going, even if something's not right."

"And that's what led you here today?"

"Exactly." Jo gave an enthusiastic nod, as if the answer should've been obvious. "I realized there are whole populations of people out there who can't speak for themselves—sometimes quite literally—in the military. They need someone on their side who knows the law."

"Hmm. So many of our students tell me they want to follow a relative into the profession. I've never heard your answer before."

"I'm not going to lie, sir. My father *is* an attorney. Once upon a time, I hoped to join his practice. But I've since realized my true calling lies with the military. I want to study the Articles of War. Focus on the rights of the enlisted."

"Interesting."

"My husband was injured at the Western Front, and I've known quite a lot of men who gave more than their fair share to this country. Since law is something I'm passionate about, I decided to focus on the military courts."

"I'm sorry to hear about your husband. And what does he think of all this?"

At one time, a question about her husband would've made the hairs on the back of Jo's neck bristle. But she'd come much too far to take offense at such an innocent question.

"He wants me to be happy," she said. "And he knows this is important to me."

"I see. Well, you made excellent marks at Bennett College, so I don't doubt you can handle the academic rigors. But, are you sure you're in this for the long haul? You won't get frustrated or overwhelmed and want to go back home?"

"No, sir. Once I've made up my mind to do something—and prayed about it, long and hard—I know how to stay the course. I'm here because I want to be here. Besides, people are counting on me."

People like Albigence, who inspires me every day. And Rebekkah, God rest her soul. The woman helped everyone, young and old, rich and poor, native and foreign-born. Not to mention the soldiers at Camp Travis, both past and future, who deserve to be heard.

"All right, then," he said. "Welcome to the law department's class of one-thousand, nine-hundred and twenty-three. God willing, I'll see you at graduation ceremonies at the very end."

"You will, sir," she said. "Trust me. You will."

ABOUT THE AUTHOR

Sandra Bretting is the author of The Missy DuBois Mystery Series, which was published by Kensington Publishing of New York. The second book in the series earned the rank of Amazon national bestseller.

Bretting also authored two standalone mysteries (*Unholy Lies* in 2012 and *Bless the Dying* in 2014) before penning *The Safecracker's Secret*, which debuted in 2022.

In between, Bretting also penned an inspirational Christian memoir titled *Shameless Persistence: Lessons from a Modern Miracle*, which detailed her miraculous comeback from a near-death experience. That book was profiled on numerous Christian radio and television stations, including the Cornerstone Television Network and the 700 Club.

A graduate of the University of Missouri School of Journalism, Bretting began her career writing for the *Los Angeles Times, Orange Coast Magazine,* and others. From 2006 until 2016, she wrote feature stories for the award-winning business section of the *Houston Chronicle.*

ACTUAL GROUP EXAMINATION "ALPHA"

(TO BE COMPLETED IN FOUR–FIVE MINUTES)

U.S. ARMY, 1917

1. How many are 50 tents and 8 tents?   ( )

2. If you save $5 a month for 7 months, how much will you save?   ( )

3. If 40 men are divided into squads of 8, how many squads will there be?   ( )

4. Mike had 12 cigars. He bought 2 more and then smoked 7. How many cigars did he have left? ( )

5. A company advanced 7 miles and retreated 2 miles. How far was it then from its first position?   ( )

6. How many hours will it take a truck to go 65 miles at the rate of 5 miles an hour?   ( )

7. How many pencils can you buy for 30 cents at the rate of 2 for 5 cents?   ( )

8. A regiment marched 40 miles in 5 days. The first day they marched 9 miles, the second day 6 miles, the third 10 miles, the fourth 11 miles. How many miles did they

march the last day? ( )

9. If you buy 2 packages of tobacco at 7 cents each and a pipe for 55 cents, how much change should you get from a five-dollar bill?   ( )

10. If it takes 7 men 2 days to dig a 140-foot drain, how many men are needed to dig it in half a day?   ( )

–U.S. Army, 1917

REVISED GROUP (TRENCH) EXAMINATION "BETA"

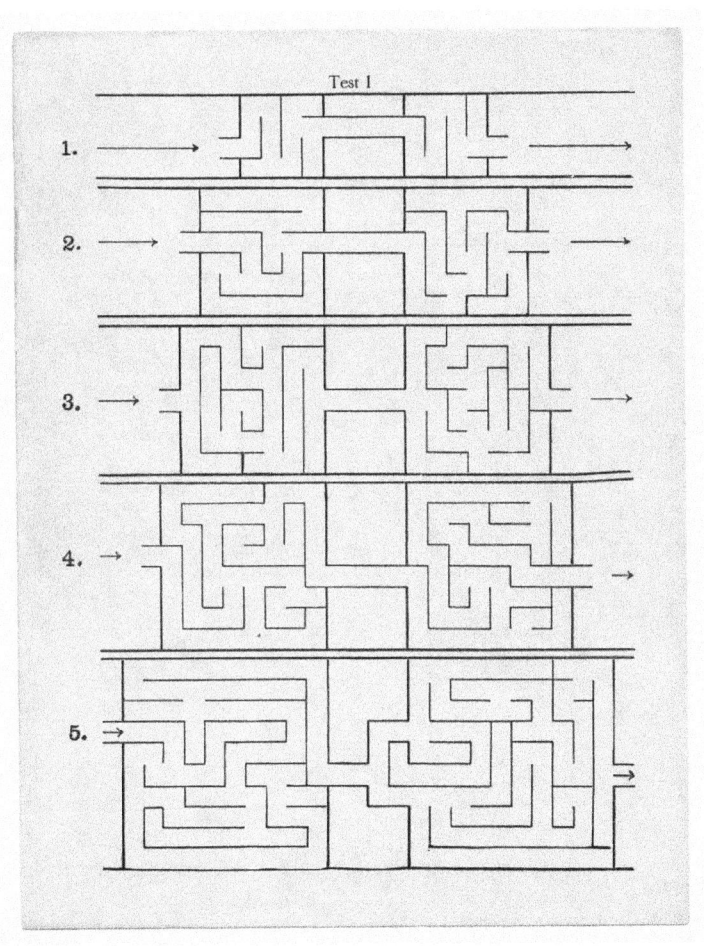

www.ingramcontent.com/pod-product-compliance
Lightning Source LLC
Chambersburg PA
CBHW071203020726
47502CB00002B/525